Praise for Susan Meissner's novels pours in
from readers and reviewers everywhere...

THE RACHAEL FLYNN MYSTERY SERIES

WIDOWS AND ORPHANS

James Scott Bell, bestselling author of *Presumed Guilty*, writes, "A powerful story of family and faith, wrapped in a mystery that touches the deep corners of the heart. Susan Meissner writes with a sure hand, and this book will make her many new fans."

Cheryl Russell at *Infuze Magazine* writes, "Susan Meissner crafts a mystery peopled with great characters (Fig is a riot!) and a plot that leads to an unforeseen, but satisfying ending. I look forward to reading the next book in the series."

Sharon Hinck, author of *The Secret Life of Becky Miller*, writes, "The characters are complex and interesting, and some of the supporting cast, like Fig, are particularly endearing. The dilemma of the story grabbed me, and I couldn't stop reading. Highly recommended."

STICKS AND STONES

Wanda Dyson, author of *The Shefford Files* and *Why I Jumped*, says, "A fantastic read! *Sticks and Stones* made me a Susan Meissner fan for life. This author knows how to combine wonderful characters, a great story, and heart-wrenching situations into a mystery that will keep you reading to the very end. And then twist your heart inside out."

Mary E. DeMuth, author of *Wishing on Dandelions* and *Authentic Parenting in a Postmodern Culture*, writes, "Susan Meissner's strength is making characters so real, you root for them as you welcome them into your life. *Sticks and Stones* is no different...Through the pages, find yourself enthralled, challenged, and uplifted."

Irene Brand, author of *The Sound of Secrets* and *A Husband for All Seasons*, writes, "*Sticks and Stones* is another fantastic, dramatic, memorable novel by Susan Meissner...[who] has a unique creativity that causes the reader to experience the pathos of her characters."

Armchairinterviews.com says, "Meissner gives us characters to cheer for and a story with enough questions to keep us turning the page... This one is well worth your time, and a place on your bookshelf."

AND PRAISE FOR SUSAN MEISSNER'S OTHER FICTION...

A WINDOW TO THE WORLD

[One of the Top Ten Christian Novels of 2005: Booklist Magazine]

Sara Mills, at www.christianfictionreviewer.com, says, "POWERFUL... When I finished the last page, all I could think was, WOW...I highly recommend this book, and applaud Susan Meissner for writing so eloquently what is almost impossible to put into words."

THE REMEDY FOR REGRET

Kelli Standish, at focusonfiction.net, says, "...Meissner's incredible gift with words has never shone truer...a must for any discerning reader's library."

IN ALL DEEP PLACES

NovelReviews.BlogSpot.com writes, "[This is] Christian Fiction the way it should be written, with threads and hints and God webs interwoven into not very rosy pictures of broken lives."

A SEAHORSE IN THE THAMES

Michelle at edgyinspirationalauthor.blogspot.com writes, "*Seahorse in the Thames* was a completely riveting and thoroughly engrossing novel unlike any I've read this past year...Meissner also tucks a wealth of life-changing spiritual material seamlessly into the pages of this novel. In many ways the message she delivers is subtle, yet it rings with such a profound and universal truth that for the believer the lesson goes straight to the heart of the matter."

DAYS & HOURS

SUSAN MEISSNER

HARVEST HOUSE PUBLISHERS

EUGENE, OREGON

Susan Meissner is published in association with the literary agency of Alive Communications, Inc., 7680 Goddard Street, Ste. #200, Colorado Springs, CO 80920. www.alivecommunications.com.

This is a work of fiction. Names, characters, places, and incidents are products of the author's imagination or are used fictitiously. Any resemblance to actual persons, living or dead, or to events or locales, is entirely coincidental.

Cover by Left Coast Design, Portland, Oregon

Cover photo © Mark Leibowitz / Masterfile

DAYS AND HOURS
Copyright © 2007 by Susan Meissner
Published by Harvest House Publishers
Eugene, Oregon 97402
www.harvesthousepublishers.com

Library of Congress Cataloging-in-Publication Data
  Meissner, Susan, 1961-
  Days and hours / Susan Meissner.
    p. cm.
  "A Rachael Flynn mystery."
  ISBN-13: 978-0-7369-1916-6 (pbk.)
  ISBN-10: 0-7369-1916-3 (pbk.)
  1. Women lawyers—Fiction. I. Title.
  PS3613.E435D39 2007
  813'.6—dc22

                                            2007011871

Printed in the United States of America

07 08 09 10 11 12 13 14 15 / LB-SK / 12 11 10 9 8 7 6 5 4 3 2 1

ACKNOWLEDGMENTS

I am grateful to my wonderful husband and children, my parents and parents-in-law, for grace extended to me during a time of deadlines and major transitions. You people are the reason *family* is such a lovely word.

I am indebted to Dione Talkington-Fletcher, an attorney whose in-depth knowledge of the Minnesota court system was invaluable to me and so graciously shared. Any liberties taken were for the sake of story and were my decision alone.

Nick Harrison, my editor at Harvest House Publishers, you are such an encouragement to me in so many ways. Don Pape and Chip MacGregor, thanks for every little and big thing you've done to affirm me; I am grateful beyond words.

And to God, the Author and Finisher of everything wonderful, You fill my days and hours with tenderness and beauty. I am Yours.

"People like us, who believe in physics,
know that the distinction between past, present, and future
is only a stubbornly persistent illusion."

ALBERT EINSTEIN

"But do not let this one fact escape your notice, beloved,
that with the Lord one day is like a thousand years,
and a thousand years like one day."

2 PETER 3:8 NASB

PROLOGUE

The light was failing as the woman folded the little girl's pajamas and placed them inside the grocery bag. The brown paper made a coarse, rustling sound and the girl, sitting on a bed with ruffled covers, wanted to plug her ears. She hated that sound, the sound grocery bags made when clothes were put inside them. The crinkly noise made her think of hurrying. Of leaving in a rush in the middle of the night, when there were no sounds in her house except the bag's crunching as clothes were stuffed in. Sometimes there was yelling before the silence. Not always. But the sound the shopping bag made, that happened every time.

The little girl wished she had a suitcase. She had seen one she liked at Sears once: pink with yellow stripes. She had been shopping with her mother and her Aunt Delia, and when she stopped in the aisle to admire the suitcases on display, her mother had shouted at her to keep up. When the little girl pulled her eyes away from the happy mannequin who stroked the suitcase handle, she heard her mother and Aunt Delia laugh. And then her mother had said, "Like you have anywhere to go."

Thinking of this, the little girl's arms flew up to her head and she clapped her hands over her ears to shut out the crinkly noise as the woman now placed a bathrobe in the bag.

The woman looked up. "What is it, sweetheart?"

The little girl, hands firmly over her ears, could hear the woman's words anyway. She could also still hear the bag and its swallowing sounds as the mother folded the top over.

"What's the matter?" The voice was pillowy soft like Wonder bread. The little girl would miss that. She would miss a lot of things about this warm house she was leaving. She was only eight. But she already knew that things at home weren't the way things should be. She couldn't put it into words, but she knew this place she was leaving was a home. And the house she was returning to was just a house. Just walls and a door.

She couldn't decide if she wanted to stay with the court-appointed mother in front of her or go home to the mother who was waiting for her. She couldn't have them both. If she had been older she might've realized she had no choice in the matter. The charges of neglect against her parents had been dropped. Again. She was going home to them regardless.

But in that moment, with her fingers curled over her ears, she felt torn by the weight of decision.

She liked the mother in front of her whom she was allowed to call Pamela. This mother smelled nice. She didn't scream. Her house was clean. There was food in the refrigerator. There were no broken windows in this house. No bugs. No sand between her sheets. Pamela tucked her in at night. Combed the tangles out of her hair without yanking. Helped her with math. Played Hi Ho! Cherry-O with her. And Rick, the dad in this house, didn't string together the names of God with stuff found in toilets to describe how angry or happy or scared he was. He didn't forget to come home at night. Rick didn't smoke. He didn't complain about the food Pamela made. He didn't hit her. He didn't hit anyone.

"Are you okay?" Pamela knelt down and put her hands on the little girl's knees.

The little girl nodded. When someone asked if you were okay, that's what you did.

Pamela reached up to the little girl's hands and gently pulled them away from her ears. "I want to tell you something and I want you to hear me so that you will always remember it. Okay?" she said.

The little girl nodded again.

"You are a very special girl. As special as a princess. I think you're very sweet and kind. And you can be anything you want to be when you grow up. Anything at all. Can you remember that, sweetheart?"

"Okay," the girl whispered.

"Don't forget."

"I won't."

Somewhere in another part of the house a doorbell rang. Pamela closed her eyes.

The little girl could hear voices. Mrs. Shaw, her caseworker. Rick. Pamela and Rick's little dog, barking. Happy barks. He thought someone had come to visit.

Pamela stood up and sighed. Then she bent over the bed and wrapped her arms around the little girl.

"Remember what I said." Pamela's cheek felt wet. "Promise?"

"I promise."

The little girl couldn't find any words to say goodbye to this woman whose house she had shared for three weeks. Somehow she knew she would never see her again.

But she would keep her promise. She would remember what Pamela had told her. In her mind, in her heart, the little girl already knew what she wanted to be when she grew up: a mother. A mother like this one whose tears were now falling on her hair, who smelled like Christmas and whose voice shimmered like a blanket made of stars.

She didn't want to be like the mother she was going home to.

Even though she loved that mother and didn't know how to stop.

She would never be like her.

Never.

The foster mother stood. She reached for the little girl with one hand and the paper bag with the other. The bag made a horrible sound.

The two stepped out into the hall. Twilight overcame the room behind them, devouring all the half-lit spaces and filling them in with shades of gray.

ONE

The infant lay on his side, half swaddled in a faded yellow receiving blanket. A tiny fist curled in mock defiance rested on his cheek, the other was hidden in the folds of the fabric. Tiny splotches of angry red dotted his newborn face—evidence of his strained entrance into the world and giving him the wrinkled look of an old man. The baby stirred for a moment in his sleep and his mother, standing over him, hesitated for only a moment before she grabbed a shot glass on the table behind her and walked away from him.

The apartment was quiet except for the low sounds of a TV that had been left on for no reason. Toys belonging to the baby's siblings lay scattered about his porta-crib, which stood at an odd angle in the living room, along with a cardboard pizza box, an empty liter bottle of cream soda, and Dixie cups that had been used as ashtrays.

A car seat sat on the floor across from the porta-crib. It was new, given to the baby's mother, Marcie, by a nonprofit group dedicated to keeping little ones safe in their mommies' and daddies' cars.

Marcie didn't have a car. A friend had brought her and her third child born in three years home from the hospital that day. There was no daddy to speak of. Nine months ago there had been, certainly. But not today.

Marcie sauntered into the kitchen and rummaged for a cigarette. She wasn't entirely sure who the father was this time. It annoyed her that she didn't know. There had been a few parties around Christmastime—nine months earlier. She had swallowed a few party drugs. Nothing too dangerous. There had been men at the parties. She just wasn't sure who she had been with. She had some inclinations of who the father was. Booth, probably. Or perhaps Vince. But neither one of them cared to find out if they were. Neither one of them believed they were. In fact, both were adamant they were not. And she simply wasn't sure.

Neither was Marcie entirely sure she was ready for another baby. She had just squeezed out her first year without so much as a whiff of meth—a feat no one seemed particularly impressed with. Not her sister. Not her mother. True, Ivy, the lady she'd met at the Laundromat and who had invited her to a support group for single moms, had been proud of Marcie's accomplishment. Everyone else seemed to think she never should have gotten tangled up with the stuff to begin with. Even the other moms in Ivy's group felt that way.

Marcie leaned against the kitchen counter and pulled a long drag from the cigarette. Her gaze fell on the porta-crib just a few feet away in the living room.

When Marcie had told her mother back in February she was going to have another baby, her news had been met with raw sarcasm. She was told she had finally found something she was good at.

Marcie hadn't remembered ever feeling as worthless as she did then. She had barely talked to her mother since. She didn't think her mother even knew she'd had the baby.

No. She probably knew. Her sister Koko had no doubt told her. She could almost hear the conversation as it took place: the condescending tone in Koko's voice as she relayed the news that Marcie had successfully brought into the world another child she couldn't care for—and her mother's head-shaking, tongue-clicking, sarcastic four-word reply: "Well, that's just great."

She took another long drag. They were wrong. She could care for this child. She just needed a little help. Was that too much to ask for?

Marcie had named the baby Leo after her grandpa, a man who died before she screwed up her life. She gave Leo her maiden name for a last name: Shipley. Made sense. She wasn't married to anyone. J.J., her three-year-old son, had his father's last name, Polk, though she hadn't seen Ronald Polk since before J.J. was born. One-year-old Hallie had the last name of the man Marcie had been married to for all of six months: Joe Hoffner. Joe was in prison somewhere.

She stubbed out the cigarette in the kitchen sink. She picked up the shot glass and the tall bottle next to it and shuffled into the bathroom.

Marcie used the toilet, wincing as her body reminded her she had just had a baby, and then sauntered into her bedroom carrying the shot glass and bottle. She needed a stiff drink tonight. Several, actually. Her life seemed as chaotic now as it was when she was trying to get off meth and wondering if the county was going to take J.J. and then baby Hallie away from her. She knew it wasn't as messed-up as that now, but it sure seemed like it. Three kids. No man. No job. No real friends. No life.

She sank onto her unmade bed, weary.

When she had arrived home from the hospital earlier that day, J.J. and Hallie had been all over her, smothering her with pleas for attention, and Koko refused to stay and help her.

"I've just spent two days with these kids, Marcie," Koko had said as she gathered up her things to leave. "I told you that's all the time I could give you. You knew that. You want more help, call Mom. Tell her you're sorry and you need her help. I've got a job."

It had been on the tip of Koko's tongue to add, "You know what a *job* is, Marcie?" Marcie was sure of it. But Koko hadn't said it. She just grabbed her keys and left, mumbling that Marcie was a fool for having another child. And Marcie had spent the rest of the afternoon with a two-day-old infant, a teething one-year-old, and a three-year-old toddler, all screaming for her attention.

She had finally resorted to screaming herself.

After a supper of Cheerios and Pop-Tarts, Marcie gave the two older children doses of cold medicine though they had no colds. And now that the antihistamine had soothed them into sleep and Leo had exhausted himself into a numbed stupor, she opened the bottle of vodka.

Marcie sat on the edge of her bed and drank.

She drank shots until she lost count.

She didn't want to think about her monotonous life. She didn't want to think about what she was going to tell the welfare office when she went to apply for more aid. They were going to want to know who the father was so that they could extract child support from him. She knew the look that would be thrown her way when she told them she wasn't quite sure who the father was. She didn't want to think about any of those things. She wanted to disappear.

Marcie drank, letting the effects of the alcohol bear her away.

When morning came, and with it a burst of sunlight and shrieks from J.J. and Hallie wanting breakfast, Marcie stumbled out of bed, unaware at first that she had not been up in the middle of the night to feed Leo. But as she used the bathroom it occurred to her she hadn't been up to feed him.

Or had she?

She couldn't remember. Her head ached.

Marcie yelled at the older children to shut up and she lurched into the living room. The TV was still on. She stepped into the open pizza box on the floor and cursed. Putting a hand onto the porta-crib to steady herself, she peered into it.

The baby was gone.

TWO

In her dream, Rachael Flynn heard a crying infant. It was a piercing, needy sound. She was standing in her loft apartment in downtown Minneapolis and her husband, Trace, and his artist friends were with her. In her dream, they were having a party or something and everyone was laughing. There were other people in the loft, too. People she didn't know. Fig, her husband's best friend, had a charcoal pencil in his hand and was drawing a sketch of Abraham Lincoln on her living room wall. Rachael was trying to yell at him to stop but her voice wouldn't carry. Then she heard the infant cry.

Her first thought was that her daughter McKenna had been awakened by the laughter. But even in her dream she recognized the cry as that of a newborn, not a one-year-old toddler. The crying baby wasn't McKenna.

"Can you hear that?" she yelled to the partygoers, but her voice was barely a whisper. No one heard her. No one turned to her.

She ran to Trace, who was seated on the couch arranging his paintbrushes in neat rows on the coffee table. "Can you hear that?"

But Trace just looked up from his brushes and asked if she liked Fig's drawing.

How could he not hear it?

"It's a baby!" Her voice was a raspy whisper.

"It's Abraham Lincoln." Trace grinned. His hair was tinted purple and glitter glistened on its spiked ends.

The wailing grew louder and Rachael shouted to the dream-room. "Doesn't anyone hear that!" she yelled, but her voice wouldn't carry.

"Rachael."

She turned and saw that the sketch of Abraham Lincoln had said her name.

"Look, Kumquat!" Fig was beaming. "He likes you!"

"Rachael," the sketch said.

The wailing seemed to fill the room.

Rachael wanted to shout, to scream, but her voice was powerless.

"Rachael!" Abraham Lincoln said.

Rachael's eyes snapped open. Early-morning sunlight oozed through the gauzy curtains at the bedroom window. Trace was leaning over her from his side of the bed, his hair a decent shade of highlighted nut brown. A tiny cross earring dangled from one ear. "Hey. I think you were having a bad dream."

A car horn sounded outside and Rachael shook the remnants of sleep from her thoughts. "I heard a baby."

"McKenna's still asleep." Trace lay his head back down on his pillow and put one arm above his head. "You were just dreaming."

"No. I heard it. And it wasn't McKenna. It was a baby. A newborn."

Trace yawned and closed his eyes. "It's probably just the cars down on the street. There must be a jam. Snarky drivers honking their horns, that's all."

Rachael sat up in the bed and listened. The loft was quiet except for the traffic on the street below. There was no sound coming from the direction of McKenna's room.

"It just seemed so real," she said, more to herself than to Trace.

"Well, I'll take the screaming baby over a traffic jam, actually. A screaming baby won't make me late for my meeting in Rochester. You do remember I have that today, don't you? Fig's taking McKenna."

She remembered. She didn't particularly like it when Trace had meetings on Tuesdays, the busiest day of her three-day workweek. She'd be in court all day. But she knew sometimes it couldn't be helped. Trace was working on a huge illustration project for a Mayo Clinic publication. He didn't always get to pick the days he met with the content providers.

And Fig wasn't a poor choice for a caregiver. He was just…Fig.

Figaro Houseman, who shared an art studio with Trace at his own loft one block away, was actually a good baby-sitter, though an unconventional one. Fig was far more outlandish than Sidney Gordon or Alphonse Brick, the two other artist friends who routinely hung out at the Flynn loft on Friday nights, and who'd also been in her dream. But Fig was also far more personable. On days when Trace had appointments and Rachael was at work at the Ramsey County Attorney's Office, Fig took on the role of McKenna's caregiver with all the willing dedication of Mary Poppins.

And all the flair of the Mad Hatter.

Rachael turned to face her husband. "Can you please remind him not to feed her Oysters Rockefeller for lunch?"

"But she likes Oysters Rockefeller." Trace opened one eye and smirked.

"Just because she likes them, doesn't mean she should be eating them."

"Fig would wholeheartedly disagree with you there."

"Fig doesn't know anything about nutrition."

"Yes, but look how happy he is."

Rachael stood up and reached for a thin cotton robe at the foot of the bed. "Happy men who eat whatever they want smile all the way to the cardiac unit."

"Well, it's a good thing McKenna's not a man then." Trace rolled over, away from her. But Rachael knew he was smiling. There was no use telling Fig to please feed McKenna the mashed-up banana and strained green beans that were packed in the diaper bag. No use at all. He'd feed her whatever fanciful idea struck him. Trace knew it.

And so did she.

She tied the robe loosely about her and walked into the master bathroom. Outside the bedroom window a car horn blared.

It sounded nothing at all like a human infant.

Whatever traffic woes had stirred Rachael awake had eased by the time she left her Minneapolis loft for the Ramsey County Courthouse in St. Paul. She arrived at the office of the prosecutor at her usual time, a tall Caribou Coffee in hand.

After nine months with the county, her role as a member of the prosecution team was finally starting to feel like second nature. She had left her job as a New York defense attorney the previous fall when Trace had been offered a multifaceted art contract with the Mayo Clinic. They both agreed it was a good time to head back home to Minnesota. Rachael's parents, reeling over the latest legal escapade with Joshua, Rachael's radically benevolent brother, were only too happy to have their more sensible-minded firstborn back home. Especially since McKenna, their first and so far only grandchild, had just been born. Rachael had been elated to work out a Monday-to-Wednesday workweek as an assistant county prosecutor. It was not the usual arrangement and she was grateful for the time it allowed her to be home with McKenna.

Making the mental shift from defender to prosecutor had been a challenge, but a welcome one. Defending young New York offenders in juvenile court hadn't exactly been her dream job. Now that she was sitting at the prosecutor's table representing the county's Human Services, she found that she was still very much embroiled in the world of troubled kids. But now she was working to protect them from harm and neglect, often the very things that had led her earlier clients to head down the wrong path.

Rachael made her way to her office, her mind on the hearings that lay ahead that afternoon. It was probably going to be a long day. She hoped Fig wouldn't decide to take McKenna jet skiing on Lake Minnetonka if she ran late.

As she rounded the corner to her office, her assistant Kate looked up from the reception desk. "You've got an EPC hearing today. It was just called in. They're sandwiching it in between your two and two-forty-five appearances."

The thought of an Emergency Protective Care hearing thrown in at the last minute on a court day didn't overly surprise Rachael or even rile her. It happened sometimes on an already-booked court day. Sometimes a child was removed from a home and quick arrangements had to be made to keep the child safe. The court only had seventy-two hours from the time authorities were notified of suspected abuse to hold an EPC hearing. It was just how things transpired sometimes.

But it always meant there was little time to study the case.

"What are the circumstances?" Rachael said as she set down her coffee cup and took the phone message from Kate.

"Not your average, I can tell you that."

Rachael looked up, wordlessly inviting Kate to continue.

"A newborn baby was found in a Dumpster in the wee hours yesterday morning."

Rachael winced. "Alive?"

Kate nodded. "He was alive."

"Where?"

"South St. Paul."

Reports of newborns being left in bathrooms and trash bins had decreased since Minnesota's Safe Haven law had gone into effect. The new law allowed a mother to abandon her newborn at a hospital or fire hall, no questions asked. But it still happened. Rachael wondered how the police had found the parents, or at least the mother, so soon. Usually it took a few days at least. But there would have been no emergency hearing set for that day if they hadn't located a parent.

"I'm surprised we didn't hear about this yesterday. So the county found the parents already?"

"Yes and no. The mother had called the cops yesterday morning to report her baby had been kidnapped."

"Kidnapped?" Rachael said. It didn't usually happen that way. Mothers who left their newborns for dead didn't call the police. They usually didn't want anyone to know they had even been pregnant. "From where?"

"From her apartment," Kate answered.

"Her apartment."

"Yep."

"So this wasn't a newborn."

"Three days old. Born at a hospital, not in a bathroom or a rest stop or anything like that. Released with his mother the day before yesterday at noon."

"I can't believe this is the first we've heard of it. Why wasn't it on the news?"

"Told you it wasn't the average."

Rachael would have to call Human Services and find out what was going on. She began to head toward her office. "Who's handling this one?" she called out. She needed to talk to the caseworker before she headed to court.

"Leslie. She said she'd be in a meeting until nine-ish."

Rachael stopped at the doorway to her office. "And the police report?"

"They're supposed to be faxing it right now."

"Make sure they send me both. I want the one detailing the finding of the baby and the one from the mother's call to the police."

Rachael crossed the threshold into her office.

She placed her coffee cup and briefcase on her desk and slid into her chair. She hadn't been at this job very long but she knew this kind of thing didn't happen very often. Mothers that dumped their newborns into trash bins didn't usually have second thoughts. And she'd never heard of one calling the police to report the baby's disappearance as a kidnapping.

The county obviously hadn't believed the mother's story: They had filed for emergency protective custody. Leslie was no doubt thinking that this mother had realized, after she abandoned her baby, that she could get caught, and that's when she called the police to report that her baby had been stolen from her.

But if she was telling the truth, her story just didn't make sense. Who steals a baby to leave it to die in a Dumpster?

It just didn't happen that way.

At that moment Rachael remembered the crying infant in her dream and she involuntarily shivered.

It was definitely going to be a long day.

THREE

The police reports lay side by side on Rachael's desk. One consisted of little more than a few paragraphs; the other, several pages.

She studied the report on the left, chronologically the first to be filed. The shorter of the two. She made her own notes on a legal pad as she read...

At 5:52 the previous morning, Charles Goodwin, an employee of Twin Cities Waste Management, had been standing in a cramped alley behind the Paradise Café off Wabasha Avenue. He was preparing to wrangle a filled Dumpster to the hydraulic lift of the garbage truck where he rode shotgun. Lenny Kobbe, his partner and the driver, was in the cab. According to Goodwin, as he placed his hands on the Dumpster's handles, he heard a raspy whimper and then a squalling sound, faint but distinguishable. Goodwin peered into the Dumpster and saw a naked male baby half-in and half-out of a tangled weave of packing material. The baby's arms were moving and the little mouth was opening and closing. "Like he was tryin' to speak, but no words would come," Goodwin had said.

He yelled at Lenny to kill the truck's engine. There was a baby in the

Dumpster! Lenny got out of the cab, saw the baby for himself, and radi-oed a 911 call.

Goodwin told police he didn't know if he was supposed to pick the baby up or leave it where he found it until help came.

"But I just couldn't leave 'im," he'd said. He scooped up the baby, and even though an Indian summer sun was already starting to warm the dank alley, he took off his outer shirt and wrapped the baby inside it.

The first policeman on the scene, Officer Alan Petrie, asked Goodwin if he saw anyone leaving or loitering in the alley.

"There weren't nobody," Goodwin had said. None of the businesses that had back entrances facing the alley were even open yet.

The baby, who appeared to be in good condition, was taken to Regions Hospital. A search of the alley revealed nothing other than a collection of other Dumpsters, disassembled crates, and rotting pallets. There were no other witnesses to question. Goodwin and Kobbe were thanked for making the 911 call and were allowed to go about their business.

The second report was filed yesterday, late morning. Police had responded to a call at eight-thirty in the morning by a south St. Paul woman who said her infant son had been abducted.

Rachael read the report and scribbled notes on the legal pad.

The call was placed by Marcie Shipley, a twenty-two-year-old single mother of three, from an apartment in a subsidized housing complex on Seventh Street. When Officer Jim Fallon and his partner arrived on the scene they found Ms. Shipley to be angry and slightly dazed. She told Officer Fallon she had put her other two children to bed at nine o'clock the previous evening. She had gone to bed herself at ten-thirty. Her two-day-old son, Leo Shipley, was asleep in a porta-crib in the living room when she went to bed. Ms. Shipley said when she got up a little after eight that morning, Leo was gone.

The officers found no sign of forced entry. Ms. Shipley said she couldn't remember if she had locked the front door when she went to bed. Sometimes she locked it and sometimes she didn't. She couldn't always remember where she put her keys, so she didn't always lock it.

"It's not like I got anything worth stealin'," she had said.

The officers asked when was the last time she had seen her baby.

"I told you! Ten-thirty!"

"You didn't get up in the middle of the night to feed him?"

Ms. Shipley had hesitated. "No."

"No?"

"Maybe I did. I was tired. I had just had a baby, you know."

"So you might have gotten up to feed him, but you don't remember if you did?"

"Well I suppose I had to. He's just two days old! But I had a few drinks before bed, so I don't…"

"You had been drinking?"

"I *said* I had a few drinks. That don't mean I was drunk."

"How many drinks, Ms. Shipley?"

"I said I had a few."

"Is it possible you called for someone to come take the baby for a little while? Perhaps a family member?"

"I already called my mother and my sister this morning! They don't have him!"

"A friend, maybe?"

"I don't have a lot of friends, okay? And the ones I got aren't the kind you hand a baby over to."

"Are you in contact with the father of the child, Ms. Shipley?"

"Look, don't you think you should be lookin' for my baby instead of asking all these questions?"

"Is it possible the father of the child took him?"

"No."

"Are you sure?"

"I don't exactly know who the father is, okay? So I think I know what I'm talkin' about when I say the father didn't take him."

At that point in the interview, Officer Fallon's partner, who was examining the house for other signs of forced entry, was radioed that a newborn had been found in an alley earlier that morning by a trash collector. The alley was less than ten blocks from Ms. Shipley's apartment building. He was instructed to have Officer Fallon ask Ms. Shipley about her whereabouts the previous night and the early hours of the morning.

Ms. Shipley had been adamant that she hadn't left her apartment, that from the time she had been dropped off at home at noon the day before to the time she called police, she had been in the apartment.

Officer Fallon had then told Ms. Shipley that an infant had been found alive in an alley that morning, just ten blocks away, and did she happen to know anything about that.

"What do you mean in an alley? What alley? Who has him?"

"No one *has* this baby, Ms. Shipley. He was found in a Dumpster. In a trash bin."

"Are you saying my baby was in a trash can? Someone put my baby in a trash can! Is he okay? Is he all right?"

The report states Ms. Shipley became extremely agitated at this point.

"Who would do that?" Ms. Shipley screamed. "Who would do that?"

The officers didn't answer her.

"You think *I* did this? You think it was me? You think I threw my baby into the trash? Why would I call you if I had done that?"

Officer Fallon ignored her question and instead suggested that Ms. Shipley get dressed so that she could accompany them to identify the baby at Regions Hospital.

"At the hospital? Why is Leo at the hospital? Is he all right?"

Officer Fallon asked Ms. Shipley if she had someone who could watch her other children for her while she accompanied them.

"Why can't you just bring Leo home to me? I just had a baby, you know. I shouldn't have to go running around. I was the one who got wronged here! You should bring my baby home to me and start looking for the person who did this."

"Perhaps your mother or another family member could watch your other children while we take care of this?"

Ms. Shipley had begun to curse. Officer Shipley asked her if she'd rather he called Human Services to come and take care of her children while she went with them. At that suggestion Ms. Shipley had backed off and grudgingly went to the phone to call her mother.

At Regions Hospital, Baby Doe was identified by his mother as Leo Shipley. Ms. Shipley asked if she could take her son home and was told Leo would be staying overnight as a precaution.

Ms. Shipley had then asked Officer Fallon if he was going to be the one to look for the kidnapper. Officer Fallon told her he would not. Detectives looked for kidnappers, not police officers.

The police report ended with a notation by Officer Fallon that an empty bottle of vodka had been found in Ms. Shipley's bedroom. And that Ms. Shipley couldn't remember how much had been in the bottle before she began to drink from it.

Rachael set the reports on top of each other and rubbed her brow. She looked at her watch. Eight minutes after nine.

She punched in the number for Leslie Tolberson at Human Services.

"Leslie. It's Rachael. You got a minute?"

"I've got a few seconds here before I have to head out. You got the message about the EPC hearing?"

"Yes. I've got the two police reports in front of me, too. What are you thinking with this?"

"Well, I'm just putting the finishing touches on my report to the court. I'll zap it over there as soon as I'm done. The thing is, Rachael, this is a weird one. But until we can figure out what really happened, we want the baby in a safe place. If Marcie Shipley is telling the truth, it will only be temporary. If she's not, well, I'm sure your office will be looking at child endangerment, attempted murder, and a few other nasty charges. We need some time to figure this out."

Rachael detected unease in Leslie's tone. "You think she's telling the truth?"

Leslie sighed. "I know how things look. Especially with this gal. She's a former meth user, a single mom, a welfare case, unmarried, and we've monitored her mothering skills before. She's made a lot of really bad choices, and I'm not saying she's Mother of the Year, but I don't know if she's the kind to leave her baby for dead. I've met some teenage mothers who've left their newborn babies in toilets. I've talked with them. Marcie's not like that. She needs a lot of help being a mother, and she definitely needs to get her act together, but...I don't know, Rachael. I never would've guessed she would do something like this."

"She had been drinking," Rachael reminded her.

"Yeah, I know. But she doesn't have a car. I just can't see her leaving her house in the middle of the night, drunk, walking ten blocks—after just having given birth—throwing the baby in a trash bin, and then walking back."

Rachael had to admit that scenario didn't seem likely.

"Who could have done it, then?" Rachael asked. "And why?"

"That's precisely why I need a little time to think this one through. I want the police to have the time to investigate this. But I can't let that baby go home with her until we know more. I have to consider that she's lying. Or that maybe it wasn't alcohol she was high on, but something else. Something that would've given her the stamina to walk twenty blocks after just having had a kid. The police are running a drug screen."

Rachael tapped the report absently with a pencil. "I suppose that's possible. What about her other children? You think they're okay at home?"

"I do for right now. I've worked with Marcie before. She doesn't exactly like me, but she's been pretty straightforward with me in the past. We'll open a file to monitor the other kids while we're looking into this. I'll tell Marcie we'll just have periodic, unannounced home visits to make sure everyone's doing okay. We're still going to file a Chips for Leo until we can figure this out. There's a lot going on here that's not in Marcie's favor. I don't want him going home until we know what's what."

"Chips" was legal speak for CHPS—a petition for a Child in Need of Protection or Services. It was the first step to legally allow the court and Human Services to step in when a child was believed to be a victim of abuse or neglect. Most of Rachael's caseload consisted of prosecuting CHPS petitions on behalf of the county.

"So where are J.J. and Hallie?" Rachael asked.

"They're with Marcie's mother. She's a piece of work herself. As is Marcie's older sister, Koko. Marcie told me they're coming to the hearing. She and her mom want to meet with the county before we go into court. Mom wants to talk conditions for getting the baby back, is my guess. Marcie's been in court before, when J.J. was a baby. She knows which questions to ask, which promises to make. If you can swing it, I'd like you to be there."

Rachael glanced down at the docket for the day. It would be a stretch to have any free time between court appearances. But she hoped it would work. She wanted to meet Marcie before they went in.

"I'll see what I can do."

FOUR

Rachael resisted the urge to pace the hall outside the courtroom. Her last case had been suddenly postponed and now she had a good twenty minutes to meet with Leslie and Marcie before Marcie's scheduled appearance. But Leslie was nowhere in sight and neither was Marcie or her mother, near as Rachael could tell. There were other women milling about the corridor. But no pair that looked like a twenty-two-year-old and her mother.

She checked her watch on reflex. She knew what time it was.

Her day so far had gone fairly well. No surprises, no no-shows. No angry parents or caregivers arguing inside or outside the courtroom. Rachael hoped the rest of the day would follow suit; she was inordinately eager to go home and mother McKenna. She had reread the police report documenting the finding of Leo Shipley three times that morning, and each time echoes of her dream filled her head.

Just like they filled her head now.

Rachael willed away the echoes of the infant's cries. Mulling over her dream would not help her get through the rest of the day. Neither would contemplating its significance. She had felt odd stirrings like this before.

On occasion she'd had a sudden and unexplainable awareness that she was suddenly privy to information no one else had.

It had happened last year when her brother Josh had confessed to shooting a man execution style and she somehow knew that he hadn't been the one to pull the trigger. Someone else had. It happened again several months later, when she had received a tip that a body would be discovered at a construction site. She had known something bad had happened at a house not far from where the body was found, even though the house was no longer there.

She had simply known it.

The insights had been like weighted shrouds about her body, something she could neither shake off nor ignore.

Josh *hadn't* pulled the trigger.

Something bad *had* happened at a house that had burned down more than a decade before.

A baby *had* been in danger.

She didn't want to consider that it was no accident that she heard a crying infant in her dreams that morning. Yet the notion that God was whispering to her again wouldn't leave her.

But I had the dream after *the baby had been found,* she reasoned inwardly. *I dreamed it this morning. Leo Shipley had already been found.*

Perhaps the dream was nothing. Just a coincidence.

Perhaps she wouldn't even mention it again to Trace. It would probably be best if she didn't. Trace wasn't too keen on her out-of-the-ordinary insights. He preferred God took care of weighty matters without enlisting Rachael's time or talents. There was no need to bring it up.

It was probably nothing.

Rachael stood and began to pace anyway.

A moment later at the far end of the corridor, she saw Leslie walking briskly toward her. Behind Leslie was a sandy-haired young woman in baggy jeans and a faded Timberwolves sweatshirt. Her hair was pulled back into a ponytail. Wisps escaped the hair band and fell messily about her face. Next to her walked another woman, older, frowning. Her steps were purposeful.

"Sorry we couldn't get here sooner," Leslie said as she closed the distance between them. "Rachael, this is Marcie Shipley and her mother, Joyce."

"Hello," Rachael said, extending her hand. Neither woman reached to take it.

"Why don't we step into this conference room?" Leslie said quickly and she opened one of several doors that opened onto the corridor.

They filed into the empty meeting room and silently pulled out chairs. Marcie seemed to hesitate for a moment and then took a chair by Leslie, facing Rachael. Her mother sat at the head of the table next to no one.

"Will you be asking the court for a public defender?" Rachael asked Marcie as she brought a file out of her briefcase and set it on the table in front of her.

"What do I need a lawyer for?" Marcie replied hotly. "I didn't do anything wrong."

"But you're going into a courtroom, Ms. Shipley..." Rachael began, but Marcie cut her off.

"I told you I didn't do anything!"

"She wants to have the Chips admit/deny hearing combined with the EPC today," Leslie said, nodding toward Marcie. "I'm fine with that."

"That's what you want?" Rachael turned her head back toward Marcie. The admit/deny hearing was usually held within ten days of the Emergency Protective Care hearing. That was the time the mother or father of the child in question admitted or denied the allegations against them. In this case, the allegation was endangerment. It wasn't unheard of to combine the two hearings, but Rachael wondered if Marcie truly understood how serious a situation she was in. If she did, she wouldn't be in such a hurry to dive into the courtroom with no one representing her.

"Of course that's what I want. Why are you people always so quick to point a finger at me? You don't even know me. I don't need ten days to figure out how to say I didn't do it. I didn't do it!"

"Well, then, do you have an idea who did?" Rachael kept her tone light, but authoritative.

"I'm no cop, lady. That ought to be pretty obvious. And how do you get off treating me like this? I know not every person whose child gets kidnapped gets treated like you're treating me. Only people like *me* get treated this way. That's the only reason you're not giving my baby back to me."

Rachael stiffened. "Not every person whose child gets kidnapped gets told their child has been found in a trash bin ten blocks from home. Not every person whose child gets kidnapped is unable to remember if they did or didn't get up in the middle of the night to feed their two-day-old infant. This isn't about people like you, Ms. Shipley. It's about you. And your baby."

Marcie opened her mouth and then shut it.

"Your baby was left for dead in a trash bin," Rachael continued. "And you cannot account for your actions the night before, Ms. Shipley, because you don't remember them. I know you think someone took your child. But you have to understand it's quite possible you could wind up being charged with child endangerment and maybe even attempted murder. We have a huge problem here. You can't remember what you did the night before. Or what you didn't do. You should ask the court for counsel, Ms. Shipley."

Rachael put the file back in her briefcase and fought down the desire to reach across the table and speak to the woman across from her in the advisory tone of another mother, and not a prosecuting attorney.

"I'm going to ask the court to rule that your baby remain in protective custody until your next court appearance, Ms. Shipley," Rachael continued. "If someone really did try to kill your child, then as long as he remains in protective custody he will be safe."

Marcie breathed in and out, heavily. She seemed to be on the verge of jumping across the table and doing who knows what. "For how long?" She did not look up.

"That's for the court to decide." Rachael's reply was gentle. "A couple weeks maybe."

Rachael looked over at Joyce Shipley. The woman had said nothing at all during the heated conversation. Nothing. But she appeared to have followed every word. She stared back at Rachael. Her gaze was hostile. Rachael turned her attention back to Marcie Shipley.

"Someone *did* try to kill my child." Marcie tossed her head and her eyes seemed to gloss over. Then she turned her gaze hard on Rachael. "You, of all people, working where you work, should know there are people out there who would do something like this. I shouldn't have to be the one to prove it. I didn't even finish high school. I shouldn't be the one to have to prove it."

"No one's asking you to prove it, Marcie," Leslie said.

"Yes, you are. You don't believe me. That's the same thing as saying, 'Prove to us you're telling the truth and then we'll believe you.'"

"Mrs. Flynn is right about keeping Leo safe until we figure this out. And while the police look into this."

"Are you saying I can't even see him?"

Leslie looked toward Rachael. "I think if the court can see you want what's best for Leo, we can arrange for some supervised visits." Rachael nodded. That was doable.

"Supervised visits." Marcie spat the words out as if they were rancid.

A knock sounded at the door. It swung open and a petite woman Rachael recognized as one of the court's guardians ad litem—an advocate appointed to guard the best interests of children involved with Protective Services—poked her head inside.

"Hey, Kelly," Leslie greeted her.

"Could I have a word with Marcie Shipley real quick? Court's running a few minutes late and I'd like to meet her before we go in."

"Sure." Leslie stood and gathered her things. "I need to apprise you of a few things, too."

Marcie stood wordlessly and made her way to the door. She cast one look at Rachael before she stepped through it. Her gaze was steel.

Joyce Shipley made no move to get up.

"Aren't you coming?" Marcie looked back at her mother sitting placidly in her chair.

Joyce narrowed her eyes at Rachael. "I want to talk to Mrs. Flynn. Alone."

Marcie huffed and sauntered out the door. Leslie cast a look over her shoulder at Rachael. Rachael, with the back of her head facing Joyce Shipley, mouthed the words, *I'll be fine.*

The door shut. Rachael turned around to face Marcie's mother. Joyce's face bore the telltale marks of a woman who had smoked heavily her adult life. Lines and wrinkles puckered the skin around her mouth. Her wiry, graying hair showed signs of a long-ago home permanent, and her eyes were neither blue nor green nor brown, but a combination shade that resembled weathered metal.

"Do you have a question for me, Mrs. Shipley?" Rachael hoped she sounded relaxed.

"No. I don't have a question for you. I've got something to tell you."

Rachael sat back in her chair and sighed. This is when the parent of an unfit mother or father usually berated her for picking on people who never had a break in life, who were doing the best job they could—no thanks to you—and who do you think you are passing judgment on other people like you're almighty God. Et cetera. Et cetera. Et cetera. "What is it, Mrs. Shipley?" Rachael braced herself for the barrage of criticism.

"Don't give that kid back to my daughter."

Rachael's first response was a wordless blink. Her second response was not much more than a whisper. "Excuse me?"

"Marcie had no business having another child. No business at all. She barely gets by taking care of the two she's got. She can't handle another one. And me and Koko can't either."

"You and Koko?"

"Who do you think comes to her rescue when she can't pay her bills or can't find a baby-sitter or can't think through the alcohol to remember which preschool J.J. goes to? Who do you think buys her diapers when she wastes her money on lottery tickets? Who do you think takes her kids when they're sick and she wants to go out? Me and Koko, that's who. Koko has a good job. Today's the third day this week she's had to ask off because of those kids. She won't do it anymore. She's had it. And so have I. I'm done raising children. If I wanted to bring up more kids, I could've found my own loser to sleep with. I'm not raising any more kids. And I know how this court thing works. You try to keep the kids in the family. You try to have the grandma or the sister with the good job take them. Well, neither me nor Koko are taking care of this baby. Marcie's a lousy mother. And believe me, I know lousy mothers. I happen to be one. So don't you go giving that baby back to her. I'll bet you a hundred dollars she was drunk when she tossed that baby in the trash. And she can't even remember it."

Joyce sat back in her chair, apparently done with her lecture.

Rachael said nothing for a moment. Joyce had given a speech Rachael had never heard from a defendant's family member before. Never. "You think your daughter walked ten blocks, drunk, threw the baby in the Dumpster and then walked back?"

"I'm not saying how she did it. I'm saying she did it. Any idiot with a car could've driven her there. She says she doesn't know who the father is, but what if she does? What if that's who took her? Or what if she just paid somebody to take her? Some drug addict who needed money for a quick fix? I'm telling you, she never should've had that baby. Koko told her to get an abortion, but Marcie wouldn't do it. You know why? Because an abortion was Koko's idea. That's right. That's how selfish and immature Marcie is."

Joyce's silence earlier in the conference room suddenly made sense to Rachael. "Your daughter doesn't know you think she did this, does she?"

"No she doesn't. And if you tell her I told you this I will deny it to your face."

Rachael wondered why it would matter. Joyce didn't seem the type to care what others thought about her. "You don't think she'll know you feel this way?"

"She'd make my life hell if she knew. I'd never hear the end of it. Marcie thinks all her problems are everyone else's fault. Well, I'm sick to death of hearing her whine. If she thinks I'm on her side, she'll actually involve me less. And that's just fine with me."

The door behind them opened and Leslie stuck her head inside. "The judge is ready for us now."

Rachael stood. Joyce stood also and started to move past her. "I swear to God, you tell her any of this, and I'll deny it," she breathed.

Joyce Shipley brushed past Leslie.

"So what was all that about?" Leslie murmured.

"I'll tell you later." Rachael grabbed her briefcase. "But I can certainly tell you why Marcie is no Mother of the Year."

FIVE

The hearing was concluded in less than ten minutes.

The petition to place Leo Shipley in emergency protective custody was read. Marcie Shipley was asked by the judge if she had been given a copy of the petition and if she had read it and understood it. She was asked if she wanted to have an attorney present.

Her answer to the judge was the same as it had been to Rachael.

"But I didn't do anything!"

The judge then asked Marcie if it was indeed her desire at that time to admit or deny the allegations of the CHPS—that she had endangered her child.

"I didn't toss my baby into the trash!" Marcie exclaimed.

"You deny the claim of this petition?"

"I didn't do it."

The judge turned to Rachael. "Your recommendations?"

Rachael stood. "Your Honor, we ask the court to rule that custody of the child Leo Shipley be transferred to the county for the duration of the petition and that the child be placed in a licensed foster care family. Ms. Shipley is unable to account for her actions the night Leo was taken from his crib and left in a Dumpster. It's the county's belief that to return the child to his mother would place him in harm's way. The county will arrange for supervised visits for Ms. Shipley in the interim and we will begin working on a case plan."

The judge addressed the guardian. "Does the guardian ad litem have a recommendation?"

Behind her, Rachael heard Kelly stand. "I believe it's in the child's best interest to remain in protective custody for the time being, Your Honor."

"I didn't DO anything!" Marcie's voice was shrill.

The judge regarded Marcie for only a second before turning his attention back to the petition in front of him. "Temporary protective custody is granted to the county. The child shall be placed in a licensed foster home. Human Services shall arrange for supervised visits for the mother. Pretrial conference is set for 30 days. That's all for today."

Marcie bolted out of her chair. "You can't do that! I haven't done anything!"

The judge's tone was calm but authoritative. "That's all for today, Ms. Shipley."

Joyce Shipley leaned across from the gallery and touched her daughter on the shoulder. "Come on, Marcie."

"I didn't do it!" The young mother's voice was trembling. Rachael wanted to block it out.

"Come on," Joyce repeated, and Marcie slowly stepped away from the defendant's table. Rachael could sense Marcie's eyes on her as she walked past. On her other side, Leslie gathered her papers together and kept her eyes on her files. Rachael turned and watched Marcie and her mother leave the courtroom. Marcie was crying and mumbling protests. She wasn't the first mother to shout out her innocence in a courtroom. Rachael had seen it dozens of times before. But something about Marcie Shipley tugged at Rachael. Something about this case troubled her. Her mind traveled to her dream. The crying infant seemed to fill the courtroom. She watched Marcie slink away in tears and she thought again of the implausibility of Marcie walking ten blocks with her son in her arms and dropping him into a Dumpster.

Rachael took off after Marcie, aware that Leslie was watching her in astonishment.

Her next case was in five minutes.

She didn't have much time.

"Marcie!" Rachael called out to the woman just on the other side of the double doors.

Marcie turned to face her. Her eyes were angry, her cheeks wet. Joyce was also looking back. Her expression was one of surprise.

"Did you give the police names of people you think might've had reason to take Leo?" Rachael said.

Marcie hesitated. Joyce cocked her head and narrowed her eyes at Rachael.

"I can't remember if they asked," Marcie finally said.

"If you think you know someone who might've done this, you should go across the parking lot to the police station and tell them."

"They won't believe me." Marcie's voice was toneless.

Rachael thought for only a moment. She had just seconds before she needed to step back into the courtroom. It wasn't her place to be giving a defendant advice. But she needed answers. "Go over there and ask for Sgt. Will Pendleton. Tell him I sent you to see him. Give the names to him. Okay? He's a detective. And he's a friend of mine."

Again Marcie hesitated. Joyce looked away. "What's the name?" Marcie asked.

"Pendleton," Rachael answered. "Sgt. Will Pendleton."

Marcie didn't thank her. She just slowly turned around and began to walk away. Joyce followed without looking back. Rachael watched them until they were out of sight. Then she turned and slipped back inside the courtroom.

Will was indeed a friend. A good one.

But he certainly wasn't used to Rachael sending over a defendant intent on proving her innocence.

And there was no time to call and tell him why she was sending Marcie Shipley to see him.

As she returned to the prosecution table, she pictured in her mind Will's ebony features crinkling into bewilderment as Marcie Shipley, a woman charged with endangering her child, tells him assistant county prosecutor Rachael Flynn told her to provide him with a list of suspects.

It wouldn't be the first time she had done something that made him tip his head in wonder.

That was something he *was* used to.

Rachael had met homicide detective Sgt. Will Pendleton a year earlier, when her brother had confessed to a murder. Her theories about Joshua's innocence had intrigued Will, and even though Josh had refused her offer of counsel, Will had let Rachael in on the investigation and had patiently attempted to grasp the notion that Rachael had special insights into what really happened. He kept her in the loop a few months later after Rachael and Trace moved back to Minneapolis and she had begun working for the county attorney's office. Rachael's heightened sensitivities regarding the discovery of a body and a long-ago burned house likewise had fascinated him, especially since it was her curious insights that solved the case.

Rachael had come to accept her inexplicable perceptions as from God, that her ability came to her by way of a grandmother who, before she died, prayed for Rachael to be used mightily of God. Trace had accepted her intermittent abilities, too, though he didn't like it when they surfaced. Fig thought it was a marvelous design by an inventive Creator. Sid and Brick were skeptical at best.

And Will didn't know what to make of it except that two homicide cases had been solved in a matter of mere weeks instead of months or years.

Rachael knew Will Pendleton would take the names Marcie Shipley offered him, even though no homicide charges had been filed and he would likely have nothing to do with the case. She also knew a voice mail from Will would be waiting for her when she returned to her office later that afternoon.

And even though she was confident she could tell Will about the dream she had had that morning, she decided as she retook her place in the courtroom, that for the moment it meant absolutely nothing.

Six phone voice-mail messages awaited Rachael after her last court appearance. She kicked off her high heels, sat down at her desk, and played them. Will's was number five.

His message was brief. "You probably know why I'm calling. I'll be in the office most of the afternoon. Give me a call when you get out of court."

Rachael listened to the last message and then pressed the speed dial for Will and waited until he picked up.

"Homicide. Sgt. Pendleton."

"Will, it's Rachael. I've some really good reasons for sending Marcie Shipley to see you."

"Good afternoon to you, too."

"Really, I do."

"And they are?"

"First of all, I had only seconds to convince her she needed to go back to the police with any names. And there are some really weird facts about her case that just don't add up. And I knew you'd see her if she told you I'd sent her."

"You know it's not my case."

"I know it's not. There are no criminal charges yet. But there might be. She could be facing attempted murder. It's highly likely if it turns out the evidence only points to her."

"But you don't think it does."

"It's just not your average abandoned-baby-in-the-trash scenario, Will. You've worked a couple of those. I know you have. This is not some teenager who hid her pregnancy from everyone, had the baby in a parking lot, and then dumped him in the nearest trash can."

Rachael heard Will inhale on the other end of the phone. One of the cases Rachael was referring to had occurred just after she and Trace moved back to Minneapolis. The abandoned baby had perished. The seventeen-year-old mother was found at a party several hours later, chasing away post-delivery contractions with beer and marijuana. Will had spent a few evenings at the loft with Rachael and Trace unwinding after that one.

"I admit this one's different," he said.

"Did you get the police report on this? Did you read it?"

"I did."

"Then you can see how quirky this is. Will, Marcie Shipley doesn't have a car. I can tell you it'd be pretty hard to walk twenty blocks after just having had a baby. Especially if you've been slamming shots of vodka."

"Perhaps it wasn't vodka she was slamming."

"Okay, but why would she wait until she's had the baby—at a hospital—and signed the birth certificate, before disposing of him? If she really wanted to leave him for dead, why not just have him in some back alley or bathroom. She *named* him, Will."

"So you think someone else did this? You think someone kidnapped her baby and threw him in a Dumpster? I gotta tell you, that's not your average kidnapped-baby scenario, either."

"There's nothing average about any of this. That's why I don't like it. That's why I wanted her to give you any names. Something's not right."

"Maybe she had second thoughts about having this kid, and made a really bad decision when she was drunk out of her mind, and then in the morning, when she realized what she had done, called it in as an abduction to avoid some really serious criminal charges."

Rachael sighed. "That's what I thought, too, until I met her."

"And now you're sure that's not it?"

"No. I'm not sure of anything. That's the problem."

Will hesitated and Rachael waited as he mulled it over. "We can check on those names," he finally said.

"I'd appreciate that. Are there very many?"

"A few. Two guys who insist they aren't the father. A Booth Rubian— don't know if Booth's his real name or not—and some guy named Vince Arigulo. And some gal at some support group she goes to. She says this gal hates her. Some support group, eh? Oh, and her sister."

"Koko?" Rachael sputtered. "Really?"

"Seems Koko advised her little sister to abort. Marcie didn't listen. And Marcie thinks Koko is not only ticked about that, but also at having to play auntie at inopportune times."

Rachael sat back in her chair. Koko? If that was possible, then it was equally possible Joyce Shipley could've done it.

No, that was unthinkable.

Still…

"Well, if you're seriously going to look into whether Koko has motive, you'd better add Joyce Shipley to that list," Rachael said.

"You're kidding, right?"

"She told me today she didn't want the county giving Leo back to Marcie, and that she and Koko are fed up with coming to Marcie's rescue. She said they're tired of taking care of Marcie's two other kids and they both wish this one hadn't been born."

"Yeah, but Grandma? That's kind of morbid."

"Will, it's morbid already."

SIX

Rachael's commute home was snarled by slow-moving traffic, an off-the-shoulder fender bender, and a lane closed for no apparent reason. As she inched her way home, her thoughts drifted from Marcie drinking herself to sleep to baby Leo lying naked in a Dumpster to the unlikely notion of Joyce Shipley leaving him there.

It couldn't have happened like that.

Not like that.

It shouldn't have happened at all.

Her mind ached with the weight of knowing Leo Shipley could've ended up like other newborns before him who'd been left in trash bins to die. It could so easily have gone the other way. If those garbage collectors had not come then, if trash pickup had been the next day, three-day-old Leo Shipley would be dead.

The bottom-line question persisted: If Marcie Shipley hadn't done it, then who? And why?

Rachael wanted nothing more than to get home to McKenna and hold her daughter tight. She didn't want to imagine someone reaching into Leo's crib, pulling him out and carrying his warm, soft body to a back alley several blocks away. She didn't want to imagine that person yanking off his diaper, pulling away the blanket, and depositing his tiny seven-pound body onto a pile of garbage. She longed to lose the image of that person walking away in the dark, deed done, to their car or a coffee shop or their warm bed. But the images clung to her as she crawled home at twenty miles an hour.

As the sun disappeared in the west, Minneapolis's reinvented warehouse district came in view and the loft's tall windows soon beckoned from several stories above her. She parked her car in the apartment garage, noting that Trace's car was still gone, and bypassed the elevator to the loft itself. She headed for street level and the sidewalk that would take her to the next block over, to where Fig was waiting with McKenna in the art studio he shared with Trace. The sidewalk, now in shadow, still radiated heat from the late September sun, but the twilight air around her was brisk. She hurried inside the lobby of Fig's building.

Rachael fished in her purse for her studio key and headed up the stairs to what had once been the mezzanine of a textile manufacturer. Two huge office spaces had been created when the factory was turned into luxury loft apartments. Fig and Trace leased one of them. A trio of reflexologists had the other. Fig's penthouse loft was above it.

Music met her halfway up the studio stairs. "Chapel of Love" wafted around her, a sonorous blending of the Dixie Cups' original 1964 recording and Fig's hefty falsetto. She opened the door to find McKenna laughing in Fig's arms as he danced and sang to her.

"Mum-Mum!" McKenna called out to Rachael as she entered the spacious room.

"Kumquat!" Fig whirled around to face her. "You're just in time!"

"Hello, Fig. Just in time for what?"

Fig set McKenna down on the polished wood floor and Rachael knelt down as her one-year-old daughter toddled toward her.

"I am picking out music!"

Rachael swept her arms around her daughter and inhaled her sweet fragrance. She lifted McKenna easily into her arms and stood. "Music for what, Fig?"

"I'm going to propose to Jillian when she returns from her gig in Morocco."

A notorious kidder, Rachael waited to see if Fig was pulling her leg. He liked to do that. But he stood there in maroon pants and tie-dye T-shirt—his curly, short hair gelled into Wolverine-like peaks—and grinned like a schoolboy.

He was serious.

"Well, that's *great*, Fig." Rachael liked Jillian. She was the only girlfriend of Fig's who hadn't scared her. Pencil-thin Jillian was a bit bohemian but she didn't take counsel from crystals or eat only yellow things, like two of Fig's other girlfriends had. Jillian was a fabric artist with one green eye and one blue eye. The anomaly fit her exquisitely. "What's the music for?" Rachael shouted above the CD player.

"For proposing."

"Music for proposing?"

"Of course."

Fig moved to the stereo behind him and turned down the volume. "Didn't you have proposing music?" he continued.

Trace had proposed to Rachael at the Minnesota Landscape Arboretum on a rainy April afternoon six years prior. He had designed a synthetic spider web and strung it between two rose bushes. The engagement ring was dangling from its glistening threads and the only audible music had been the drumming of raindrops on her umbrella.

"Um, well, kind of." McKenna began to finger one of Rachael's diamond stud earrings.

"You think 'Chapel of Love' is too cheesy?" Fig dropped the grin.

"No. It's just…it's just a little premature. It's more like a wedding song, not a proposing song."

"Hmmm. Good point." Fig furrowed his brow. "I need to find my CCR albums."

Rachael gently moved McKenna's finger away from her earring. "CCR? You mean Creedence Clearwater Revival?"

Fig looked up. "Well, sure."

Rachael offered Fig a weak smile. "Maybe you should pick *where* you're going to propose first. You know, if it's on a lake you might want something soft and jazzy."

Fig studied her a moment. "That sounds boring."

McKenna wriggled in her arms and Rachael set her down. "Well, to some it would, I guess."

Again Fig was silent as he looked at her. "What's the matter, Kumquat? You look sad."

Rachael looked up in surprise. "I do?"

"Yes."

"Tough day at work, Fig. That's all." Rachael plopped down onto one of two sofas, both named the Idea Couch. McKenna waddled over to her and climbed on her lap.

"All your days are like that, Rachael."

Fig didn't often use her name. It was mostly Kumquat or Raquel or some strange word in a language she didn't even recognize. Rachael fingered her daughter's golden wisps of hair. "Not all of them are. But today, yes. A baby was found in a Dumpster. Alive. But still. If someone hadn't found him…"

Before Fig could respond, the door behind them opened and Trace entered the studio.

"Hey!" His voice was cheerful, his arms full of drawings and a large black portfolio.

"Da!" McKenna gurgled.

"Gotta work on that second *d*, kid." Trace approached the black Idea Couch, dropped his artwork, and scooped McKenna into his arms.

"Hi, honey." Rachael smiled up at him. She knew it looked rather feeble.

Trace looked from Rachael to Fig and back again. "What's with you guys?" He turned back to Fig. "Did you tell her? About proposing to Jillian? She doesn't think it's a good idea?"

"It's not that, Tracer. Rachael's cool with it. She just had a bummer day at the brig."

Trace swiveled his head around. "Another one?"

"It's not always that bad!" Rachael sat forward on the couch, irked at feeling so defensive.

"Someone dumped a baby in the trash," Fig continued.

Trace looked back at his wife. "Dead?"

"No," Rachael said. "He was found in time. But it's the weirdest thing. The mother called it in as a kidnapping. She says she didn't do it. That someone stole her baby from its crib and *that* person threw him in the Dumpster."

"Stole him? And threw him away?" Trace looked dubious. "Why?"

"I don't know. I don't know what to think. She insists it was someone else who tried to kill her child. That someone came into her apartment while she slept, took her baby, and tossed him in a trash bin ten blocks away."

"Whoa." Trace set McKenna down and picked up his artwork.

"I know. It's crazy. And it doesn't look good for her. She's young, single, a high school dropout, been involved with Protective Services before. I really don't think she has any idea how to parent one child, let alone three."

Trace seemed to stiffen. Rachael realized too late she had made a generalization that wouldn't sit too well with Trace, given his upbringing.

"That doesn't mean she did it," he said quickly.

"I know it doesn't," Rachael answered back.

"Is she in jail?" Fig asked.

"No. She's not in jail. But the baby's going into foster care until we can figure this out."

An awkward silence followed. Rachael wasn't going to volunteer any more information. Fig apparently didn't know what else to ask and Trace's face was stony.

"So are you going to propose tonight?" Trace asked Fig, in an abrupt shift in conversation.

"No, no. Not yet. Haven't picked out the music or the food or the beret or anything."

"You do have a ring?" Rachael cast a quick look at Trace. He was looking down at their daughter.

Fig smiled. "Oh yes! A lapis lazuli and an emerald twined together in white gold. Blue and green. Just like her eyes! Here. I'll show it to you."

Trace coughed. "I've seen it. I'll take McKenna on home. See you in the morning, Fig Newton." Trace put his artwork under one arm and grabbed McKenna with the other. The little girl giggled.

"Sure. Later." Fig watched Trace disappear out the studio door. When it had shut behind him, Fig turned to Rachael. "Guess he had a bad day, too?"

"I don't think so, Fig. It was me. Sometimes I'll do or say something that will remind him of his mother. And not in a good way."

Fig tipped his head. "Not in a good way?"

Rachael turned to face him. "His mother was young and single and very much in need of help and guidance when he was born. She never really got it. He doesn't like it when people assume the worst about people they don't even know."

"Oh, yes. He and I have talked about this before. About how he feels about his mother. And what happened to her. You know, Trace is the closest thing I have to a brother. I wish I had known his mama. She must have been amazing to have raised such a great guy."

Months could go by before Rachael thought about Trace's mother, Elizabeth, even though she and Trace had given their daughter Elizabeth's maiden name. It was different for Trace. Rachael knew he thought of his mother far more often than she did. Elizabeth McKenna Flynn had died when Trace was sixteen, and the circumstances had been difficult. She had jumped from a bridge into an icy river. Trace was convinced it had been accidental, that she had fallen. Others—including his stepfather, Thomas Flynn—had doubts. Trace hadn't been particularly close to Thomas. Elizabeth's death and their differing views on how she died drove the wedge even further. Elizabeth had met Thomas when Trace was seven, long after her most difficult hurdles had been crossed: an unplanned pregnancy in her freshman year of college, a man who walked out on her, parents who rejected her, and no financial means. And she had crossed them alone. A drawing of a sparrow in a storm, which now hung matted and framed in their dining room, gave evidence of where Trace's artistic abilities had sprung. Rachael knew it was also how Elizabeth McKenna Flynn had seen herself: small, defenseless, trampled, yet nevertheless watched by God.

Elizabeth was not like Marcie Shipley.

"I wish I had known her, too, Fig."

Trace's mood had brightened by late evening and Rachael had nearly decided to say nothing about her comment at the studio earlier that evening. But as the evening wore on, the urge to apologize swelled.

She waited until they were reading in bed. The lights were low, and McKenna had long since been put to bed.

"Trace, I didn't mean to insinuate earlier tonight that only women who have it all together make good mothers..." she began, but he cut her off.

"Rach, don't worry about it. It was nothing. I overreacted."

"But that's not what I meant."

"I know it's not."

"It's just that I see *so* many who don't and..."

"We don't need to talk about this, Rach. Really, we don't. It's no big deal. I know what you see every day."

The last sentence silenced her.

I know what you see every day.

He knew without her saying a word that she had been feeling like she walked past the same train wreck every day—the same shattered bodies, the same stains, the same ruins. It all looked the same.

"What do I see every day?" she murmured a moment later.

"What?"

"What do I see every day?"

Trace shrugged as if to say, *You know better than I what you see every day.* "Broken lives, broken homes, broken kids. Isn't that what it's like?"

She nodded wordlessly. For six years—first in New York, and now here—she had been involved in some way, shape, or form with juvenile court. Six years and she was just now beginning to notice its effect on her, the effect of dealing with the same miseries, day after day, month after month.

It hadn't begun to slowly eat away at her until this year.

Starting when McKenna was born.

When she became someone's mother.

It was a long time after the light was turned out before Rachael fell asleep.

SEVEN

Marcie Shipley's file from Human Services was thick in Rachael's hands.

"It goes way back," Leslie had said when she handed the file to Rachael the day before. "I copied everything for you, from all of her Human Services files. At the back there are notes from some of her juvenile records—just the ones that would have bearing on her parenting skills. Or lack thereof."

"Juvenile records? You mean investigations into neglect by her own mother?"

"Actually, Joyce Shipley was never in court for neglect, though I get the idea she probably should have been. She's written a few bad checks and was suspected of welfare fraud once, but a petition of neglect was never filed against her. Those notes on the juvenile side are Marcie's. She was in court twice for being truant. Joyce let her drop out of high school when Marcie got pregnant at sixteen, so her truancy problem ended then, you could say. She miscarried that baby at fourteen weeks but she never reenrolled in school. Joyce said she'd be better off getting her GED at night school than hanging around the crowd she did at school. But she never earned her GED. She was picked up once for underage consumption and another time for use of a controlled substance. I remember Joyce being fairly ticked when Marcie pulled stuff like this. But Marcie just wouldn't listen to her, and Joyce didn't know how to make her listen. It's nothing you haven't seen before."

Rachael had thanked Leslie for making the copies and placed the bulging file in her briefcase to study on Thursday, one of two work days a week she spent at home with McKenna.

Now with McKenna tucked into her crib for an afternoon nap, Rachael spread the file out on her dining room table and began to read. She started with the notes at the back. With Marcie's past.

The truancies in her freshman year of high school seemed to be the beginning of Marcie's unraveling. The girl would show up at school in the morning, but at some point in the day would disappear. Detentions went unserved, interventions went ignored, her grades slipped. A court order to attend school with no unexcused absences produced the desired results, but the file closed at the end of the school year. When Marcie began her sophomore year, the court order was no longer in place. She began to leave again in the middle of the day. Joyce Shipley was called to a meeting with school officials to discuss Marcie's self-destructive behavior. Joyce was quick to point out that she dropped Marcie off at school every morning and it was the school's fault for not keeping track of Marcie during school hours. *Mother refuses to assume any responsibility for her daughter's actions, nor does she appear to have a plan to discipline Marcie,* Leslie's notes indicated.

Then later in the school year, Marcie found herself pregnant. Joyce's willingness to let her daughter drop out of school and stay out after she miscarried sealed the girl's fate into a world with no options. A year later, she was sentenced to community service when she was picked up for underage drinking, which she only completed half of, and was required to attend chemical dependency classes when she was later charged with possessing and using marijuana. When she turned eighteen, the court let the community service hours go, since Marcie had attended the classes.

Then her adult file began. At nineteen, she bore her first child, Jackson James. The father, Ronald Polk, skipped town two months before his son was born and that was the last anyone had seen of him. Just two days after J.J. was born, the first investigation into Marcie's skills as a parent began. Traces of amphetamine had been found in her blood by the hospital. The hospital had reported it and a file was opened, but the case never went to court. When questioned, Marcie said that she had been to a party the night before J.J. was born and had had a headache. She had asked a friend for an aspirin.

"They must have given me something else," she had said. "I wasn't taking anything while I was pregnant. Nothing. I didn't even smoke."

Marcie was monitored by Human Services for the next few weeks as a precaution. Leslie made several unannounced visits to the new mother at her apartment.

Rachael studied Leslie's notes:

Marcie seemed to be at ease with me visiting her. The apartment was fairly clean, though the air smelled of cigarette smoke. She said her boyfriend, whom she insisted was not the father of the baby, sometimes smoked when he came over. I reminded her that he should not be smoking around the baby and she told me she would make him step outside the next time he comes. The baby seems to be thriving. Color was good. Crib and bedding looked clean.

I asked her if she had any questions about how to care for J.J. and she said sometimes he cries for no reason and she doesn't know how to get him to stop. I asked her what she has tried. She said she's tried rocking, patting his back, a bath. I asked her if she'd like our public health nurse to stop by and give her some help there and she gratefully accepted. That was encouraging. I asked her if she was using anything and she said no. When I asked her if she would give me a urine sample, she did without so much as a complaint. The analysis came back clean.

There were two more home visits by Leslie over the next month. Marcie appeared to be handling motherhood fairly well. Leslie's notes stated that Marcie was getting some help with child care from her mother and her older sister, Kimberly, whom the family called Koko. *The family seems a bit confrontational,* Leslie wrote. *Not with me, but with each other. Joyce and Koko are critical of just about everything Marcie says or does. They are also at the apartment a lot. Odd, because it's like they really don't want to be. Still, J.J. looks healthy. He'd had a diaper rash, but Marcie did what the public health nurse suggested and the diaper area looks good.*

Apartment still smells heavily of smoke. Reminded Marcie to have friends take their cigarettes outside.

Leslie had requested another urine sample. Marcie had given it to her. It came back clean. The case was closed the next day.

The next handful of pages detailed Marcie's history with child support officers, medical assistance, her subsidized housing arrangements, food stamps, and financial aid. She had never been able to hold down a job, had never been able to help the county secure child support from J.J.'s father, and had never earned her GED.

A second investigation into Marcie's skills as a parent began when her daughter Hallie was three months old. At this point, Marcie had already divorced Hallie's father, whom she hastily married when J.J. was ten weeks old. She filed for divorce within the year, after he was found guilty of armed robbery.

This time, an anonymous tip had been called into Child Protection Services: Marcie's children were often heard crying in the apartment. Sometimes it appeared that no one was home with them. The intake worker gave the tip to Leslie. Rachael read carefully Leslie's notes:

Responded to a call from a neighbor in Marcie's apartment building who reported she often hears the children crying and no other sounds from within. Neighbor suspects the children are left alone for periods of time. Sometimes hears Marcie yelling at J.J. Loud noises, too, as if something is being thrown against a wall.

Found Marcie at home when I came, unannounced. She was surprised and angry to see me. Said at first that she wasn't going to let me inside, then relented when I reminded her it would be a snap to get a court order, and that I just wanted to check to see how she was doing. She was sullen, eyes were bloodshot, the place was a mess. J.J. is walking, looks good, no apparent signs of maltreatment. Let me hold him, showed signs of interest in me. Brought me one of his toys. The baby was asleep. Also appeared to be healthy, no visible signs of neglect.

I asked Marcie if she had left the children alone in the apartment. Her first response was to ask who told me she had done that, because they were liars. She vehemently denied she's left her children alone. Seemed resentful that I would accuse her of leaving a toddler and three-month-old alone.

I asked her if her children cried a lot. She said all kids cry. Sometimes J.J.

cries when he doesn't get his way. Sometimes he cries when he's tired. The baby cries when she's hungry and when she wakes up and lots of times for no reason at all. She told me if I had any children of my own I would know this. I asked her if the kids' crying frustrated her, if she sometimes felt like it was too much to handle. She told me what frustrates her is people who stick their noses into other people's business. She asked me if her mother or sister called it in, because they didn't know what they were talking about.

I explained that we would be monitoring her for a little while to make sure everything was okay. She told me I was wasting my time and that there were plenty of other rotten parents I should be spying on. I asked if she was staying clean and she said, "Are you?" I asked if she would submit a urine sample and she told me she wasn't going to be peeing into any more cups. Pee had nothing to do with children crying, and wasn't that why I was there?

I told her that her eyes looked red, that that's often an indication some-one's been using something, and that I just wanted to make sure she wasn't putting her kids in danger. She said, "My kids are just fine. And so am I. I am doing just fine on my own. I don't need any help from you."

Leslie made three more visits over the next six weeks. She was unable to substantiate the neighbor's claims.

The investigation was closed.

The next set of papers in Marcie's file were recent additions, placed there the day Leo Shipley was found naked in a trash bin.

Rachael reread the emergency protective custody petition, though she knew its content well. She had argued it in court two days earlier.

Based on Ms. Shipley's inability to account for her actions the night her son was removed from his crib and left in a trash receptacle, and in light of prior investigations into her parenting abilities, it is the county's recom-mendation that the infant Leo Shipley remain in protective custody pend-ing the outcome of an investigation into the matter.

The judge had ruled in the county's favor.

And now the county had a matter of days to decide if there was enough evidence to prove to a judge that Marcie had willfully endan-gered the life of her child.

She leaned back in her chair.

Rachael had worked with young women like Marcie, young women who became mothers far too early in life. She knew some of them did the best they could and it still wasn't good enough. She knew that others truly had no idea how to embrace responsibility. And others, like Elizabeth McKenna, just needed some help.

The kind of mother she didn't know was the kind who wanted her child dead.

She'd never met a mother like that.

But she knew someone who did.

She picked up the phone to call Will.

EIGHT

"So what do you want to know?" Will didn't sound perturbed over the phone, but Rachael could tell the Bonnie Drury case she was asking him about was still fresh in his mind. And still bothered him.

She had read about the case, knew it was Will's, and knew the attorney who'd prosecuted it. The case in question involved eighteen-year-old Bonnie Drury, a high school senior who had given birth to a daughter in a truck stop bathroom on an icy January night. The six-pound girl, whom a coroner later concluded had been born alive, had drowned in the toilet where she had been abandoned. Bonnie, who had been on her way to a high school basketball game, was late to the game that night. But she only missed the first half. She'd had to go home to change after spilling a Coke on herself as she drove. Or so she had said when friends asked where she had been.

No one knew she had been pregnant. She had hidden the pregnancy from everyone with the help of winter attire and a healthy dose of denial.

Later the next week, Bonnie had awakened in the middle of the night drenched in sweat and burning with fever. Unable to get her daughter out of bed, Bonnie's mother called for an ambulance. It hadn't taken the emergency-room staff long to determine a section of placenta was rotting away in the young woman's uterus. It had taken a little longer for Bonnie to admit that yes, she had had a baby. But she feigned amnesia when asked where the baby was.

The police were summoned and put two and two together rather quickly. The dead infant found the previous week, a few minutes from Bonnie's home, shared her blood type.

Will paid Bonnie a visit as she recovered at home from her infection. He asked her where she had been the night that baby had been discovered. Bonnie feigned amnesia again.

"Your friends say that you were at a basketball game with them," Will had said.

"Okay. So maybe I was."

"They said you got there late because you had to go home and change."

"I spilled a drink on my shirt!"

"So you do remember that night."

After several seconds of thorny silence, Bonnie had proceeded to tell Will she had been raped nine months earlier and that she hadn't told anyone because she was afraid the attacker would find her and kill her. She had tried to pretend there was no baby. Ignoring the pregnancy helped her forget the attack.

"But surely you knew, as the baby began to grow and as you felt her move, that she was real," Will had said.

"I pretended she wasn't."

"So you do remember the night you had her."

"Not all of it. I was in a lot of pain."

"You drove yourself to the truck stop."

"I was driving to the basketball game."

"In pain?"

"I didn't know I was in labor. I just thought I had stomach flu or something."

"So when did you realize you were in labor?"

"When I stopped at the gas station on the way. I thought I was going to be sick."

"And then what happened?"

"Well, I guess I miscarried there."

"Miscarried?"

"I don't know. I was sick. There was blood. It was like I was sick. Everything just fell into the toilet."

"The baby fell into the toilet?"

"It was like I was sick."

"Did you check to see if the baby was breathing?"

"I told you I was sick. I don't hardly remember anything."

"So you left the truck stop, went home and changed, and then met your friends at the basketball game."

"I guess."

"Sounds like you remember a lot."

Will had then reached in his pocket and showed Bonnie a picture of the toilet and the baby curled up inside it, under a sea of bloody water.

"That's your daughter, Ms. Drury. She drowned in that toilet."

Rachael knew that what Bonnie had done next haunted Will. Bonnie had shrugged.

Two days after Will visited Bonnie Drury at home, a classmate of Bonnie's called Will, debunking Bonnie's story.

"I bet you a hundred bucks that baby was mine," Gary Wiesenthal told Will. "Bonnie broke up with me back in September. She never told me she was pregnant. I bet you there was no rape, either. That kid was mine. And I wouldn't have let her do what she did."

Will asked Mr. Wiesenthal if he would submit to a paternity test. He did. The test was conclusive that he was the father.

Armed with the new evidence, Will paid another visit to Bonnie Drury. She finally caved in and admitted she had not been raped, and that Gary Wiesenthal was in fact the father.

"And you admit you left your child to die in a toilet," Will added.

"The baby was born dead!" Bonnie had countered.

"Your baby was born alive and drowned in that toilet, Ms. Drury."

Then he had read her her rights.

It had not taken long for the case to go to court or for a jury to render a decision. Bonnie Drury was found guilty of voluntary manslaughter and child endangerment. She was sentenced to ten years in prison.

Working for the office of the prosecution and being a personal friend of Will's, there wasn't much Rachael didn't know about the case. But she had never asked Will how Bonnie felt about what she had done, or how Bonnie felt about what happened to her daughter.

She knew how Will felt about it.

Rachael phrased her next question carefully. "I want to know if Bonnie knew what she was doing when she did it. Did she really know that when she left the bathroom, her child would die? Does she have any regrets?"

Will was quiet. Rachael wished she could see his face. She rushed to explain herself. "I mean, I know you can't know exactly what she was thinking, but you spent so much time on this case, you probably have an idea what was going through her mind."

"You're thinking this will help you figure out how Leo Shipley ended up in the trash." Will's tone was thoughtful.

"I'm thinking it will help me figure out if Marcie Shipley could have done it."

"As long as you understand this is just me thinking out loud, Rachael. I'm not a psychologist."

"I understand. I'm just looking for some perspective here."

Will sighed. "I believe Bonnie does have regrets, but not the kind you're looking for. When she told me she pretended the baby wasn't real, she was being totally honest with me—one of the few times she *was* totally honest with me. She never thought of the child growing inside her as a human being. She told herself over and over there was no baby. Even when she saw a picture of her little girl in the toilet, it was as if she were looking at slaughterhouse waste. Yeah, she has regrets. She regrets that her little illusion was shattered, that's she's in prison for killing someone. It's hard to pretend there was no baby when you've been found guilty of killing it."

Rachael pondered the young woman's ability to turn her back on her own child. She just didn't get it. When she thought of McKenna sleeping in the next room, it didn't seem possible.

"But how does a mother do that? I mean, it just seems to go against every maternal instinct I have. Is she mentally ill?"

"I don't know how a mother could do it. You'd have to talk to a criminologist or maybe God Himself, Rachael. And Bonnie was found competent to stand trial. There is absolutely nothing in her medical history to indicate she suffered from mental illness."

"Did she ever say why she did it?"

Again, Will was quiet for a moment before he answered. "She didn't want the inconvenience or the responsibility of being a mother, and she didn't want people talking about her at school or her mother giving her a hard time."

"But she had kept the pregnancy a secret. She could've just gone to a hospital, had the baby, and relinquished it."

"She never thought of the baby as a baby, Rachael. The pregnancy was always just a nuisance to be ignored."

Rachael tried to picture Marcie thinking this way, behaving this way. It just didn't fit the little she knew of her. "Are they all like this, Will? Do all the mothers who abandon their infants in trash cans and toilets think of their babies as nonhuman?"

"Well, if you think about it, how else could they do what they do? How else could they treat a helpless child like garbage? They would be monsters if they didn't."

In her mind, Rachael pictured Bonnie Drury expelling her child into the toilet. There was blood. There was dirt. It was a truck stop bathroom, for pity's sake. Then she imagined Marcie Shipley reaching into a crib, removing the child she had borne and named and whose cries she had heard on and off for two days. She pictured her removing the blanket from his warm body and somehow getting him inside a Dumpster ten blocks away.

And then calling the police the next morning to report him missing.

Made no sense.

None at all.

Unless Marcie had been out of her mind drunk.

Or high.

Or was mentally ill.

"Rachael?"

"Sorry, Will. I'm just at a loss with this one."

"None of your heavenly insights this time?" He said it as part joke and part admiration. Will had made it clear he was a bit in awe of Rachael's intermittent and unexplainable episodes of heightened acuity.

The fact was, Rachael didn't know if the dream she had several days ago meant anything at all, if it had anything to do with what happened to Leo Shipley.

It certainly didn't explain anything.

She hesitated. "No."

NINE

The drawing of the sparrow filled Rachael's line of vision as she tore a chicken nugget into tiny pieces and placed them on McKenna's high-chair tray.

Matted in charcoal gray and framed in black, Elizabeth Flynn's pen and ink sketch contrasted with the beige wall of the dining room on which it hung. Rachael had never minded the contrast before. She didn't exactly mind it now, either. It was just that the difference between the two was so stark, and she hadn't really realized it before.

Elizabeth had drawn the tiny black-and-white bird on a nest of twigs. Its body was crouched, hunkered down, as the leaves on the branches around it fluttered and rain beat down. The sky above the nest was thick with rain clouds. A tiny sliver of light was etched into the angry bank of swirling thunderheads. It was the only color in the drawing; a tiny splinter of red-orange.

God in his heaven was looking down on the beleaguered sparrow, peeking at it through the darkness.

But not sweeping the darkness away.

"Ta tin!" McKenna touched Rachael's arm with a sticky hand, drawing Rachael's eyes away from the drawing.

"You want more chicken?" Rachael picked up another chicken nugget and began to pull it apart. She placed the pieces on the high-chair tray, but her eyes were on the sparrow fighting to stay atop its nest.

The little bird's eyes were closed, unaware it was being watched.

"Un-un." McKenna held up a juice cup. Rachael rose to fill it, contemplating the little she knew about Trace's mother.

Elizabeth McKenna had been eighteen and away from home for the first time at college when she met a senior whose last name Trace didn't even know. His birth certificate listed the father as unknown. Elizabeth had struggled with depression on and off in high school and had routinely been unable to meet her parents' high expectations. She wanted a career in art. They wanted her to pursue a business degree. There was no money to be made in art, they said. And she wasn't that good, anyway. The invitation to physical intimacy had been a temporary tonic, a way of escape. In the arms of a lover, Elizabeth found she could forget her parents' demands and the accompanying downward pull of her spirit into despondency. But at the end of her freshman year when she wound up pregnant, the father, with his new college degree and dreams of independence, disappeared. And Elizabeth's pious parents, first ashamed of their daughter's bouts of depression and now ashamed of her pregnant and unwed state, refused to acknowledge her or her need.

Trace had told Rachael how his mother lived in the basement of a house full of spoiled brats, as he called them, nannying for the family who let her live there while she carried and bore her child. She lived with the family for six years, for room and board, and eked out a living by selling drawings and paintings at swap meets and flea markets. When bouts of depression would come, Elizabeth would often paint for hours on end to ease her mind. Sometimes she sought solace in an empty church. Trace remembered bringing crayons and a Spiderman coloring book to the big church down the street from the house where they lived. He used the bench of a wooden pew as a tabletop and colored while his mother knelt, rocked, and sometimes whispered her lament.

"We were poor and she was sick," Trace had told Rachael once. "But I didn't know how bad things were until she met Thomas Flynn and married him. When we were finally in a house of our own and I had my own toys, my own bike, and she could afford medication for her depression, it finally dawned on me how bad off we had been. She never let on."

Thomas Flynn adopted Trace, and Rachael knew their relationship as father and son had been amicable in the early years. Trace had been starved for a father figure in his life. But his primary devotion was to his mother. As he grew, Trace discovered Thomas didn't understand Elizabeth's melancholy moods and thus minimized them. Trace grew up with them and knew they were part of who she was. And that she had nurtured and treasured him despite them.

Rachael now returned the cup to her daughter.

Her analytical side was conjuring a scale. On one end was Trace's mother: young, single, and pregnant with a child she would end up loving extravagantly. On the other was Bonnie Drury: young, single, and pregnant with a child she would abandon in a toilet.

Somewhere on that scale was Marcie Shipley. If Marcie was at Elizabeth's end, then someone kidnapped her child with the sole intention of ending his life. If she was at Bonnie's, she was something of a monster.

The front door to the loft opened then and Trace stepped in followed by Petra Salvo, a high school junior and one of Brick's students.

It was Friday night and Fig had invited Trace and Rachael, along with Sid and Brick, to his loft for dinner. Petra was McKenna's babysitter.

"Hello, Petra." Rachael wiped her hands on a dishtowel.

"Hey, Mrs. Flynn. Heya, McKenna." The teenager tossed a backpack onto a dining room chair and walked toward the high-chair.

Trace still stood by the door. "You ready?" he said to Rachael.

Rachael nodded. She bent down and kissed the top of McKenna's head. "Call if you need anything, Petra. We're just a block away."

"Yep. Tell Mr. Brick I brought my art history study sheet, which everyone totally hates, and I am studying it after McKenna goes to bed, so if I flunk the test Monday, it's not my fault."

Trace laughed. "Whose fault would it be then?"

"His!" Petra laughed back. "For making a lousy study sheet."

Rachael cast a look back at Elizabeth's drawing as she grabbed her purse on the dining room table and walked toward the door. "Thanks, Petra."

"No prob."

Rachael slung her purse over her shoulder and her eyes met Trace's. He had seen her glance at the drawing.

He opened the door for her and they stepped out into the hallway of the sixth floor.

"You okay?" Trace put his arm around her waist as they walked toward the elevator.

"I'm fine," she said quickly.

Fig's menu for the evening was inventive as always, beginning with a tureen of bubbling whiteness that Fig happily announced was a Scottish staple.

"What is it?" Molly, Sid's wife, ventured a look inside the massive pot as everyone took seats at Fig's dining room table. Her petite features were crisscrossed with dread.

"Cullen Skink! I'm trying out all Scottish recipes tonight. Jillian's half Scottish, you know. I've decided to propose after I've made her an exquisite meal honoring her lovely heritage. Romantic, eh? But I have to try them all out on you guys first."

"Fig."

"What?"

"What *is* it?"

"I told you. It's Cullen Skink."

"*What is it?*" Each word fell from Molly's lips as if stapled to the air. Rachael peered into the pot as well.

"Isn't a skink a kind of rat?" Brick's tone was contemplative. A notorious brooder, Alphonse Brick appeared ready to sample his first rat. His Mediterranean features looked mellow by the light of Fig's many candles.

"I think it's a lizard," Trace said.

Rachael felt her face drain of color.

"I'm not eating a rodent. Or a lizard." Sid shifted his ample weight in his chair. "Not eating it. I don't care how romantic you think it is, lover boy."

"Me neither!" Molly whispered.

"Some rodents and lizards are quite tasty, but I assure you there are no rodents in this pot." Fig stirred the contents with a ladle. "Skink is Scottish for soup, lads and lasses. This is made with haddock. You know. The fish."

Sighs of relief circulated and Fig served the soup into bowls. "Now I'll just get the mince and tatties while you try that." He turned and scurried back to his kitchen.

Brick looked up from his spoon. "Mince and tatties?"

"What are mince and tatties?" Molly's brow was crinkled with fresh worry.

"Probably muskrats and tapeworms," Sid grumbled.

Molly's spoon clattered to the table.

"Meat and potatoes, you cowards!" Fig called out.

"Want me to ask him meat from what?" Trace whispered to Rachael.

"And I've some lovely leeks and asparagus in lemon sauce," Fig continued.

Sid turned to Trace. "I haven't had lovely leeks in a long time. Too long."

"I hope it's just vanilla ice cream for dessert," Molly murmured, tentatively tasting the Cullen Skink.

"Vanilla ice cream isn't for proposing," Fig said, suddenly behind her with a serving tray.

"It isn't?" Molly blinked up at him.

"No. I've made an *Ecclefechan* tart for dessert."

"Of course you have," Sid said, raising his water glass. "You know, Fig, I'd be happy with just a bowl of Lucky Charms."

Fig shook his head. "You are so unromantic, Sidney. It's a wonder you managed to nab such a pretty wife." He took a seat beside Molly. "And that Lucky Charms fellow isn't Scottish, pal."

Sid grinned. "He's not?"

"Leprechauns are Irish, dude." Brick lifted his spoon to his lips.

Rachael sipped her soup in silence. It was savory and creamy and warmed her. She hadn't realized she felt chilly.

"What's the matter, Kumquat? You don't like the skink?" Fig's voice was full of concern.

"No. I mean, yes. Yes, I do like it," she stammered. "It's really very good, Fig."

"You haven't said a thing since you got here."

There was no point in sharing what was on her mind. The cases she worked on weren't exactly the topics of dinner parties. And what would be the point anyway? If there was a case to be built against Marcie Shipley, it was her call, no one else's. She willed the corners of her mouth to spread into a grin. "I'm just enjoying everyone else giving you a hard time, Fig. Nothing you fix really surprises me anymore."

Fig's eyes widened and then he cocked his head. "Is that a compliment?"

"Definitely."

As they began to walk the block home three hours later, Trace reached for Rachael's hand. "Want to talk about it?"

She leaned into him as they walked. "We don't have to."

"I don't mind. You may as well get it off your chest."

Rachael inhaled deeply. Maybe it would help to talk it out. "It's this thing with Marcie Shipley."

"The mom of that baby the garbage guys found?"

"Mmm. I've never met a defendant who I've been so unsure about, Trace."

Trace was silent for a moment. "Does this have something to do with why you were staring at my mother's drawing?"

She nodded. "I don't think Marcie's the kind of mother that yours was. I don't think she's that gifted, but she's not like the women who leave their babies for dead, either."

"So that's good, right? That means it's not so bad."

Rachael sighed. "It means someone else took her baby and tossed it in the trash."

"Well, yeah. I guess so."

"Who would do that?"

"That's Will's job to figure out, Rach. You don't have to find out who did it if it wasn't her."

They walked in silence.

"Will thinks she did it and doesn't remember it," she continued. "Or that she doesn't want to remember it. That maybe she was high on something. She has used meth before."

"Okay."

"But she passed the test. They screened her the day her baby disappeared. It couldn't have been meth. It would've shown up in the test."

"So…"

"So that means it was something else. Something that she mixed with the vodka. Something that didn't show up in the test."

"Okay."

"But then how did she wind up ten blocks away, Trace? And how did she get back home? She'd have to be lucid. She'd *have* to be."

"Yeah. Okay."

"But that's just it! If she *was* lucid, she'd remember it."

"So then she's lying."

In that moment, Rachael realized what bothered her the most about Marcie's case. It was why she had stared at the drawing of the sparrow earlier in the day, why she wasn't part of the conversation at dinner, why this case was needling her.

She wanted to believe Marcie was telling the truth.

And reason was leading her down another path entirely.

"Yeah, she'd be lying," Rachael murmured.

"And you don't think she is."

"I don't know what to think."

TEN

A dozen copper-colored files lay across Rachael's desk, all needing attention, and each one detailing the life of a child whose world had been turned upside down. She'd be in court all the following day, standing before a judge and making recommendations for each of the children whose names were typed across the file tabs. Mondays were defined by the number of folders on her desk, the number of children whose lives hung in the balance.

So were Tuesdays.

She lifted her coffee cup to her mouth and drank. She doubted she would be able to leave her desk for lunch today. Too much to do.

Maybe she could get Kate to pick up a sandwich for her.

The intercom on her phone beeped.

"Yes?"

"Um, Rachael. There are two people out here who would like to see you." Kate sounded polite but hesitant.

Rachael checked her day planner. She had no appointments scheduled.

"It's Marcie Shipley and an Ivy Judson," Kate continued.

Marcie.

Coming to see her?

"Is Leslie with them?"

"Uh, no."

Rachael hesitated. The timing was terrible. She had a mountain of paperwork to wade through. And it wasn't normal to meet with a defendant outside the courtroom. But if Marcie had information…

She wondered for a split second if she should call Will. But she dismissed the urge as quickly as it came. She didn't want to scare Marcie off. It would be just as easy afterward to tell Will what Marcie said.

"Is the conference room available?" Rachael stood and grabbed a notepad and pen.

"Yes."

"All right. I'm coming."

Rachael stepped out into the hallway and then the reception area. Standing in front of Kate's desk was Marcie Shipley and a slightly overweight woman who looked to be in her mid-fifties. She was dressed in a pair of sunshine-yellow pants and an oversized sweatshirt printed with gigantic pansies. Her face was weathered by early wrinkles, but her face looked kind.

"Hello, Marcie," Rachael said. "What can I do for you?"

Marcie seemed nervous. She tugged at a lock of hair that had escaped her ponytail and smoothed it behind her ear. "Hey, this is my friend Ivy. I wanted you to meet her."

Rachael turned to the woman standing next to Marcie. "Hello."

"Hello, I'm Ivy Judson. I'm a friend of Marcie's."

The woman stuck out her hand and Rachael shook it.

"Is there something you'd like to tell me, Marcie?" Rachael kept her tone gentle. "I don't usually visit with people outside the courtroom."

"Yes. Yes there is."

"Here. Let's go in the conference room." Rachael led them to a room off the hallway containing a long table and padded chairs. The woman with Marcie had a noticeable hitch in her step. "Please have a seat."

As soon as Rachael had taken a chair, Marcie began.

"Look, I know what you've seen in my file. I know I've got a past and some of it's not pretty. But you need to know I could never do what you think

I've done. Never. I know I've blown it sometimes but I really am trying to do what's right for my kids. Ivy here, she can tell you how hard I'm trying."

Marcie's eyes had swelled with moisture. In court, Marcie had been defiant, frustrated. Today she appeared anxious.

"Marcie, I…" Rachael began, but Marcie cut her off.

"If you could just let Ivy tell you what I've been doing, how hard I've been working."

Rachael turned her head to look at Ivy. The woman was serene and relaxed in her chair. She smiled at Rachael.

"Are you a neighbor, Mrs. Judson?"

"Please just call me Ivy. No, I'm not a neighbor. I'm just someone who wants to help young mothers like Marcie here. It's hard to be a single mother in the big city. I'm sure you know that. So I have a support group that I invite young single moms to. We talk about ways to keep our kids safe, how to make wise choices, how to make plans for the future. It's a wonderful little group. And Marcie's been in it for six months now. She came all on her own, you know."

Rachael hadn't heard Ivy Judson's name come up before. "You work for a social service agency?"

"Oh, no. I don't work for anyone. I do this for free. Because I love these girls and their kids. They just need some help and guidance. We all need that. Some people get it from their families. But some don't."

"And you've been helping Marcie?"

"Yes. And she's been coming all on her own!"

"I take it you have a social work background."

"No, no. These girls don't need another social worker. I'm a mother. I've been where they are. I was a single mother. I raised two kids on my own. I know how hard it can be."

Rachael had worked with several Ramsey County support agencies in the last year, most of them staffed by professionals. Oftentimes the court ordered parents to attend parenting classes and support groups. But it seemed Ivy Judson's group was something altogether different.

"She's not like some people that just look down on you and tell you everything you're doing wrong," Marcie said. "Ivy's the only person who's ever found something nice to say about me."

"And how did you find Ivy's group?" Rachael opened her notebook. It was time to jot down what she was hearing.

"I saw a flier on the bulletin board at the Laundromat."

"I put fliers in Laundromats because I know a lot of young mothers use them," Ivy said, smiling. "I offer free child care so these moms can come and just relax for a little while and talk about what they're struggling with and how to be good moms. Sometimes we talk about discipline, sometimes about menu planning, sometimes about deadbeat dads who don't care about their kids. They need to talk about these things, you know. It's not easy raising kids on your own."

"Yes," Rachael said. "You say you offer free child care?"

"My next-door neighbor, June, she watches the kids when we meet. She loves kids. She has ten grandchildren and sixteen great-grandchildren and none of them live close by. She used to be head of the nursery at her church, but then they asked her to retire. She still loves kids, though. She plays games with them and fixes them healthy snacks. No store-bought cookies at June's."

"And how often do you meet?"

"Once a week. On Wednesday mornings." Ivy looked down at Rachael's pad of paper. "Why are you writing this down?"

Rachael looked up at her. "Does it bother you that I'm writing it down?"

"No. I'm just wondering why you are."

"You came here to speak on Marcie's behalf. This is the sort of thing where I take notes. I'm sure you can understand that."

Ivy smiled. "You're thinking, 'What does a fifty-two-year-old single mother know about running a support group,' aren't you?"

"No."

"It seems the professionals in law and government are always thinking we single moms don't know anything. I may as well tell you I'm on disability, too. I have a bad back and bad veins in my legs. And I know what most folks think of people on disability, that we're lazy and like to live off other people. But I'm telling you that what happens in my living room is *good*. It's good for these girls, and it's good for their kids. I give back as much as I take. You just ask these girls."

Ivy was still smiling, but Rachael sensed that the woman had defended herself on many occasions.

"I'm sure it's something you're very proud of," Rachael said.

"Darn right."

"How long have you had your group?"

"About a year or so. I started it not long after I moved to St. Paul." Ivy sat back in her chair. The defensive look was gone from her eyes.

"So Marcie's been coming for six months."

"That's right. And do you know she got herself off that meth? All by herself. We threw her a party, the other girls and I."

Rachael turned to face Marcie. "You were using when you started going to Ivy's group?" Rachael had been under the impression Marcie's meth days ended when Hallie was a baby.

"No. I stopped long before that. But no one seemed to care. My mom didn't care. Koko didn't care. Leslie didn't seem to care. Ivy was the only one who thought I had done something big."

"See, we take care of each other in my group." Ivy tapped the table with a stubby finger. "That's the difference between what I do and what the county does."

"And what does the county do?" Rachael said.

"You point fingers." Ivy sat back in her chair again. "No offense, but you do. You say you want to help, but all you do is point out everything that's wrong. And nothing ever gets done."

"I see."

"I'm not saying I'm a worker of miracles. There's a limit to everyone's abilities. But at least I see change."

"And you've seen change in Marcie?"

Ivy looked over at Marcie and beamed. "Marcie's had her struggles, but she's trying so hard to be a good mother. And she comes all on her own."

"Please, Mrs. Flynn." Marcie sought Rachael's eyes. "Let me have Leo back. I didn't throw him in that Dumpster. I swear I didn't. I'd like to strangle the person who did. I want him home with me. He belongs home with me."

"There is a lot the county has to consider, Marcie. Not just what's best for you, but what's best for Leo."

"But he's my son. I'm his mother!" Marcie turned to Ivy, pleading silently for her support. Ivy reached over and put an arm around Marcie's shoulder. "Come to Ivy's group. Come see what I'm learning. You'll see."

Rachael stammered. "I...I don't know if that's a good idea."

"She can come and just watch for a little bit, can't she, Ivy?"

"Sure. Sure she can."

Rachael shifted her body in her chair. "Perhaps."

"I'm going there on Wednesday. Here—gave me that pad." Marcie motioned for Rachael's notes, and Rachael pushed the notepad toward her and the pen. Marcie wrote down Ivy's address in fat, loopy script. She pushed the notepad back.

"All right. I'll *try* and make it. But I'm not making any promises." Rachael rose from her chair. "Now I'm afraid I have to get back to my desk. Thanks for coming by, Marcie. Nice to meet you, Ivy."

Ivy stood, smiling and pushing her chair in.

Marcie turned to her friend. "Can you wait for me outside? I just need to tell Mrs. Flynn something confidential."

Ivy hesitated just for a moment. "Of course." The woman turned and walked out of the room. When she was gone, Marcie turned to face Rachael.

"There's another reason I'd like you to come on Wednesday."

"And what's that?"

"One of the women in the group hates me. I can't say that around Ivy 'cause she thinks we're all wonderful."

"One of the other women hates you?"

"She hates me."

"And you think this woman had a reason to want to harm Leo?"

Marcie squared her shoulders and tossed her head back slightly. "She *hates* me."

Rachael frowned. Ferreting out suspects wasn't in her job description. She wasn't a detective. Marcie should be telling Will or another cop about her suspicions. "You should tell the police this, Marcie. Not me."

"I did tell the police. They just asked me if Sharell ever made any threats to me. She didn't. But that doesn't mean she didn't do it."

"It really isn't my place..."

"Hey. Aren't you the one who's gonna give my baby back to me or not?

You just come and meet her. Then you make up your own mind whether or not you think she could've done it."

Rachael spent a wordless moment in thought. Will didn't like it when she played detective. Neither did Trace. Neither did her supervisor.

Marcie reached out and touched Rachael lightly on the arm. It was a tender touch and surprised Rachael. "I didn't throw my baby in the garbage. I didn't do it."

The young mother turned and walked out of the room.

ELEVEN

Ivy Judson's duplex was located on a busy St. Paul street that at one time was only bothered by light residential traffic. But over the decades as Minnesota's capital had expanded and its population swelled, boulevards that stretched from one residential block to another became thoroughfares and parking lots for the urban workforce. Rachael had to park a block away from the salmon-colored duplex.

She hadn't mentioned to her supervisor where she was headed when she left the courthouse. Nor Will. Nor Leslie. She wasn't keeping them in the dark, Rachael told herself as she got out of her car. She just had an annoying hunch Marcie was innocent, but it was a hunch only. And hunches didn't stand up in court proceedings.

Rachael had purposely worn a pair of plain black slacks and a pale-pink Oxford shirt, leaving her suit jacket back at the courthouse. She didn't want to look lawyerish at Ivy's. A nice suit was a dead giveaway. And alarmed people into silence.

Rachael crossed the street, closing the distance to the duplex. She had arrived ten minutes after the support group started. That was intentional, too. She wanted to be the last to arrive.

Ivy's stoop was swept clean except for a tiny pile of overturned Matchbox cars near the front door. Road dust lay on their lacquered sides. They appeared to have been napping there for a while. As she pressed the doorbell she could hear the sounds of playing children next door, in the second half of the duplex.

The door opened and Ivy smiled. "Well. You *came*. Come on in, Mrs. Flynn."

"Hello, Ivy." Rachael stepped inside. The front entry led to a living room decorated in shades of lilac and mint green. Within it were seven young women, six of whom lifted their heads in guarded interest. Marcie, sitting on the end of Ivy's sofa, had raised her head as well. But her face wore the look of someone who had just won a hand at cards. Rachael had come.

"Gals, this is a lady from the county." Ivy's voice was genial but laced with something akin to contempt. Rachael couldn't quite define it in her mind. And each girl had clearly flinched the moment Ivy had said the word *county*. "She came to see our Marcie here, to see what Marcie's been learning here at our little group. Her name's Mrs. Flynn."

"You the one who took her baby away?"

Rachael turned toward the voice. A woman of Latino descent, leaning forward in a kitchen chair across from the sofa, was staring at her.

"Now, now, Danitra. That won't help our Marcie," Ivy soothed. Then she reached out and placed her hand on Rachael's back. "Here. You take my chair, Mrs. Flynn." She directed Rachael to an armchair in the circle of women.

But Rachael didn't move. "That's very kind. I won't be staying very long."

"Good," someone murmured. But Rachael couldn't tell who it was. She looked over at Marcie who was staring at a tall, dark-skinned woman sitting directly across from her. Marcie looked back at Rachael and inclined her head toward the woman.

"Well, shall we introduce ourselves?" Ivy said happily.

"They don't have to do that." Rachael didn't want to raise anyone's defenses.

"We don't mind, do we? We've nothing to hide here." Ivy pointed to the couch. "You already know Marcie. Next to her is Liza and then Arden. Over there is Danitra and Rose and Toni. And that's Sharell."

Rachael studied the women as their names fell from Ivy's lips. Liza looked to be the youngest and was the only one smiling at her. She was blonde, petite, and wore a row of tattooed *L*'s on the underside of her arm. Arden, short and obviously pregnant, sported a hair color that defied description. Hues of orange, brown, and lavender sprouted from her head. Rachael turned her attention to the other side of the circle. Danitra's soft brown eyes had not left her. The young woman continued to stare, expressionless, as Rachael took in the rest of the group. Rose and Toni, both brown-haired and of average build and countenance, looked away from her, seemingly bored. Sharell, tall and willowy, did nothing to hide her displeasure that Rachael was in the room.

"You sure you don't want to sit down?" Ivy asked.

"No, but thank you very much."

"Well, all right. What would you like to know?"

Rachael cleared her throat. "Well, I'm here because I was invited. What would you like me to know?"

Sharell's head whipped around to face Marcie. Everyone turned to face her. Marcie shifted her weight on the couch.

"Does anyone feel like sharing with Mrs. Flynn what we do here? How we've been here for Marcie?"

"Why can't Marcie just tell her herself?" Sharell said, toneless. "No reason we all have to hear it. It's not our problem."

"Sometimes it's helpful to have someone else back you up, Sharell." Ivy looked around the room. "Anyone?"

"I don't mind saying anything," Liza replied. "I don't mind it. I like to talk."

"Good Lord," Sharell grunted. She heaved her tall body back into her chair.

"Well, go ahead, then, Liza." Ivy's smile was broad.

"This is a great group," Liza beamed. "Ivy's been so nice to each one of us. She lets us talk about what we're going through. She cares for us. She makes us feel good about who we are. She's been like...like a mother to me. My mother, she never understood me. Never tried to. I'm like an insult to her. But Ivy, she understands me. She doesn't think I belong in some nut house…" Liza's voice dwindled away and her eyes grew glassy.

"There, there. That's so nice of you, Liza dear," Ivy cooed. "But what can you tell Mrs. Flynn about Marcie?"

Liza wiped her eyes and looked at Marcie sitting next to her. "Marcie's been real nice to me. She doesn't mind sitting next to me. She braids my hair sometimes and that feels nice."

Sharell snorted.

Liza looked up and seemed to freeze in mid-sentence.

"Did you want to say something, Sharell?" Ivy asked.

"I have nothing to say about any of this." Sharell tossed a hand up in the air. "If I'd known we was gonna give out medals to Marcie, I'd have stayed home."

"No you wouldn't have," Toni mumbled. "This is the only time you can get away from your kids."

"Shut your mouth." Sharell spat the words out.

Across from her, Rachael saw Marcie look her way.

"Girls, girls, listen to me," Ivy said gently. "We've all been where Marcie is, haven't we? We know what it's like to have government people tell us we don't know how to be good moms."

Every eye in the room turned to Rachael.

"We know what it's like to have them want to take our kids away," Ivy continued. "We know how frustrating it is. Marcie needs us now. That's what a support group is for. To support each other, hold each other up when times get tough. So what can we tell Mrs. Flynn about our friend, Marcie?"

"She's not my friend," Sharell mumbled.

"She's a good mother." Liza seemed to have found her voice again.

"She's no different than the rest of us." Danitra pitched her head Marcie's direction.

"Well, then you're saying she should have her kid back," Toni interjected. "If she's just like the rest of us, she should have her kid back. We all got *our* kids."

"Not all of us do," Danitra said, staring at Liza. "Not all of us got our kids."

Liza seemed to shiver where she sat. Arden reached out and touched her knee.

"Let's not get into things we know we can't change, Danitra." Ivy's voice had taken on a strange edge. Rachael turned to look at her. Her face for the first time was stern. Perhaps she was rushing to protect Liza or cutting Danitra off from saying any more. But then her features seemed to soften again. "Let's concentrate on how we can help Marcie."

Sharell surveyed the group. "Whatever mess Marcie is in is her own fault. It's about time she got that through her thick head."

"Sharell."

Sharell turned to Ivy. "Every time something happens to Marcie, it's always someone else's fault. I'm sick of it. We all have to take responsibility for our actions. All of us. Well, I've had it up to here with Marcie blaming everyone else for her problems. Every one of them is her own fault. You want us to support her? You want us to be there for her? How about we tell her the truth for once." Sharell turned to Marcie. "But you don't want to hear the truth, do you, Marcie? You just want to go on pretending the world owes you. The world don't owe you nothing! You drink, you use, you never worked a day in your life, and you don't even know who fathered this baby that just *disappeared* from your house. And you blame everybody else for it all. I don't want to hear any more about it." She turned her head around to face Ivy again. "We either move on to something else or I'm outta here."

"Marcie, how do you feel about what Sharell just said?" Ivy had watched a lot of TV to come up with that response, Rachael thought. She waited to hear what Marcie would say.

Marcie appeared unruffled and Rachael knew why. Sharell had done exactly what Marcie had hoped she would: demonstrated her keen hatred for her.

"I don't think Sharell wants to talk about this anymore." Marcie's tone was gentle. Liza cocked her head. Even she didn't appear to be buying it.

"Oh, give me a break!" Sharell exploded. "You're only saying that because *she's* here." Sharell pointed with her thumb toward Rachael. "If she weren't here, we'd spend the whole time talking about you. And only you." Sharell turned her head around to face Rachael. "The best days in this group are the ones she doesn't come to."

Rachael looked at Marcie. "I thought you came regularly to this group, Marcie."

"We all lead busy lives. She comes when she can," Ivy said quickly. "She always comes if she can."

"She comes when she's not drunk," Sharell grumbled.

"You're a liar," Marcie breathed.

"And you're pathetic."

"All right, ladies." Ivy raised her hands like a priest offering a benediction.

"Perhaps I should go." Rachael reached for her car keys in her pocket.

Marcie looked up at her, concern written on her face. It was clear Marcie was unsure if Rachael had seen enough.

"But you just got here," Ivy said, obviously unflustered by the last few minutes of discussion.

"I'm sure everyone would just like to be able to do what you normally do. I feel that I'm in the way." Rachael looked up at the circle of women. "Thanks for letting me visit. It was nice to meet you all."

"Bye!" Liza called out cheerfully. No one else said a word.

"Well, it was nice to have you." Ivy opened the door for Rachael, her ever-present grin wide. "You come back anytime."

"Thanks, Ivy."

The door shut behind her and Rachael stood for a moment on Ivy's porch, processing what she had just heard. She had no idea what to make of it. Sharell clearly didn't get along with Marcie, but the woman would have had absolutely nothing to gain by taking and abandoning Leo Shipley in a Dumpster. Unless she hoped Marcie would go to prison for it and would therefore no longer be a part of Ivy's group. But was Sharell that dependent on the group that she would murder a child so that she could be in the group and free of Marcie's presence at the same time? It didn't seem likely.

As she stood there, the door next to her opened and a silver-haired woman emerged holding a scatter rug full of crumbs.

"Good morning!" the woman said to Rachael. She began to shake the rug over the stoop railing onto a fading, twisted juniper.

"Hello." Rachael knew she had to be looking at June, the woman who cared for the kids in Ivy's support group. J.J. and Hallie were no doubt inside her house at that moment. "You must be June."

"Why, yes I am. You a friend of Ivy's?"

"Um, well, more like an acquaintance."

"You one of the mothers in her group?" The woman's face was creased with doubt.

"No. Actually, I work with the county. One of the moms is in a difficult spot. I'm just trying to make sense of things."

"Oh. You mean Marcie."

"Do you know Marcie well?"

June gave the rug one more toss. "Well, I only see her when she drops her kids off and then when she picks them up. But her kids are sweet little things. They sure don't look like they're being neglected in any way. They run to her when she comes for them."

"Do you know what happened to her baby?"

"I heard about it."

"May I ask you if you think Marcie could've done it? You don't have to answer me. I'm just trying to do the right thing here."

June was silent for a moment. "I honestly don't know, miss. I don't want to think that she did. But sometimes desperate people do desperate things, you know? These are tough times we're living in. I imagine if it was late at night, and if she'd been drinking or something, she might've done something like that, but I don't think she meant to hurt him. That's the difference, you know."

A second question was in the air between them before she had time to consider if she should ask it. "Do you have any reason to think Sharell could've had anything to do with this?"

"Sharell?" June's eyes grew wide. "If you're asking do I think Sharell did it *for* Marcie, I'd say no. I don't think those two get on very well. And there'd be no other reason for her to be involved."

"You watch Sharell's kids, too?"

"Oh yes. Two little boys. Good kids."

"Would you say she's a good mother?"

"Well, yes. I mean she's not perfect. None of those gals are. But they're trying, you know. They come to Ivy's group because they want to be good mothers." June peeked her head back inside her house. "I need to get back inside."

"Of course. I took too much of your time. I'm sorry."

"It's quite all right."

Rachael took a step and then turned back around. "This is wonderful, what you're doing for these women. Really. I wish there were more people who stepped in like this to help young mothers."

"This was all Ivy's idea. She's the visionary. She's a saint, is what she is. No one loves people like Ivy does."

"Well, thanks again," Rachael called out.

"Goodbye."

Rachael walked briskly up the block to her car, tossing the new information around in her head.

She had come for answers.

She was instead leaving with more questions.

What was Marcie truly capable of doing? No one was claiming she was a perfect mother, not even Marcie. Was she pointing fingers at Sharell to take the focus off herself? Or was Sharell's disgust with Marcie truly so deep that she'd want to harm her child? Or did the father of the baby want to rid himself of any responsibility and claims of paternity? And beneath all these questions was the niggling fact that Joyce Shipley was sure Marcie had done it. Marcie's own mother actually had the lowest opinion of her daughter's parenting skills.

It was often the least likely suspect who committed the crime, and that's usually who Rachael zeroed in on first. But who was the least likely?

As she crossed the street, Rachael withdrew her cell phone from her pants pocket and pressed the speed dial for Leslie at Human Services, hoping the social worker wasn't out on a call.

Rachael needed to start somewhere with what she'd just witnessed. Leslie might be able to shed some light on Ivy's group and the women who attended it. If Ivy's group had indeed been around for a year, perhaps Leslie had heard of it.

Rachael didn't know the last names of any of Ivy's young mothers, but she hoped Sharell wasn't a terribly common name.

TWELVE

Leslie picked up on the second ring. "This is Leslie."

"It's Rachael. Hey, are you busy this afternoon? I'd like to run some things by you."

"Hi, Rachael. If you come over right after lunch we can talk. But I've got appointments the rest of the day. What's up?"

Rachael pressed the button on her power lock and opened her car door. "I'm working on Marcie Shipley's case. I've got some information I think we need to look at."

"Really? What is it?"

Rachael slipped inside her car, closed the door, and leaned back into the seat. "You ever heard of Ivy Judson?"

"Ivy who?"

"Judson. She has a little support group on the south side for young single moms. She's not attached to any agency or anything. It's just something she does on her own."

"Oh, that's the group Marcie was talking about, right? This gal has it at her house."

"That's the one."

"You know, I think we've got another young mom in the system here who goes to that group. She's not one of mine, but I know who works her case."

Rachael sat forward. "Is her name Sharell?"

"No. I think it's Liza."

Rachael made a mental note to ask who handled Liza's case. "Does the name Sharell ring a bell? I don't know her last name."

Leslie paused on the other end. "I don't recall that first name, but I can ask around. Why? What's up?"

Rachael raised her eyes to the rearview mirror. The duplex looked rosy in the late morning sunlight. "Marcie told me one of the girls in Ivy's group, a gal named Sharell, hates her. She thinks this Sharell might've taken Leo."

Leslie's laugh was mixed with disbelief. "What on earth for?"

"I don't know. To teach her a lesson. To punish her for being a whiner. To get her out of the group. Or maybe there's a huge reason Sharell hates her that Marcie hasn't told me."

"So you've talked to Marcie about this?"

Rachael picked at a thread on her blouse. "She came by the office on Monday. With Ivy."

"Really?"

"She wanted Ivy to tell me what a good mother Marcie is, that she's attending the group, that she got off meth all on her own, that she's made a huge turnaround in her life and is therefore incapable of having done anything to harm Leo."

"Wow. So you believe all that?"

"Do you?"

Leslie exhaled heavily. "I don't believe anything without checking it out."

"Neither do I. That's why I'm calling you."

"Well, come on over after lunch and we'll see what we can find out. Unless you want to come right now. Are you at the courthouse?"

"No, actually I'm not." Rachael inserted her key into the ignition. "I'm just leaving Ivy Judson's."

"You *went* there?"

"Yes, I did. And please don't give me a hard time about it. I wanted to see it for myself. And I was only there for a few minutes."

"And what did you see?"

"Enough that I want to find out more about this woman named Sharell."

"Okay. See you right after lunch?"

"Yep. See you then." Rachael clicked off the phone and eased away from the curb.

The salmon-colored duplex fell away from view.

Leslie handed Rachael a Vikings coffee mug and took a seat across from her at her desk at Human Services.

"Thanks." Rachael sipped the coffee. Leslie had added caramel flavoring. It was good.

"Okay. I ate my lunch at my desk and I came up with a few things." Leslie took a sip from her own mug and set it down next to a muddy-brown file folder. "I thought Ann here in the office might know your Sharell since she's the caseworker for Liza Cooley. They're in that group together and perhaps her name's come up before."

Leslie sat forward. "Ann has only worked with Liza for the past eight months, but she does know Sharell. She worked with her two years ago. It was just for a short period of time. And it was for reasons completely different than what we've been monitoring Marcie for. Ann said Sharell Hodge was married to an abuser. The police had been to her apartment several times on domestics. Gordon Hodge was arrested at one point and charged with battery, but Sharell later dropped the charges and settled for a restraining order instead. Gordon Hodge was your typical power monger and continued to try and see her, made threats, the usual. Sharell wasn't completely innocent, either. Several of those initial domestics, she was the one who threw the first punch, broke the first window, yada yada. And she had been known to be verbally abusive to neighbors she didn't like. There were restraining orders out on her, too."

"But what about her kids? She has two little boys, right?" Rachael took another sip of the coffee.

"She was never charged or suspected of being abusive to her boys. There were a couple times when she requested respite care, and we gave it to her. Ann said Sharell hit some low points where she felt she just couldn't care for her boys. But she came to us and asked for help and actually admitted she was afraid she might hurt them. She agreed to take anger management and parenting classes. And Ann said Sharell never showed evidence of chemical dependency, so we never had to cross that ugly road with her. The boys were in respite care twice for two weeks each time. After they came home the second time, Sharell had in-home visits from Ann and a parenting specialist twice a week, sometimes three. That went on for four months. By that time, she and Gordon had divorced and he had moved to St. Louis. There hasn't been another file open on Sharell since then. She's on welfare and medical assistance but there hasn't been a Chips or even a need to monitor her for almost two years."

"Is that Sharell's file?" Rachael pointed to the folder under Leslie's hand.

"Yes."

"Is there anything in there about why Sharell was so angry?"

"It's nothing new, Rachael. She grew up in a tough neighborhood, was abused by an uncle, practically raised her two siblings, barely eked out a high school diploma, married a loser, and has never found her way out of poverty. It's the same stuff that makes a lot of people you and I work with angry."

"So there's nothing in there to suggest she's manic-depressive or schizophrenic or homicidal?"

"No, not at all. Well, I take it you met her. Did you think she was any of those things?"

Rachael's mind conjured an image of tall, slender Sharell—sharp-edged, cynical, a survivor. Bad-tempered, but not malicious. At least she didn't come across as malicious. Sharell didn't appear to need the group so badly that she'd kill someone's child to get rid of a member she didn't like. She instead came off as a person who had been forced to learn self-sufficiency. Besides, Sharell had told Rachael just that morning that she was going to leave Ivy's if the conversation remained centered on Marcie. Sharell clearly liked the group—otherwise she wouldn't come—and perhaps it was the only time she could get away from her kids. But she didn't come across as someone so dependent on the group—or so disgusted with Marcie—that harming Leo was her only course of action. If Sharell had intended to hurt Leo, it had nothing to do with Ivy's group.

"No," Rachael said. "I wouldn't have thought she was any of those things. Insensitive and ticked off, yes. But not crazy."

Leslie tapped another file on her desk. "Now, Liza's a different story."

"Liza?"

"Ann said she's quite likely schizophrenic or bipolar. It's hard to say. She's never been properly tested. The few tests she's had were inconclusive. Ann's been a little concerned that Liza thinks of Ivy Judson as a professional therapist. And she's not, of course. She's not a professional anything."

Rachael thought back to how quickly Liza's moods had swung from one extreme to the other in the few minutes Rachael had been at Ivy's. Cordial one moment, weepy the next, stunned the next, and then cordial again. She also remembered Danitra's comment that not everyone in Ivy's group had their kids with them and that she had been looking at Liza when she said it.

"Where are Liza's children?" Rachael asked.

"Child. A baby girl. She's with Liza's parents in Plymouth."

"What happened?"

"I guess Liza ran off with a guy her senior year of high school. That was last year. She came back six months later pregnant. Her parents took her in, but they tried to overmanage her life, so Ann says. A few weeks after the baby was born, Liza ran off again, this time with the baby. She was found under a freeway overpass three days later. She was practically catatonic. And the baby was severely dehydrated. She was sent to a mental hospital for two weeks and the baby went back to Liza's parents. When she got out, Liza voluntarily signed over custody to her parents. At least that's what the paperwork says. Liza says she was drugged and forced to sign the papers. Anyway, that was when Ann got on board with her. Liza wants her baby back. The parents want to terminate her parental rights.

It's a mess. The thing is, Ann thinks Liza *was* heavily sedated when her parents had her sign those documents."

"So where is Liza living? I take it not with her parents."

"No. She's living in an apartment here in St. Paul with a couple of friends from high school. She's working at a tattoo salon, lovely place, but Ann says she's got to hand it to her. She's working. She shows up every day. And she's seeing a mental health counselor. And taking medication for her mood swings."

Rachael took another sip of her coffee. This new view of Liza troubled her. In a sense, it introduced another wrinkle. Another possibility. If Liza had looked at her friend Marcie, who always sat by her and sometimes braided her hair, and saw that Marcie had a brand-new baby that she got to keep, what would she do in a dark, wild moment?

What was she capable of doing?

Could jealousy have pushed her over the edge?

"What are you thinking?" Leslie's voice pulled Rachael out of her tumbling thoughts.

"Just wondering if Liza maybe, was, you know, jealous of Marcie's new baby. And maybe..." Too outlandish to even say.

"And maybe Liza took Leo and dumped him?" Leslie's eyes were wide.

"Ridiculous, I know."

"Well, nothing in our business surprises me anymore. It could've happened that way, I guess. It just doesn't seem likely. And I have to say that most of the time when a child is abandoned like this, a parent is to blame."

Rachael fingered the coffee cup handle. "Has Marcie been to see Leo?"

"I took her to see him yesterday."

"And?"

Leslie shrugged. "Marcie cried when she held him. She nursed him. She kissed him over and over. And she cried when we left."

"Do you think it was an act?"

Leslie was quiet for a moment. "No. I don't."

"The thing is, Leslie, I can't see myself going into court and telling a judge Marcie shouldn't get her son back because we think she threw him in a Dumpster. We don't have a shred of proof that she did it. All I have are hunches."

"And what are your hunches telling you?"

Rachael ran her finger along the rim of the cup, touching the place where her lipstick kissed it. "That she didn't."

THIRTEEN

Will Pendleton sat across from Rachael at his desk at the St. Paul Police Department, sipping a peach Snapple. She had brought it to him.

"This isn't a bribe, is it?" He winked and held the drink high. His dark-brown features were creased in amusement.

"Hardly. I know you can't be bought with one peach Snapple." Rachael winked back and took a sip of her lime-laced Diet Coke.

"Something's on your mind, though."

She kept her eyes on the soda can in her hands. "I went to Marcie's little support group this morning."

"Rachael."

She looked up. "I know I should let the police do the investigative work, Will. But there would be no real reason for the police to look into this. I just have this gut feeling that Marcie is innocent. I only went there because Marcie told me there is someone who attends that group who hates her. Hates her enough that Marcie thinks she could've taken Leo."

"That sounds like reason enough for the police to look into it."

"Marcie hasn't a snippet of evidence that Sharell did it, though. And she told me she did mention it to the cops. She was asked if Sharell has

90

ever made any threats. Sharell hasn't. I don't think anyone's followed up on it, Will. And I can't say as I blame them. That's not much to go on."

"Still, it's not a good idea for you to be running around talking to people who could be potential suspects, unless you want to wind up on the other side of the witness stand. Like we haven't had *this* discussion before." Will saluted her with his drink and took a sip.

"I *wasn't* running around. And besides, those girls wouldn't have opened up to you or some other cop."

Will smiled. "And so they opened up to you, Ms. County Attorney?"

"Okay, okay. Most of them were restrained around me, too. But Marcie wasn't. And Ivy wasn't. And Sharell wasn't afraid to show me how she feels about Marcie. I was only there for a few minutes. And I saw enough to make me curious about the other girls who attend that group."

"You mean you have suspicions about more than one?"

"Well, yes I do."

"And I suppose you want us to check them out?"

"I know this isn't a top priority case, but I have to come up with a convincing argument against Marcie and I have to do it by next week for the Chips hearing. I don't have one, Will. There are plenty of hurdles I'd have to cross to prove she endangered her child. And if she didn't leave Leo in that Dumpster, then someone else did. I know it's not my job to figure out who that person is, but I have to consider it. I have to know whether or not it's even conceivable that someone else could've done it."

Will pulled a blank pad of paper close to him and picked up a pen. "What are their names?"

"Sharell Hodge and Liza Cooley. Marcie gave you Sharell's name already. She probably has a record. She's been involved in some domestics, and she's had a restraining order out on her."

"That's not the same thing as a criminal record, Rachael. You know that."

"Yes, of course. But it bears witness to her character. It matters. *You* know that."

Will smiled. "And this Liza Cooley? Who is she?"

"She's only nineteen, and she's got some significant mental health issues. Her baby girl was taken from her when she was found with her daughter under a freeway overpass. She had been missing for three days.

The baby was severely dehydrated. The grandparents have custody at the moment."

"And you're suspicious because?"

"I'm just wondering if she might have taken Leo because she's jealous. Perhaps she was angry that Marcie got to keep him."

"So she took Leo and threw him in a Dumpster?"

"Maybe."

"Wouldn't it make more sense for her to take Leo and keep him for herself?"

"Yeah, it would make more sense. But she's not well. Her caseworker thinks she might be schizophrenic or bipolar or maybe some combination of both. Liza wouldn't necessarily do what makes sense."

"Anyone else?"

"Have you guys checked out who might be the father?"

Will put his pen down. "I don't know if those leads have been followed up on. I can check."

"Can you? Like right now?"

"Right now."

"Please?"

Will put his Snapple on his desk and stood. "I'll be right back."

He returned a few minutes later, accompanied by a woman Rachael had seen in the department before but had never met. The woman looked to be about her age, a little taller. More freckles. Rachael stood to greet them.

"Rachel, this is Lindy Kirby. She's working the case. Lindy, Rachael Flynn."

"Hello." Rachael reached for Lindy's outstretched right hand. The woman's grasp was firm. In her left hand she held a file folder.

"I hear you've got some questions for me?"

"If you don't mind."

"Not at all." Lindy pulled up a chair and Rachael sat back down. Will walked back to his desk, grabbing his Snapple as he retook his chair.

"Will has told you I'm on the Chips for Leo Shipley?" Rachael said.

"He said you were wondering if we've come up with anything on criminal charges."

Rachael leaned forward. "Yes. If you've been able to build a felony case against her, I'd like to know what you've got. To tell you the truth, I'm having a hard time proving she actually dumped her baby in a Dumpster."

"Hard time proving it or a hard time believing it?" Lindy's tone was civil.

"Both. She doesn't fit the usual profile, she doesn't have a car, and she had just given birth. And she insists she didn't do it."

"We've been considering those things, too."

"Lindy, Marcie mentioned to me that the two men who might've fathered the child were both pretty adamant that they didn't want anything to do with this baby."

"Yeah, she told us that, and we did look into it. One of them, Vince Arigulo, left the state three months ago. He's got a pretty tight alibi. He was in South Dakota the night Leo Shipley was abandoned, and the woman he's living with will attest to it."

"And the other one?"

"That'd be Booth Rubian." Lindy opened the file she held in her hand and handed Rachael a standard mug shot. Booth Rubian wore a look of defiance before the camera lens. His chin and cheeks were peppered with stubble and his light-brown hair fell about his face in a tangle. As Rachael's mother liked to say, he looked like trouble.

Lindy went on. "Booth Rubian has spent some time in jail over the years—aggravated assault, driving with a suspended license, driving with an open bottle, possession. He's not exactly the kind of guy you want to bring home to mama. He lives in Mendota Heights, so he's not too far from Marcie's neighborhood. He said he was at home asleep the night Leo was taken. His brother lives with him and works nights, so the guy doesn't have the best alibi. The brother left for work at ten-thirty and Booth was home. When the brother got home at a quarter to six the next morning, Booth was in his bed asleep."

"That's not an alibi at all." Will sat back in this chair and laced his fingers across his chest.

"No, it's not."

"Does he have a car?" Rachael asked.

"He does."

"Does he deny being Leo's father?"

"Well, he can't know for sure because he and Marcie did have intercourse. He admits that. But he was quick to say he wasn't the only one Marcie has been intimate with. He said there was a party back in December, and that Marcie was there and high on something. And that a lot of other men were there, too. He refused to take a paternity test. It would have to be court-ordered before he'd agree to one. And Marcie didn't list him as the father on the birth cert, so it might be tough to get a judge to sign off on it. Marcie listed the father as 'unknown.' And you know what? I don't think she does know. Not for sure."

"What if we did get a court order and he did have to submit to a test? And what if we all found out he *is* the father? Does he know the county could garnish his wages for child support?" Rachael said.

"Yeah. I think so," Lindy said. "He already has two children in another county. So I think he understands how the system works."

"So he knows that if he's Leo's father, a court will order him to pay child support for the next eighteen years?"

"I'd say he knows that. I wouldn't be surprised if Vince Arigulo left Minnesota precisely because of that. I think he was surprised we found him so easily."

Rachael turned to Will. "What do you think?"

Will unlaced his fingers. "Anything is possible, really. It's possible Mr. Rubian had nothing to do with this and possible he had everything to do with it. It's even possible that he and Marcie were in cahoots. Perhaps Rubian told her from the beginning he wasn't going to be a father to this child and she decided after she had Leo that she really didn't want to be a mother to him. So she contacted Rubian. Maybe she was drunk when she called him. He drove over to her place in the middle of the night, and they either dumped the baby together, or she told him to dump the baby wherever he pleased. In the morning, when she realized what she had done, she called the police and cooked up the abduction story, not implicating Rubian in the slightest, of course. In fact, maybe she has you looking at Sharell to keep your eyes off Rubian."

"Sharell? The woman in her support group?" Lindy looked from Rachael to Will.

"Rachael met Sharell Hodge today." Will cocked his head toward Rachael. "She went to that Ivy Judson's support group."

Lindy turned her head back to face Rachael. "You did?"

"I was only there for a few minutes. Marcie wanted me to meet Ivy so that Ivy could essentially be a character witness for her. I met Sharell while I was there. Marcie told me earlier that Sharell hates her. She thinks Sharell hates her enough to want to harm her baby."

"I talked to Sharell Hodge a few days ago," Lindy continued. "Marcie gave us her name when she insisted her baby had been kidnapped. I didn't tell Ms. Hodge I was questioning her motives, but I think she picked up on it. I just asked her if she knew anyone, anyone in the group perhaps, who would've had a reason to harm Leo Shipley."

"What did she say?" Rachael said.

"She said the only person in the group who has a reason to harm Leo Shipley is Marcie Shipley."

"Why? Why does she think that?"

"Because, Sharell said, Marcie Shipley never learns from her mistakes, never takes any responsibility for her mistakes, and doesn't deserve to be a mother."

"How would Sharell know all this?" Will interjected.

"Because, and again this is from Sharell, Marcie talks at the support group. A lot. She tells the group that she leaves liquor lying around, that she forgets to lock her front door, that sometimes she leaves a mark when she spanks J.J. too hard, that her male friends leave their crack at her house, that sometimes she wants to just get on a plane—without her kids—and start over. Maybe Marcie thinks confession is good for the soul, but Sharell is clearly disgusted with her."

"Disgusted enough to do something about it?" Rachael asked.

"Sharell has nothing to gain by killing Leo Shipley," Lindy replied. "If she wanted to be the cause of Marcie's undoing, all she would have to do is call Child Protection Services and rat Marcie out."

"But what if she thinks all that will happen is that Marcie will get a slap on the wrist?" Will said. "I mean, Marcie's been monitored by Child Protection Services before. She knows how to do and be what the county expects."

"Okay, but why kill Leo?" Lindy countered. "What does she have to gain by it? And it's no secret she doesn't like Marcie. Why do something so terrible when people already know you don't like the victim?"

Rachael's head was spinning. "So is Booth a suspect?"

Lindy lifted her shoulders. "Potentially."

"And Marcie?"

"I'd say Marcie and Sharell both are. And Will tells me you've got another name for me. Liza Cooley? She might be one, too. We just don't have enough information to label anyone a suspect at the moment. Certainly not enough to arrest anyone."

Lindy stood.

Rachael stood as well. "Thanks, Lindy."

"Anytime."

Lindy turned to go.

"Lindy, when you talk to Liza, can you be gentle with her? I don't want her to think we suspect her of anything. She likes Marcie. And she's not... she's not well. Mentally. If she did drop Leo in that Dumpster, she may not remember it. Or she might've blocked it out."

Lindy started for Will's door. "I understand." She turned and left.

Rachael sat back down and picked up her Diet Coke. The names swirled around in her head. Marcie. Booth. Sharell. Liza. And what about Joyce and Koko? They had made it clear they didn't want Marcie to have another baby. Could either one of them have done something so heinous to their own flesh and blood?

Or was it none of these? Was it just an evil stranger who preyed upon a three-day-old infant for no other reason than the thrill of the abduction and the baby's ultimate, horrible end? "Too many suspects, Will," she murmured.

He smiled back at her. "Too many is always better than none at all."

FOURTEEN

Trace cupped his hand over the phone and called out to Rachael across the kitchen. "Fig wants to know if he can bring the hors d'oeuvres."

Rachael stirred a pot of marinara sauce bubbling on the stove as McKenna, at her feet, emptied a cabinet of mixing bowls. The Friday get-together with Fig, Sidney, and Brick was at their place that night. "We're just having spaghetti. Did you tell him that?"

Trace smirked at her. "I did. He told me not to tell you that, in Italy, spaghetti *is* the hors d'oeuvre."

Rachael tapped the spoon against the side of the pot. "No, it's not. It's a side dish."

"Da!" McKenna announced, holding up an orange measuring cup.

"I think he would still win any argument about there not being a main dish," Trace replied.

"If you serve it as a main dish, it's a main dish." Rachael placed the spoon atop a ceramic tile on the counter. "Cup," she said to McKenna, and then lifted her head to look at Trace. "I suppose he's not bringing just cheese and crackers?"

But Trace only smiled and pulled his hand away from the phone.

"That'd be great, Fig. Oh, sure. No, I'm sure Rachael will like that. See you at seven."

He placed the phone handset back in its cradle and walked over to his daughter, scooping her up in his arms. McKenna squealed.

"Well?" Rachael said, unable and unwilling to put her hands on her hips.

"Chicken-liver crostini."

Rachael winced.

Trace lifted McKenna high above him. "What? It's Italian, Rach. It's perfect."

She leaned against the counter and watched McKenna grin and coo above Trace's head. "Molly and Sid won't eat it."

"They will if they don't know what's in it."

Rachael laughed. "Molly won't eat anything of Fig's without asking him what's in it."

"That's why Fig's going to tell everyone you made them."

"Oh no he's not!"

"C'mon. Be a pal. Molly and Sid are culinary cowards. Fig's just trying to wake up their boring palates."

Rachael turned to a cabinet behind her and opened it. "That's Fig talking. Besides, I don't want Fig saying I made something when I didn't. That's a lie." She withdrew a stack of plates and placed them on the countertop.

Trace came up behind her with McKenna in his arms and kissed the back of her neck. "That's Rachael the lawyer talking."

Rachael hesitated for a second and then eased her body backward onto her husband's chest.

McKenna reached out a stubby hand to touch her face. "Nom!"

"That's just who I am," Rachael murmured.

The three of them stood there for a moment, within each other's loose embrace.

"So you want to keep doing this?" Trace's voice tickled her ear.

"I like standing in the kitchen with you and McKenna."

Trace laughed. "I think you know what I mean."

"I'm guessing you mean me working. Or you watching McKenna the days I'm working?"

Trace tipped his head against hers. "All of it. These cases you work on, they drain you, especially the tough ones. I see it when you're not at the office. Your mind is always on them. Like this one right now with that baby. Maybe it's time for a little break."

Rachael let Trace kiss her temple. She closed her eyes, letting his words sink in. "And McKenna? You think McKenna suffers because of it?"

"No. No, I don't. But McKenna's not an infant anymore, Rach. She's walking, getting into things at the studio. When I'm alone with her there, I don't get anything done. Fig doesn't complain because Fig wouldn't, but he spends a lot of time chasing after her, too."

Rachael turned her head to look at her daughter. McKenna had her thumb in her mouth with her cheek against Trace's collarbone. The little girl smiled at her around the shape of her thumb. "So you're saying it's not working anymore."

"I'm saying we need to start talking day care or hiring a nanny. And I know how you feel about crowded day-care centers…" Trace's voice trailed off.

"So you're thinking I should quit."

"I'm not asking you to quit," Trace said quickly. "But we're going to have to do something. I can't get any work done in the studio when she's there. And I hate to even say it, but I am on a contract."

Rachael sighed. "I know you are."

"I'm only suggesting you think about taking a little break because you seem like you need it. And we need to do something about McKenna."

Trace was right. Lately she had been unable to leave work where it belonged. And she did spend her waking moments at home consumed by the cases she was working on. But how could she not? The cases mattered. Each one was far more than just the court file that held the documentation. The cases were about children in crisis. And the work she did on their behalf had formed her adult identity. She had thought of nothing else besides juvenile law and its exercise since high school.

"I don't know what I'd do with myself all day if I didn't have this," she whispered. "I don't know if I could give it up completely."

"We're only talking a little break, Rachael. Until McKenna's a little older and we feel okay about leaving her with someone. Besides, I bet you could find a less stressful outlet for your passions. You could volunteer for the

Legal Aid Society or be a consultant or work for the county as one of their contracted experts."

Rachael smiled up at him. "You've been thinking about this for a while."

He grinned back at her. "Haven't you?"

She rested her head back on his chest. "It's just I think of that baby, Leo Shipley, and every other child whose little lives are so complicated by the mistakes and crimes of people who are supposed to care for them. Some of these kids are so neglected, Trace. You wouldn't believe some of the things people do to their children."

"Someone else can do that job for a while, Rach. There are others who feel the way you do, who know what you know, and who can argue it in court."

Rachael was silent for a moment. "I need to think about this. Pray about it. There's just too much happening right now for me to think clearly."

"It's that one case, isn't it? The one with the baby?"

"It's just all so gray. Nothing about it is black and white, Trace. Except that a baby was left for dead in a trash bin. I can't seem to get a grip on the mother's personality. I don't think she did it, but who else would?"

Trace began to sway with Rachael and McKenna in his arms. "Ah, well, you should have come to the Artners in Crime at the beginning of this abandoned-baby investigation, *cherie*."

Rachael laughed lightly. "*Artners* in Crime?"

"That's Fig's creative mind at work. Fig thinks he, Sid, Brick, and I could figure this one out for you. Just like we did those other two cases. Your brother's and that Randall Buckett's. You know. When we drew the sketches of how the crimes might've gone down."

"You guys didn't figure it out! Even I didn't figure it out with just the pictures you drew."

"Okay. So I exaggerate. But you have to admit when we drew the different scenes, you began to put two and two together. Both times. It's true. Admit it."

He had a point. Twice the artists had helped her flesh out two cases that had her and the police stumped. Twice she figured out the case before the police did. "Okay. The drawings helped."

"So. The Artners in Crime are on tonight?"

Rachael pulled away from Trace to stir the sauce. "Maybe the guys won't want to do it."

"Fig already told me he does. Brick will do whatever Fig does. And Sidney will do it so he can complain about it."

"Fig." Rachael shook her head and set the spoon down.

"He gets into this, Rach. It makes him feel like he's doing something important."

"All right. But no names. I'm not giving out any names."

Trace set McKenna down. "No names."

"And you guys have to promise not to say a word about it to other people. Especially Sid. He can't say a word to his friends in the newsroom."

"Done. And you'll think about the other thing?"

Rachael picked up the spoon to give the marinara another stir, though it didn't need it. "I'll think about it."

"So, what's that on top of the bread?" Sid's wife, Molly, whispered to Rachael as she peered at the embellished slices of toasted baguette resting on a stoneware platter.

"Don't ask," Rachael murmured back to her. She and Molly were standing in the kitchen as Rachael put the finishing touches on a Caesar salad. Sid, Brick, and Trace were admiring a drawing Fig had just brought into the open living room.

"If I can't ask, then I won't eat it," Molly said.

"You won't eat it either way, Moll."

Trace looked up at her from across the room. "Rachael, come see Fig's drawing."

Molly and Rachael made their way into the living room. Fig, beaming in a pair of deconstructed jeans and a seventeenth-century-style swashbuckler tunic, stood next to an easel. Resting on the wooden frame was a sepia and white drawing of Jillian under a willow tree. The only color was in her eyes. One green, one blue.

"That's lovely, Fig," Rachael said.

"Look closer, Kumquat."

"Excuse me?"

"Come." Fig held out his hand, took hers, and led her to within inches of the drawing. "Look closer."

Rachael bent at the waist and examined the ink. Within the strokes of the drawing were words: curled script in Jillian's hair, in her flowing skirt, up and down her slender arms, in the willow branches above her head. "Oh my goodness, Fig. What does it say?"

"Look and see!" he whispered.

Rachael cocked her head, moved in closer, and read the flowing words on Jillian's outstretched left arm. "You are my sun and moon. My east and west." In Jillian's long hair: "My life began when you became a part of it." And in her skirt: "You are heaven's gift to me."

She looked away from the messages clearly meant for Jillian to read. "It's really beautiful, Fig."

"Look here." Fig pointed to the squiggly drop of sunlight in Jillian's open palm.

Rachael squinted and saw two words: "Marry me."

The drawing was Fig's proposal.

Rachael looked up and smiled at him. "Very clever, Fig."

"Think she'll like it?"

Rachael looked back at the drawing. "She'll love it."

"When does she get back from Morocco?" Molly was kneeling at the drawing, studying the love lines.

"Ten days!"

"So are you all set, Fig Newton?" Trace patted his friend on the back.

"I've got everything but the iguana." Fig clapped his hands once. "Now then. Enough gawking at my drawing. I don't want you to see what's written on her ankle. Let's try that appetizer. I'm starving and I bet Rachael's made something delicious!"

Fig strode confidently into the open kitchen leaving his friends to wonder if the iguana was to be an engagement gift to Jillian or a dish to be eaten.

The aroma of garlic and basil hung in the air long after the plates of spaghetti were consumed and the crème brûlée eaten. A few slices of chicken-liver crostini lay untouched on the platter. Rachael made a second pot of coffee as Trace got out sketch pads and a Kerr jar full of art pencils. He placed them on the now-cleared dining room table.

"We've all promised to take any information you give us to our lonely graves, haven't we, Sidney?" Fig poked Sid with a red-barreled art pencil.

"I know how this works." Sid pushed the pencil away.

"Okay. Give us the partics, Kumquat. Don't worry about names. We'll invent some good ones. Then you and Moll go knit a sweater or something. I can't draw if you're looking at me."

"Why is it you can sculpt while people look at you but you can't draw?" Brick's brow was creased in consternation. "That makes no sense."

"We're talking about Fig, Brick," Sid muttered. "Do the math."

"Okay!" Fig seemed to have happily ignored the question and the answer. "We're ready, Rachael. Fire away."

Rachael took a breath and then began to describe what she knew. "The baby is three days old. He was found by sanitation workers in a Dumpster ten blocks from his mother's apartment. The mother doesn't have a car. She is young, single, and she was drinking the night the baby was taken. She has used drugs before but she tested clean and she says she hasn't used anything since she found out she was pregnant. She can't remember getting up to feed the baby in the middle of the night. She can't remember locking the front door. She has two other kids, and none of them have the same father.

"Her mother and her older sister have helped her out through the years but they are both clearly tired of it. Both of them feel that this gal is in way over her head and isn't responsible enough to raise a third child. The sister had told her to get an abortion. The mother told me not to give the baby back to her daughter.

"The father is believed to be one of two men. The mother isn't sure. She had been to a party nine months earlier and had taken some kind of party drug and she doesn't exactly remember who she was with. Both the men in question claim not to be the father. One left the state and was two hundred miles away when the baby was dumped. The other lives nearby.

He has a car. And he has two kids from another relationship, so he knows how much child support is. He has a record. And he wants nothing to do with this baby. He refuses to take a paternity test.

"The baby's mother belongs to a support group for young, single moms run by a do-gooder who once upon a time was a single mother herself. At this group there is a woman who clearly dislikes the mother of the abandoned baby. Loathe might be a better word. There is also a young woman there who suffers from mental illness whose baby girl was taken from her by the county. She likes Marcie a lot, but she's suspected of being schizophrenic or bipolar or maybe a mixture of both.

"The mother of the abandoned baby insists she didn't do it. She wants her baby back."

Rachael stopped. The artists were staring at her.

"This one's too hard," Sid said a second later, putting his pencil down. "This isn't about drawing a scene. It's about drawing a motive. Who can know that with just three minutes of information? Who can draw that?"

"Oh, put a lid on it, Sid," Fig scolded, turning over a fresh piece of paper. "Just because something's hard doesn't mean it can't be done."

"Doesn't mean it can, either," Sid grumbled. He picked up his pencil. "And would it be too much to ask for some plain cheese and crackers?"

FIFTEEN

An hour and a half after Rachael and Molly were sent away to let the artists work, they were called back.

"We drew names!" Fig announced as he led Rachael to the dining room table, cleared of everything but five sketches turned upside down. Molly filled in a gap at the table by Sid and leaned in for a better view. "We named the baby Tiny Tim," Fig continued. "Mom is Babs, dad the loser is Rufus, psycho girl at the group is Sybil, angry girl at the group is Zena, and disgusted sister is Cruella."

Sid, seated at the table, looked up at Rachael. "Can you tell who picked the names?"

Brick, sitting next to Sid, turned to him and frowned. "Hey, I picked the name Tiny Tim." He looked up at Rachael. "Fig picked the others."

"And don't even bother telling him that he spelled *Xena* wrong," Sid continued.

"I don't like anything spelled with an *X*." Fig shrugged. "*Z* is a much prettier letter. *X*'s are for tic-tac-toe and pirate treasure."

Rachael smiled. "Those are very interesting names, Fig."

"Yes, they are. Okay, so Sid the whiner got Rufus the loser, Tracer drew

Sybil in all her forms, Brick got Zena with a Z—which is cool because he's always been a little afraid of warrior princesses—and I got Cruella. Nobody pulled Babs out of my beret, so we took turns on her drawing. Ready to see what we've come up with?"

Fig turned over the first drawing, a series of cartoon boxes with Sid's name scrawled at the bottom. In the first panel a man—whom only Rachael knew to be Booth—was shown in Marcie's apartment, standing with his hands in his pants pockets, and looking aloof and disinterested in his surroundings. In front of him was Marcie, disheveled, bleary-eyed with one hand raised in exasperation. In the other she held a liquor bottle. Above her head was a dialogue bubble: "I never wanted this baby! This is all your fault." In the second frame, Booth calmly told Marcie, "No one forced you to have the kid." Next, Marcie wagged a finger at Booth. "It's *your* kid! And where were you when I could've done something about it? Nowhere!" A shrugging Booth said, "It ain't my kid." In the fourth panel, Marcie had sunk into the couch with the bottle inches from her lips. Above her head was a dialogue bubble: "You knew I had taken something that night at the party. It wasn't consensual. Yeah, I know what that word means. A good lawyer would, too." By frame number five, Marcie had passed out on the couch. Booth was looking at the crib in the far corner of the room. The sixth frame showed an open front door, a night sky beyond it, and a blanket lying where it fell by the legs of the crib.

"So, why wouldn't she just tell the police it was, um, Rufus who took the baby?" Rachael looked up at Sid.

"If she were rip-roaring drunk she might not have remembered he was even there."

"And his motive for killing the baby would've been the threat of a date rape charge, not child support."

Sid lifted his shoulders. "If the baby is the only evidence against him, then yeah, that makes more sense to me than ditching the baby to avoid his pay being docked. A guy like that could dodge child support. He wouldn't have to commit murder to do it. But I got his name. Fig made me draw him."

Rachael looked down at the cartoon blanket lying in a tumble on the floor. It could've happened that way. Could've. But why would Booth have come to Marcie's apartment that night? What brought him there?

He wouldn't have come unless Marcie begged him. Or threatened him.

Rachael moved on to the next drawing and turned it over. The broad strokes and semi-impressionistic faces were clearly Brick's.

He had drawn Sharell, tall and imposing, with X's dangling from her ears.

"What are those?" Fig peered down at the drawing and the woman's head.

"Earrings." Brick popped a cracker in his mouth.

Sid laughed. "Good one, Brickman!"

The drawing was simple, no props in the background, not even a baby. Brick had drawn Sharell in a standing pose with a fist raised and an expression of loathing on her face. As Rachael looked closer, she could see that Brick had scrawled words into the woman's flesh and clothes.

"I borrowed Figgy's idea." Brick pointed to the word *disgust* scrawled across the woman's torso. "This chick has to have some pretty powerful emotions boiling inside to want to kill another woman's child. So I just kept piling them on."

Rachael rotated the drawing, seeing words materialize as the paper turned on the table: Fury. Rage. Resentment. Vengeance. Defiance. Wrath. Fear. Blame. Bitterness. Hostility. Vexed.

Rachael noted with a slight grin that Brick had drawn the x in *vexed* with particular flourish.

"I wonder why this woman would hate her so much," Rachael said, as she righted the drawing.

"Guess you'd have to go back in time and figure it out," Brick replied. "I think it would have to be way intense. Not just a cat fight over who got the best parking place at the support group. I'm thinking Babs here did something or threatened to do something to the warrior princess. Something big."

"Okay, now look at mine!" Fig turned over the third drawing.

Fig had drawn Koko as the famed Cruella DeVil, down to the two-toned wild hair and flowing furs. His drawing showed her zooming away from a Dumpster in a classic convertible, head thrown back and laughing wickedly. An emaciated alley cat, peeking out from behind a crumbling box, was hissing as Koko-as-Cruella sped away.

"That's horrible, Fig!" Molly exclaimed. "Disgusting!"

"Yes, it is!" Fig replied, matching her tone.

"No woman would do that to a baby for such a silly reason as being fed up with baby-sitting!" Molly continued.

"Indeed!" said Fig.

"So why did you draw it, Fig?" Rachael asked.

"To show you how it couldn't have happened, Kumquat. I don't think the sister did it. She'd have to be a monster. And even monsters have reasons for doing horrible things. Usually it's because they're hungry. I don't see that she has a reason. Do you?"

Rachael didn't even know what Koko looked like. It was hard to picture the woman leaving her nephew to die in a trash bin when she stood to gain nothing. If it was freedom Koko wanted, all she had to do was to refuse to help Marcie any longer. The same held true for Joyce.

"No, Fig. I don't."

"Well, then! There you go. Moving on!" Fig turned over the next drawing. The finely etched anatomical features were Trace's, perfectly proportionate and hauntingly beautiful. Rachael would know her husband's interpretation of the human body anywhere.

Trace had drawn Liza, aka Sybil, in three phases. In the first she was bent over in grief, clutching her shoulders as if to hug herself. At her bent knees was a pair of baby booties—a symbol of the child she bore but from which she was separated. Underneath the drawing was the word *despair*. In the second, Liza was shown reaching into a crib in a darkened room, her face expressionless, except for her eyes, which were almost feral. Beneath that drawing was the word *desperation*. In the third, Liza was drawn with an arm around Marcie, her smile an unmistakable mix of sincerity and compassion, her eyes liquid with sympathetic tears. Below the drawing was the word *disconnect*.

The eyes told the story more than anything else. Liza, if she was indeed schizophrenic, moved in and out of control. In and out of hostility. And she was likely unaware of the constant shifting.

"That gal kind of gives me the creeps," Sid murmured as he stared at Trace's sketches of Liza's three faces.

"Me, too," Molly whispered. "Her eyes are so spooky, Trace."

"What do you think, love?" Trace said to Rachael.

Rachael fingered the penciled face of Liza, devoid of emotion, as she reached into Leo Shipley's crib.

"I think we could be on to something here," Rachael said, never taking her eyes off the drawing.

Sid sat back in his chair. "Lover boy wins again."

Brick tossed his pencil on the table and leaned back, too. "She always likes Trace's stuff better than mine."

Rachael raised her head. "That's not true, Brick. Yours is really good, too."

"Yeah. Uh-uh."

"Don't go getting out the snacks for the pity party, you two!" Fig scolded. "We still have the last one." He turned over the fifth sketch.

"Oh, that!" Sid snorted. "That's practically all yours, Fig!"

"Not so, Squidney. You wanted Babs to have a beret like mine and I gave her one. Here we go, Kumquat. Last one."

Rachael looked at the drawing Fig had uncovered. The artistry was indeed mostly Fig's. Marcie wore Fig's beret on her head, but the loopy, elongated eyes were surely influenced by Brick and her lovely hands were courtesy of Trace. The rest of the drawing was Fig in motion. He had drawn her in two frames. In the first, Marcie rode a Harley with plumes of fire for exhaust while holding a bundle in her arms, and in the other, she rode a unicorn back to her apartment. No bundle.

Rachael looked up at Fig. "This makes no sense."

"That's because she's on drugs."

"But she tested clean the next day."

"Aren't there ways to beat those tests, love?" Trace said.

"I've heard there are drugs you can take to mask other drugs," Sid added.

Rachael knew this to be true. It was easy to buy masking agents, especially on the Internet. But being able to take those cleansing drugs the morning Marcie woke up and figured out what she had done meant she had to have them on hand.

"How would she have known she was going to need those masking drugs?" Rachael wondered aloud. "She's not working so she's not subject to drug testing. She wasn't being monitored by Human Services for drug use. Why would she have had them on hand?"

"Maybe she called a friend who she knew would have some, before she called the police," Molly ventured.

"Maybe..." Rachael absently rubbed her temple. Marcie didn't come across as that organized. The young mother would have to be a fairly analytical thinker to assume the police would suspect her and press her for a drug test. That image didn't measure up to the Marcie that Rachael had met.

And if Marcie had been on some kind of drug, that again brought up the question of how she got to the Dumpster and back home again. Was she lucid enough to call a cab? Or had she indeed walked twenty blocks round trip? Without being seen?

"So?" Fig said.

Rachael looked up from the drawings. "You guys did a great job, really."

"Have it all figured out?" Sid said genially, and the room erupted in easy laughter.

Everyone in the room knew she didn't.

"Thanks, everybody. You're the best." Rachael pulled the drawings close to her.

"No problemo, Kumquato!" Fig looked around the table. "Hey. Anyone want me to warm up Rachael's appetizers?"

"Molly and I know where those little slabs of science experiment came from, Fig," Sid replied, cocking his head. "Nice try. No, I don't want you to warm up *your* appetizers."

And neither did anyone else. The friends slowly moved away from the dining room table—Brick to the drawing of Jillian where he announced loudly that "I love your mutant pinkie toe" was scrawled across the subject's ankle; Sid, Molly, and Fig to the living room sofa where Fig began to lecture on the merits of an exotic diet; and Trace to Rachael's side at the table, where he told her gently to leave the drawings and come join the others.

The dream came to her that night, many hours after the evening had ended and the artists had left. The loft was awash in silence.

Rachael stood in a dark alley, shivering. Fig's alley cat was perched on a sagging box, watching her with languid eyes. She sensed movement behind her, but when she turned she saw nothing but darkness. She reached out her hands and felt a cool surface. Hard. Smooth. The trash bin.

The baby within it began to wail.

Terrified, Rachael reached inside the Dumpster, though she could see nothing. Her hands flailed and her fingers clutched at discarded fabric. Yards of it. The baby would suffocate.

The cries intensified.

She couldn't find the baby. She banged on the side of the Dumpster and tried to scream for help, but her voice was silent in her throat.

The cries were piercing, growing louder, filling the whole alley.

With one hand, Rachael banged the Dumpster in frustration and with the other she fought through heavy fabric, looking for the baby. She couldn't find him! The cries enveloped her, stung her.

Arms were suddenly on her shoulders, pulling her away from the Dumpster.

"No!" she screamed and her voice broke through. "NO!"

"Rachael!"

The baby's cries were instantly silenced and Rachael awoke with Trace's arm around her.

She was standing at the picture window in her bedroom; a loosely hung curtain half off its rod, clutched in one hand. Her other hand, covered by Trace's, was flat against the window.

The glass was marked with a tattoo of body heat where she had been pounding, pounding, pounding the window with an open palm.

SIXTEEN

Trace handed Rachael a mug of green tea and she wrapped her fingers around it, leaning back on the couch in her living room and letting the warmth of the cup permeate the skin on her palm.

He sat down next to her with a cup of his own, bringing it to his lips as he eased his body next to hers, but never taking his eyes off his wife. Rachael could feel his eyes on her.

She looked up at him. "I'm sorry, Trace."

Trace reached out his free hand and laid his arm across her shoulder. "Nothing to be sorry for, Rach. You had a bad dream. No one has to apologize for having a bad dream."

"But I scared you. I'm sorry for that."

He squeezed her shoulder and laughed, but the sound of it was filled with uneasiness. "Yeah, you scared me. I really thought you were going to break the window. It's a long way down." He sipped his tea. "Good thing the glass is double-paned."

"I'm really sorry." Tears stung at Rachael's eyes. She wasn't sure why.

"You don't have to be sorry. It's not your fault. It was a dream." Trace's voice was gentle. Soothing.

"It seemed real," she whispered.

"But it wasn't real."

"There was a baby in the Dumpster, Trace. I heard him. There was all this material on top of him and he was going to suffocate. I couldn't get it off of him."

"Rachael. You were sleepwalking. You got tangled up in the curtains. That's all."

Rachael exhaled heavily and enclosed her cup with her other hand. "I've never done that before. I've never sleepwalked. And it seemed so *real.*"

Trace leveled his eyes at her. "It was just a dream."

Rachael looked up at him. "It was more than a dream."

"What are you saying?" Trace's voice had taken a slight edge. She knew she was making no sense.

"I've had nightmares before, Trace. They weren't like this. I could hear this baby. I felt the damp of the alley. I could smell it."

"So, what are you saying?" Trace repeated, and apprehension now laced his words.

"I don't know, Trace. I just…It wasn't like a normal dream. It was like it was real. Like I was really there. I could feel it all. Touch it all. The Dumpster, the cold, my fear, the cat…"

"The cat."

"Fig's cat. It was like I could reach out and touch it."

"Fig's cat?"

She was talking nonsense. It didn't feel like nonsense but she knew it sounded like it. "That scrawny alley cat Fig drew in his sketch. By the Dumpster. That was in the dream, too."

"Rachael."

"I know how that sounds. But, Trace, I'm telling you this wasn't an ordinary dream. It was different somehow. I haven't felt like this since last spring. Back when I was working the Randall Buckett case. Remember? Whenever I was near that house…"

She didn't finish. She didn't have to. Trace knew which house she was talking about—the one on Randall Buckett's street, the one that had burned down years ago and yet still had called out to her, coaxing her to consider what had happened inside before flames swept it away.

"But you didn't dream anything beyond what you already know, hon," Trace said. "You dreamed of a baby in a Dumpster in an alley. That's already happened. And the baby *was* found in time. There's nothing there that you don't already know. *I* could've had that dream. Fig could've."

She said nothing and sipped the tea. It was sweet and pungent. Calming.

"It just feels different," she said. "Like I was meant to notice something."

"Well, what?"

She hadn't a clue. "I don't know."

They were silent for a few moments as they drank.

"So what time is it?" she finally said.

"Four."

"I…I don't know if I want to go back to the bedroom, Trace."

"You want to stay up?" Trace's eyes widened.

She felt her face flush. She felt like a child afraid of the monsters under her bed. "No. I just don't want to go back to the bedroom. I don't know. I just…I just don't want to."

He took her tea from her and set his cup and hers on the coffee table. "Well, it's a good thing we spent the big bucks on a comfy couch, then." He pulled her close to him and Rachael drew up her legs onto the couch, easing her body into the crook under his arm. Trace let his head sink back into the throw pillows behind him. He closed his eyes.

"I'm sorry I scared you," Rachael whispered.

"Put a lid on it, Kumquat." Trace stroked her shoulder with his thumb.

Rachael snuggled into Trace's warm torso and soon felt the slow rising and falling of his chest under her cheek.

She closed her eyes. But she did not sleep.

Rachael drove to the courthouse on Monday morning in a slow drizzle and tedious traffic. Neither complication annoyed her. Her mind was on other things. Friday night's dream had consumed her thoughts over the weekend, despite her attempts to appear as if all was well. She found herself throughout Saturday contemplating what she had done to the curtain, how she had pounded the window, how the baby's cries had filled her head. She called the St. Paul Police Department twice to see if there had been a second baby discovered in a Dumpster. There hadn't. She spent the day distracted, pausing often to gaze at the drawings the artists had made for her and which she had left on her dining room table.

On Sunday, a day on which she usually resisted any mental interruption of a work thought, the situation had not changed. She and Trace usually alternated where they attended worship together as she liked traditional services and Trace and Fig liked something a little more unconventional. It was her Sunday to surround herself with cathedral ceilings, massive organ pipes, and stained glass. But her mind wandered as the service progressed.

She could remember nothing of the sermon she heard, nor which hymns had been sung.

Trace hadn't been fooled by the "I'm just tired" excuse she gave him as they left the church. She was glad he hadn't told her to stop dwelling on the dream because it would've been excellent advice impossible to follow. Telling a person to stop thinking about something was like telling him or her to stop feeling something. A ridiculous request.

Trace did tell her to put the sketches away Sunday afternoon and to join him and McKenna on the roof to watch Fig experiment with jujitsu. And she had complied. But she got them out again after Trace went to bed, studying the drawings, contemplating whether God was indeed whispering something to her. She found herself whispering back.

No answers had come, however. She had awakened Monday morning sure of only one thing: There was no way she could prove a case of endangerment against Marcie Shipley. The woman may indeed have abandoned her baby in that Dumpster but there wasn't evidence to sustain it. The police hadn't charged her with anything yet. And it might be weeks or months before they did. If they did. There would be no hearing. And she wasn't going to ask for a continuance. She was going to have the CHPS petition against Marcie dropped.

And that meant Leo would be returned home.

She knew she was in effect declaring that someone else snatched Leo and dropped him into a trash bin. But it wasn't her job to figure out who that was. That was for the police to tackle.

Rachael exited the interstate and turned her car toward the courthouse. Her first order of business would be to call Leslie to set up a meeting to discuss the conditions for dismissing the CHPS and bringing baby Leo back home. There would indeed be conditions.

Moments later, Rachael pulled into the Ramsey County Courthouse parking lot. She grabbed her umbrella, briefcase, and travel mug of coffee and dashed toward the entrance.

Once inside, she made her way briskly toward the prosecutors' offices, intent on making the call to Leslie as soon as she got to her office.

But as she swept past Kate's desk, her assistant reached out her hand. She held a yellow phone message in her hand. "Oh. And there's someone here to see you." She nodded toward a set of chairs in the waiting area.

Seated there and looking up at her was Ivy Judson.

Rachael checked her surprise and walked over to her. "Hello, Mrs. Judson."

Ivy's smile was wide, but Rachael noted there was no easy confidence behind it. Not like before. She stood. "Mrs. Flynn, I hope you don't mind that I've come down here. I just need to talk to you."

Rachael couldn't help but wonder if Ivy had come to reveal something that would throw a wrench into her carefully constructed plans for the morning, plans that had been percolating in her harried brain all weekend long. But she hoped she hid her uneasiness. "Certainly. Why don't you come back to my office?"

"Thanks. Thanks very much." Ivy stood and moved toward Rachael, the hitch in her step causing the woman to rock as if she were swaying to music.

They headed to her office. Inside, Rachael pointed to a chair facing her desk. "Please, have a seat."

Ivy pulled the chair up close to the desk. She set her purse down by her feet as she sat, and then smoothed the top of her black polyester pants.

"What can I do for you?" Rachael clasped her hands together. She wouldn't start out taking notes. She wanted Ivy to be able to speak freely.

Ivy cleared her throat. "Well, I've been meaning to call you since you visited our group the other day."

She stopped.

"Yes?" Rachael said.

"See, I didn't want you to come away with the wrong idea about my girls."

"Wrong idea?"

"I mean, I know my girls can come across a little—oh, what's the word?—self-centered, but they're all of them facing some pretty tough circumstances, you know. And they've gotten used to just being themselves at my place. They don't have to put up a false front at the group. They can just say whatever's on their mind. It helps them sort things out. And they learn from each other that way."

"I can understand that, Mrs. Judson."

"Oh, can you please just call me Ivy?"

"Of course."

"See, I know you didn't want to stay long that day, but I just wanted you to know my girls are up against some tough odds. They've been through a lot. Each one of them."

Ivy was trying to communicate something.

"What's really on your mind, Ivy?"

The woman shifted in her chair. "The police were talking to Sharell and Liza. About Marcie's baby. About what happened to him."

"Yes?"

"Well, they're both upset, as you can imagine. And when my girls are upset, I'm upset."

"I know it can be a scary thing to have the police asking questions, but they have to ask them, Ivy. I'm sure you understand that."

"Yes, but why are they asking my girls? Why would they know anything?"

"The police have to rule out that they don't. The only way to do that is to talk to them. If they know nothing, they have nothing to worry about."

"Yes, but do the police really think Liza or Sharell could've done something like this?" Ivy shook her head as if the very idea were laughable.

Rachael leaned in. "Do you?"

"What?"

"Do you think either one of them could've done it?"

Ivy opened her mouth and then shut it. She looked away from Rachael for a second, biting her lip, and then swiveled her head back. "If you only knew how hard these young girls have it. And how it hurts them to have you pointing your finger at them."

"No one is accusing Sharell or Liza of anything."

"Yes, but when the police ask questions like that, it feels like it to them," Ivy huffed.

"But it had to be done." Rachael unlaced her fingers. "Leo Shipley could've died. Whoever put him in that Dumpster committed a terrible crime that could've led to tragic results."

Ivy silently dropped her head to study her hands in her lap.

"Your neighbor told me as I left your place how much you love children, Ivy," Rachael continued. "I'm sure you wouldn't have wanted Leo Shipley to die in that Dumpster."

The woman snapped her eyes shut and her bottom lip began to tremble. "No, of course not," she whispered. Then she looked up at Rachael, and her eyes were glassy. "It's just I love my girls. And their babies. They try so hard."

"I can see how much you care for them."

Ivy drew a finger across her eyes, to flick away the tears. Rachael reached for a tissue box on her credenza and pushed it toward her. The tissue made a pajama-soft sound as Ivy pulled it from its box.

"Thanks," Ivy said.

Ivy dabbed at her eyes and Rachael studied her.

"Would you mind answering a question, Ivy?" Rachael said, using as gentle a tone as she could.

Ivy, clutching the tissue, looked at her, brow crinkled. "What question?"

"Do you think Sharell or Liza could've done this?"

Ivy stared at Rachael, the tissue frozen in her hand. Then she reached down for her purse and stood. "You people really don't care what I think." Her laugh was humorless. "You've never cared before what I think. And I have to go."

Ivy took a step, the hitch in her step more pronounced than before.

"Could Marcie have done it?" Rachael said, rising from her chair.

Ivy took another step. "I'm not the one who should have to answer these questions. I have to go." She didn't turn her head.

"Ivy, please. Wait." Rachael came around from behind her desk. "I really *do* want to know what you think."

Ivy turned slowly. "I think these girls got a rotten hand dealt to them, Ms. Flynn. The lives they're living aren't all their fault. That's what I think." She turned and took another step. Rachael reached out and touched her on the arm.

"Is that really all you want to tell me?" Rachael said.

Ivy hesitated only for a moment. "Yes. Yes it is." She took another step and then turned back around. She stood framed in the doorway. "I'm all they have, Ms. Flynn."

Then she walked out of Rachael's office.

Rachael gazed at the doorway for several long seconds after Ivy had disappeared through it. Rachael wasn't convinced that the woman knew who had left Leo in the Dumpster, but she was certain of one thing: Ivy had her suspicions. Just like she did.

The phone on her desk split the silence. Rachael stepped back behind her desk and lifted the receiver. "Rachael Flynn."

"Hey, it's Leslie. I thought you were going to call me first thing."

Rachael sighed and flicked a stray hair out of her eyes. "Sorry. Just had a little unplanned visit from Ivy Judson. She was waiting for me when I got here this morning."

"Are you kidding?"

Rachael sank into her chair and reached for the travel mug of coffee. "No, I'm not."

"What'd she say?"

Rachael mindlessly traced her finger around the lid of her mug. "She's got an interesting case of mother hen syndrome. She's watching out for her girls, I guess. You know, I get the impression she's afraid one of her girls *does* know how Leo ended up in that Dumpster."

"Really? You might want to pass that on to the police."

"Mmm. I will."

"Well, guess who was waiting for *me* when I got to the office this morning?"

Rachael rubbed an eyebrow. "I've no idea."

"Koko Shipley."

An unbidden image of Cruella DeVil filled Rachael's head and she mentally shooed it away. "What did she want?"

"She wanted to tell me how to do my job."

"Terrific."

"Now she wants to come see you so she can tell you how to do yours."

Rachael sat forward in her chair. "What?"

"I convinced her to wait in the conference room here while I called you. I thought maybe if you're not busy you could come over here and we can sort this out."

"Sort what out?"

"Koko knows the Chips against Marcie's probably going to be dropped and Leo will be returned home. She has some choice words for that plan."

Rachael exhaled heavily. "What has she got against her sister?"

"Oh, everything I guess. Mostly she doesn't like the way Marcie mothers her kids. Koko's apparently got that job nailed, too. Motherhood, I mean. Even though she doesn't have any children. So. Want to come over? We have to chat anyway."

Rachael took a swig from the travel mug. The coffee inside was cold. She winced and set the mug down.

"I'll come. See you in a few."

SEVENTEEN

Koko Shipley did not stand when Rachael reached out her hand to greet her. Nor did she welcome Rachael's handshake.

"Nice to meet you, Miss Shipley. I'm Rachael Flynn."

The woman looked down at the outstretched arm across the conference table and then raised her eyes to Rachael's. Her highlighted brown hair was pulled tightly back from her face and bound with a shimmering plastic band. Broad hoop earrings lightly touched the shoulders of her brown leather jacket. Her eyebrows and eyelids were heavily lined, giving her an intense look that might have made her stunning had she been smiling.

"I know who you are," she said.

Rachael withdrew her arm.

Leslie, next to her, cleared her throat. "Can I get anyone some coffee?"

"None for me, thanks," Rachael replied, her eyes on Koko. It wasn't the first time she'd met a hostile family member of a person whose child had been removed from the home. But it was the first time the hostile family member was furious that the child was being returned. It was usually the other way around. Rachael sat down. Leslie took a chair next to her. Koko ignored the offer of coffee.

An exchange of niceties prior to getting down to the crux of the matter didn't appear likely. Rachael dove in.

"Miss Shipley, I understand you don't approve of the county's plan to return your nephew to your sister?"

"You got that right." The woman's annoyance was palpable.

"I'd like to hear your concerns."

"My concerns? Are you telling me *you* don't have concerns? Do I really have to spell it out for you?"

Rachael felt a bubble of indignation rise within her. She mentally massaged it away. "Miss Shipley, if you have information about your sister that affects this case and this child, then this is the time and place to share it."

"You people are unbelievable." Koko shook her head.

And you are unbelievably rude, Rachael thought.

Leslie opened a notebook. "Why don't you just say what you came here to say, Miss Shipley."

The woman sighed heavily, rolled her eyes, and moved forward to rest her elbows on the table. "My sister is a walking disaster of a mother. Surely that's obvious. She never should have had any of those kids. She may be stuck with the older two, but she doesn't need that baby and that baby sure doesn't need her. And I tell you what. I don't need her having any more kids, either."

"What makes you say she's a disaster as a mother?" Rachael opened her notebook as well.

"Like you can't see it?" Koko swung her head from Rachael to Leslie and back to Rachael. "She's hopeless! She's a high school dropout who's never worked a day in her life. She doesn't have a husband, or money, or an ounce of self-respect. She drinks, she takes drugs when she doesn't even know what they are. And she's always in some kind of crisis. I've had it up to here with her and her choices. Up…to…here." Koko saluted the top of her head.

"Are you saying Marcie neglects her children? Have you witnessed her neglecting, abusing, or mistreating her children?" Rachael asked calmly.

"Because if you have, you really should file a petition of suspected neglect and list every incident."

"She already told me that!" Koko waved a hand in Leslie's direction.

"Well? Have you?" Rachael replied.

"Hey! It's not my job to keep Marcie in line! It's your job!"

"And I told *you* that we do not take a child away from his mother without substantiated evidence that the child is in danger." Leslie's voice was composed but commanding. "We've been monitoring your sister since Leo disappeared and we've not seen any evidence that her children are being neglected."

"She threw her baby in a Dumpster!"

"Do you have proof that she did that?" Rachael asked.

"Proof? I can't believe we're having this conversation. Proof? Who else would have done it? You people make changing a lightbulb an act of Congress!"

Rachael leaned fully forward in her chair. "You're right. It would be a lot easier if we could just base all our decisions on what we think without having to prove anything, but I don't think you'd be very happy in a world like that, Miss Shipley. If you have proof your sister dropped her baby in that Dumpster, if you saw her do it or if she told you she did it, that is proof. What you suppose about how the baby got there isn't proof. And neither is what I suppose about it."

Koko was silent.

"Did you see her do it? Did she tell you she did it?" Rachael asked.

Not a word.

Leslie stepped in. "Have you witnessed Marcie neglecting her other children? Does she leave drugs or alcohol lying around the house? Does she hit her children? Mistreat them? Does she knowingly or unknowingly put them in harm's way? Have you actually witnessed any of these things? If you have, we really want to know, because to tell you the truth, we have no evidence of any of this, Miss Shipley. Since Leo has been in foster care, Marcie has complied with every request we've made of her. She had more than one random urinalysis and she came up clean. We've made surprise visits to the house and have found nothing to indicate her children are in danger. And you can be sure that when Leo is returned, there will be conditions. We will continue to monitor your sister and check in on her kids."

Still not a word.

"Look, I can tell you're worried about your nephews and niece," Rachael began but Koko cut her off.

"Look, those kids are not my problem. And you don't know anything about me. And I'm telling you right now, I don't want to be a part of any arrangement to get Marcie out of this mess. Neither does my mother. So don't you go making us a part of it, you understand? Don't you go writing us into your little case plan."

"Don't worry, Miss Shipley, you won't be in it," Leslie said, looking down at her tablet and scribbling a notation.

Koko sat back in her chair, apparently appeased on one matter. But her silence this time was momentary. She clearly was not happy with the other matters.

"The dumbest thing you could do is give that baby back to my sister."

"So you've said, but as we've told you there is nothing presently to indicate that your sister is incapable of caring for her children," Leslie replied.

Koko snorted but said nothing. Rachael sensed loathing from the woman across from her, the same disdain she had felt from Sharell Hodge. It nagged at her. She wanted to know why.

"Miss Shipley, can I ask you a couple questions about your relationship with Marcie?" Rachael said.

"What kind of questions?" Koko didn't bother to hide her annoyed skepticism.

"Well, were you close growing up?"

"Does it look like we were close?"

"How much older are you?"

Koko huffed. "I'm twenty-seven. She's twenty-two. I think you can figure that out."

"Have you always felt this way about her?"

"*What* way?" Koko tossed a hand in the air, suggesting Rachael had posed a ridiculous question.

"You can hardly stand her. That's pretty obvious. Has she done something to you to make you feel this way?"

Koko smiled, but there was nothing comical in its shape or depth. "In case you haven't noticed, my sister is a leech. She sucks the life right out of anything she touches. She takes and she gives nothing back. She's been that way since the day she was born. Marcie will never leave the system. Never. She'll be with you till the day you retire. Both of you. And she'll just take from you, from everybody, for as long as you let her."

For a moment, Rachael sat in stunned silence. "Why do you think she's that way?"

"Because she likes it." Each word was delivered separately as if independent of the others.

"She likes being that way?"

"That's right. And I'm sick of it."

Koko leaned back, practically daring Rachael to pose another question.

"Can I ask why you came down here, Miss Shipley?" Rachael asked as hospitably as she could. She hoped it didn't sound flippant. She really wanted to know.

"Can't you tell?"

"No, not really. You don't like your sister, you say you don't care about her kids, and that you're sick and tired of coming to her rescue. I'm just wondering why you bothered to get involved here at all."

Koko stood, grabbing her purse and placing it on her shoulder.

"See that my name stays out of that plan," she said calmly and headed for the door to the room.

As she opened it, she turned her head toward Rachael. "And my reasons for what I do and don't do are none of your business."

Monday afternoon's preparations for court kept Rachael busy—too busy to fully digest Koko's caustic observations and too busy to sneak in a call to Will. She wanted his advice about what she was planning to do, and his affirmation. But every time she picked up the phone to call him, she was interrupted by another phone call or a colleague with a question. Finally at four-thirty, she told Kate to hold her calls and she closed her office door. She pressed the speed dial for Will at the police department.

"Hey, Rachael. What's up?"

"The usual. Unsolvable case, lots of restless nights, too many questions, not enough evidence, a host of suspects."

"No revelations from on high this time?" He was joking. Sort of.

"Maybe. No. I don't know."

"That almost sounds like 'yes.'"

Rachael exhaled heavily. "I don't think Marcie Shipley dumped her baby in the Dumpster, Will."

"You told me that already. Last week."

"I still think it."

"If it makes you feel any better, Lindy Kirby isn't convinced she did it either."

"So what *does* she think? If Marcie didn't do it, then someone else had to have done it."

"That's not your problem, Rachael. Seems like I've said that to you before. Haven't I?"

She ignored him. "Does Lindy think it was just some random snatching by a lunatic who wanted to kill a baby?"

"I don't know. I just know there isn't enough evidence to charge anyone with anything. She told me she talked to those women at the group. They didn't give her any reason to think they had anything to do with it. Course they could be lying."

"That just makes it more complicated, not less."

"For us, not for you."

Rachael toyed with the phone cord, pondering. "We've got nothing to keep the Chips against Marcie, Will. I can't prove Leo is in danger if he's returned to her."

"Well, if you can't prove it, you can't. And at the moment there certainly aren't charges from our office to fall back on. So there you go."

She sighed. "I just needed to hear you say something like that."

"Okay, then. I've said something like that."

She grinned.

"Rachael, your instincts have served you pretty well," Will went on. "Usually better than mine serve me. If you really think she's innocent, and you can't prove it otherwise, then I'd say you're doing the right thing."

"Thanks. Um, I don't suppose Lindy's in the office right now?"

"Nope. She left at three."

"Will she be in tomorrow?"

Will feigned an exasperated tone. "Wednesday, Rachael. She'll be in on Wednesday."

"Hey, I just want to talk to her about Sharell and Liza and what they said to her."

"Even though I told you Lindy didn't get anything from them?"

"I just need to know what they said, Will."

Will was silent for a moment. "You would've made a great cop, Rachael. You never give up."

She smiled. "So you've said."

An easy silence rested between them. Then Will spoke up.

"So, was that a 'yes' before?"

"What?"

"Are you getting, you know, odd hunches that you can't account for?"

There wasn't a hint of mockery. She appreciated that about Will. He wasn't much of a believer in anything extraordinary. But he'd never made light of the insights she sometimes had. "I don't know. I had a weird dream. I've had two weird dreams, actually."

"Dreams? What kind of dreams?"

Rachael felt her face flush. "I...I had a dream that a baby was crying the morning Leo was found. *Before* I learned he had been found. I had another one a couple nights ago. But this time I was sleepwalking when I dreamed it. I was out of my bed, looking for this crying baby and pounding on the bedroom window. Scared Trace to death."

Will said nothing on the other end.

"Probably just two really bad dreams. And bad timing. That's all," Rachael said.

"Probably," Will finally replied, but his voice was thoughtful.

"Well, thanks, Will."

"Okay, then. Catch you later."

"Bye."

Rachael hung up the phone and stared at her desk. Her day planner was open to Wednesday, the day the meeting with Marcie had been set to go over the conditions for Leo's return. The day Leo would be brought back home. She stared at the penciled-in date.

Leo would be going back home.

Images from her dream began to sneak into her head as she looked at her handwriting and she stood abruptly to scatter them.

She walked over to her office door and opened it wide, willing the confusing fragments of the nightmare to disappear down the hall, away from her work area and the file that bore Leo Shipley's name.

EIGHTEEN

Burning toast set off the loft's smoke alarm.

And set McKenna to screaming.

Rachael hurried into the kitchen from the hall bathroom to remove the offending piece of blackened bread, tossing the smoldering rectangle onto the countertop. She grabbed an art journal off the island in the middle of the kitchen and waved at the gray swirls of smoke as McKenna howled in her high-chair.

"It's okay, baby!" she soothed in McKenna's direction. The alarm continued to screech its warning, despite Rachael's frenzied arm-waving. Trace appeared from the upstairs bedrooms.

"Here, take this!" She handed him the journal and moved to take McKenna out of her high-chair.

Trace looked down at the magazine in his hands. "I haven't even looked at this issue yet," he mumbled.

With McKenna in her arms, Rachael grabbed another magazine off the countertop. *Bon Appétit.* A Christmas present from Fig. "Fine. Use this one."

Trace switched magazines and reached up to fan away the curling plumes.

The smoke alarm fell silent and so did McKenna.

"So. You're having a new kind of toast?" Trace quipped. He tossed the magazine on the counter and peered at the crispened slice of bread.

"I'm sure Fig would say there's a culture somewhere in the world where burnt toast is a delicacy." Rachael reached for McKenna's cup off the highchair tray and handed it to her daughter.

"Want me to make you a less carbonized version?"

"You're sweet. Thanks, but no. I'm late. McKenna's lunch is in the fridge. Mac and cheese. You'll have to warm it up. And try not to let Fig doctor it up with hollandaise or Tabasco or lemon curd." Rachael wiped McKenna's fingers with a washcloth and set her down on the floor.

"Okeydoke. I'll tell him to just stick with the chutney." Trace grabbed a bowl from a cabinet. "Oh, and remember you said you'd try to come home a little early today. I have to take those proofs over to the printers this afternoon."

"Right, right," Rachael muttered. Of all the days Trace had an appointment, it had to fall on a Tuesday. Court day. "If the judge is running on time, and if there are no surprises, I should be able to be home by four."

"Peachy." Trace poured milk on his cereal.

Rachael handed McKenna a set of measuring spoons, kissed the top of her head, and grabbed her travel mug of coffee. She kissed Trace on his neck. "Gotta go."

"*Ciao.*"

Rachael smiled back at him and sailed out the door.

The day's docket was full, but to Rachael's surprise and subdued delight, it was proving to be a smooth day in the courtroom. No no-shows, no last-minute changes, no delays. As the day progressed, Rachael imagined she would have time to get started on the motion to dismiss the CHPS against Marcie before heading back to the loft at a quarter to four.

By three o'clock her last case had been heard. Rachael made her way back to her office to tie up a stack of post-court items and hammer out the dismissal.

She was immersed in a sea of open petitions when her phone rang. "Rachael Flynn."

"Hi, Rachael. It's Lindy. Will said you wanted to talk to me?"

"Lindy! I didn't think you were going to be in today."

"I had a few things to take care of. Just ran into Will and he told me you're set to dismiss the Chips on Marcie Shipley."

Rachael pushed aside the other paperwork and fished for the Shipley file. "Any reason why I shouldn't?"

"It's still an open investigation as far as I'm concerned. Marcie Shipley insists an intruder took her baby. And we finally have one neighbor who says she saw someone near Marcie's front door the night Leo disappeared."

"Really? What time? Man or woman?"

"It was sometime after three-thirty. She couldn't say if it was a man or a woman. She said it was too dark."

"But this woman is sure she saw someone?"

"She's sure."

"What was she doing up at three-thirty?" Rachael scribbled the time on a blank piece of paper in Leo Shipley's file.

"She was getting a drink of water. Heard a noise outside. Looked out her window."

"Did she think it was odd that someone was at Marcie's door at three-thirty in the morning?"

"Actually, she thought it was Marcie. And she didn't think that was weird because when Marcie goes out, she tends to stay out late."

"Didn't she know that Marcie had just had a baby?"

"She wasn't aware that Marcie had given birth already. She and Marcie aren't close. And this woman is not her next-door neighbor or anything. She lives across the parking lot from her. Whatever she saw, she saw from a limited vantage point."

Rachael tapped the file with her pencil. "Did she see a car?"

"She didn't watch long enough, Rachael. She just saw a figure at Marcie's door. She thought it was Marcie coming home late. She told me she didn't notice if there was a car or not."

"Well, what was the noise she heard? Was it a car door?"

Rachael heard Lindy chuckle on the other end of the phone.

"What?" Rachael said.

"Will said you were...thorough."

"Can't help it. I'm a first-born," Rachael replied. "So, was it a car door?"

"She said it could've been. But she's not sure, Rachael."

"Hmm."

"Will said you wanted to know how it went with Sharell Hodge and Liza Cooley."

"I do."

"There's not a lot to tell you. Both of them say they were home in bed the night Leo was taken. Both of them denied having anything to do with his disappearance."

In her mind, Rachael pictured the two drawings: one of Sharell as warrior princess, and the other of Liza in metamorphosis. "Were they surprised you wanted to question them?"

"Sharell was positively ticked. She really, really doesn't like Marcie Shipley. I didn't say I came to ask about her whereabouts the night Leo disappeared, but she guessed it. I started out telling her I just needed to talk to Marcie's friends and acquaintances to see if any of them knew of someone who would want to harm Marcie's baby. And right away she said, 'You mean, you want to know if I'm the one who did it?'"

"Just like that?"

"Sharell's not just street-smart, I'd say she's smart, period. Every question I asked she knew what I was really trying to get at. I finally told her we could just cut to the chase if she wanted. She said something like, 'Ask your blankety-blank questions and get the blankety-blank out of my house.'"

"So?"

"I asked her if she knew how Leo Shipley ended up in that Dumpster. She just said no, plain and simple. I asked her if she had anything to do with Leo Shipley getting dumped in that Dumpster. And she said, 'I think I already answered that.' She told me she was at home the night Leo disappeared, asleep in her bed and her children were with her. I asked her if she has a car and she said yes. Then I asked her why she hates Marcie Shipley so much."

Rachael poised her pencil over the paper. "And?"

"She said Marcie Shipley blames all her problems on everyone else. She plays the victim card over and over and over again. Nothing is ever her fault."

Lindy stopped.

"That's it? That's why she hates her?" Rachael exclaimed.

"I know. Doesn't seem like enough of a reason to despise someone, does it?"

"No."

"I didn't think so either. I asked her if that's all there was to it. She said Marcie is also prejudiced against black people. Fond of making racial slurs, likes to pin the blame for all the problems on the street on the black community, that kind of thing."

Rachael frowned. "That still doesn't seem like enough."

"I know what you mean. I think maybe Marcie threatened Sharell somehow. I asked Sharell point-blank if Marcie had ever made threats and she just shrugged and said Marcie's not smart enough to know how to make a threat."

"Do you believe her?"

"That Marcie's not smart enough?"

"No. That Marcie didn't threaten her somehow."

"I don't know. Like I said, Sharell is smart. She knows we're looking for someone with a motive."

Rachael tried to remember all the words Brick had drawn into his sketch of Sharell. Vengeance had been one of them. A smart woman—a smart, angry woman—could choose vengeance.

And vengeance was as good a motive as they come.

"Did she say anything else?" Rachael asked.

"Nope. I left after that. I went to see Liza. And I gotta tell ya, she was pretty clueless the whole time I was talking to her. She didn't get that I was trying to discover if *she* had anything to do with Leo's disappearance. When I finally got around to asking her if she knew how he came to be in that trash bin, she was, like, flattered I had come to her for insight on how the heck a baby ended up in the garbage."

"So, I guess she wasn't much help."

"She told me baby snatchers are always looking for infants to sell on the black market. She said someone tried to take her baby once, to sell it to a rich couple in Hollywood who couldn't have children."

"Oh, dear," Rachael sighed.

"Yeah."

"So, did you ask her why a baby snatcher would take Leo and then toss him in the trash?"

"Ah, well. Baby snatchers who are about to get caught have to ditch the merchandise."

"She said that?"

"Pretty much."

"Does she really believe Leo was taken by baby snatchers?" Rachael slumped in her chair, wearied by the new information that seemed to throw another veil on the truth.

"I don't think so, Rachael. I think she was just trying to come up with an idea for me because I asked for one. I think she *wanted* to help me. She seems pretty compliant."

"She's also quite possibly schizophrenic."

"I know what you're thinking, but we don't have near enough cause to demand she be properly diagnosed. No judge would sign off on it. She has no obvious motive. She denies knowing anything about Leo's disappearance. And she answered all my questions."

Rachael exhaled heavily. "All right. Thanks, Lindy. Would you let me know if you find out anything new?"

"Will do. And I assume Marcie's getting new locks on her front door?"

"It's going to be one of the conditions of Leo's return."

"Okay. See ya."

Rachael hung up the phone, pursing her lips together as she digested what Lindy had told her. Her eyes fell upon her watch as she laced her fingers together and drew them up to her chin.

She gasped.

It was twenty minutes after four.

NINETEEN

By the time Rachael arrived at the studio it was ten minutes to five. She had called Trace twice on the road and twice got his voice mail. She tried calling the studio, too. No answer.

She could tell the studio was empty before she even unlocked the door.

Inside, the massive room was still and silent. McKenna's toys lay strewn about. Works in progress lined the walls, were propped against pillars and hung from nails. A half-finished sculpture of a kneeling soldier occupied a circle of late afternoon sunlight. Next to the statue lay a pile of plastic Fisher-Price farm animals.

A few feet from the door stood an easel. Rachael's name appeared in purple ink at the top of the sketch that rested on it.

Rachael moved closer. The drawing, obviously drawn in a hurry, was a note prepared for her in Figgy fashion. He had sketched McKenna pushing Fig in an oversized stroller, while Fig tossed toys out of it. Dashing ahead of them was Trace, with a sheaf of drawings in his arms and dragging a puppy pull toy wrapped around one ankle.

She inwardly thanked Fig for coming to Trace's rescue, dismissing her concern about where Fig may have taken McKenna on their walk. Fig had recently decided he didn't like cell phones and presently didn't own one, so there was no way she could reach him. She would simply have to wait for him to return.

Rachael picked up the purple ink pen that Fig had left resting on the easel. She drew a lopsided stick figure wearing a skirt and carrying a briefcase. "Sorry," she wrote.

She turned to go and then hesitated, turned around again, took a step forward, and began picking up McKenna's toys, dropping them one by one into a wicker basket by the window.

"I'm sorry, Trace." Rachael held out her arms to take McKenna from him as Trace walked into the loft.

"S'all right. It's a Tuesday. Court day. It happens." He eased their daughter into Rachael's arms.

"But I was done in time to leave. That's the thing. I just lost track of time and then I got a phone call…I'm really sorry."

Trace paused and then shrugged. "I should've tried to find a different day to do this. Tuesdays are nuts for me and Fig, anyway."

Rachael kissed McKenna's temple. "McKenna gets in the way." It was not a question. She set the little girl down and watched her toddle away.

"She doesn't mean to. But she does." Trace tossed his keys onto the island counter in the middle of the kitchen. "Thought any more about a nanny?"

"No. Not really," she admitted.

Trace turned to the fridge, opened it, and pulled out a carton of orange juice. "So are you going to?" He almost sounded a tad annoyed. Almost.

"I will. I promise."

Trace took a swig from the carton.

"Did you get your artwork to the printers in time?" she asked.

Trace nodded and took another drink.

"Fig didn't mind taking McKenna?"

"He cancelled an appointment. But you know Fig. He said he didn't mind. He probably doesn't."

Rachael sighed. "I'll have to find a way to make it up to him."

Trace put the container back in the fridge. "Just don't draw him any more pictures." He turned and winked at her.

A smile formed on her lips. "And why not?"

"He said you stink at art." Trace closed the fridge door and began to walk toward the living room.

"So where did he take McKenna?" she called after him.

"Tapunui's."

"Do I want to know what that is?"

Trace swiveled his head around and grinned at her. "*That* is a man. Tapunui is a friend of Fig's from Tahiti."

Fig had quite a collection of friends from exotic places. It was one of the ways he unintentionally satisfied his infatuation for unusual cuisine.

"I suppose they had a snack there," she said, her eyes on McKenna as she toddled into the living room mumbling "da ba da ba."

"Poison," Trace mumbled over his shoulder.

An odd joke. "Poison?"

Trace turned back around. "I said *poisson, cherie.*"

Poisson. Fish. "Any species I'd recognize?"

"*Poisson cru, madam.*" Trace sank into a couch and grabbed the TV remote away from McKenna before she put it into her mouth. "Raw. Marinated in lime juice and coconut milk."

"And McKenna ate it?"

"*Oui.*"

Trace hopped off the couch as McKenna made a beeline for the open staircase. They needed a gate now that McKenna was walking.

They needed a lot of things.

As soon as the Leo Shipley case was closed she would begin looking for a nanny.

Or a new job.

Marcie Shipley was late.

The meeting to go over the conditions of Leo's return had been set for Wednesday morning at nine thirty. When there was no sign of Marcie at nine forty-five, Leslie left the conference room where she and Rachael were waiting and called Marcie's apartment.

No answer.

"I can't believe she's doing this," Rachael breathed when Leslie returned to the conference room.

Leslie shook her head. "Every time I think I understand a person, he or she makes a special attempt to surprise me. But you know what? She'll have an excuse. I bet you ten bucks she'll have an excuse for how this isn't her fault."

Rachael heaved a sigh. "If Koko were in this room she'd be screaming, 'I told you so.'"

Leslie grimaced. "I so don't want her to be right. For lots of reasons."

Rachael studied the conditions she had prepared for Marcie to sign. She had prayed over them, stewed over them, and was certain they were fair and judicious. Leslie thought so, too. So had Tim, her supervisor. But she was unnerved by the words that stared back at her. It was almost as if something wasn't right. Like she had missed something. Something big. Like these conditions weren't going to protect Leo Shipley.

Like he was still in danger.

Remnants of her second dream wafted across her and she involuntarily shuddered.

But I don't think Marcie did it! Rachael wordlessly chided herself. *I don't have sufficient proof that Leo is in danger if we give him back. I don't have any proof.*

The phone in the room buzzed to life and a voice split the quiet. "Your nine thirty appointment is here, Leslie."

"Finally," Leslie grumbled. She opened the door and marched out of the conference room.

Rachael absently sipped her coffee and waited. Three minutes passed and the door opened. Leslie held it ajar as Marcie stepped into the room, followed by Ivy Judson.

Marcie looked bored. Ivy smiled when she saw Rachael, seemingly quite happy to have been invited to tag along to Marcie's meeting.

The women came into the room and sat down at the table. Leslie rolled her eyes as she took her seat.

"Where've you been, Marcie?" Rachael said simply. "This meeting was set for nine thirty."

"My mom didn't come to get me," Marcie muttered. "I told her I needed to be here."

"And you arranged for her to come get you and bring you?"

"She knew I needed to be here." Marcie sat back in her chair. "I called her at work this morning when she didn't come and she acted like we'd never talked about it. Typical."

"And did you? Did you talk about it?"

"I already told you that I told her. I told her last week I needed a ride."

Leslie caught Rachael's gaze and mouthed the words "ten bucks."

"So you called Ivy?" Rachael continued.

"And I was happy to help her, Ms. Flynn," Ivy chirped. "Don't you worry about that."

Rachael smiled at Ivy but immediately turned her attention back to Marcie. "And where are J.J. and Hallie?"

"Oh, they're with my neighbor. You know. The one you met. June." Ivy said it as if the question had been posed to her.

"You would like Ivy to be here while we go over this?" Rachael asked Marcie.

"Well, sure. Why not? She's the only person who even cares about me."

"That's fine with me if she's here," Leslie chimed in.

Rachael cleared her throat. "All right then." She slid a document from in front of her across the table to Marcie. A copy still lay in front of her. "These are the conditions under which Leo will be returned to you."

Marcie barely glanced at the piece of paper. "Can I get him today? I want him today. I don't think I should have to wait another day."

"Let's go over these first, all right?"

Marcie pursed her lips together and leaned forward, tipping her face close to the paper.

"I'll read them out loud so there's no mistaking what's expected of you," Rachael continued.

Marcie sighed. "Leslie already told me what was going to be on here. I already did some of it. I got a new lock."

"That's true. She did." Ivy's tone was motherly. "I made sure she did."

Rachael smiled faintly. "Shall we begin? Number one is you abstain from alcohol and mind-altering chemicals."

"That means drugs, dear," Ivy said softly.

"I know what it means," Marcie grumbled.

"Will you have trouble complying with this?" Rachael said.

"It's not like I'm an alcoholic. And I don't do drugs anymore."

"But you had been drinking the night Leo was taken. You were completely unaware when someone came into your home and took him. Isn't that right?"

Marcie exhaled heavily. "Yeah. Okay. Fine. No booze."

Rachael went on. "Number two is to get a new lock on your front door..."

Marcie butted in. "I told you I already did that."

"And that you *use* the lock," Rachael continued. "You have to use the lock, Marcie. You need to lock your door when you go to bed at night. Actually you should lock it whenever you and your kids are in the apartment."

"I know how to lock a door." Marcie's tone was thick with annoyance.

"But you don't always do it, dear. That's what she's saying," Ivy soothed. "You just need to put a little note by the door to remind yourself, that's all."

"Number three is that you continue to submit to random UAs and house checks by the Department of Human Services for the next six months." Rachael didn't look up from the copy of the document.

"As long as it's just Leslie. I don't like it when you send over a caseworker I don't know."

"I think we can arrange that I'm the one to make the visits, Marcie," Leslie replied.

Rachael went on. "Number four, you do not allow friends or family to consume alcohol or drugs around the baby or your other children. And everyone must step outside to smoke."

"I don't hardly smoke at all anymore!" Marcie exclaimed.

"She means your friends, honey," Ivy murmured.

"Number five," Rachael continued. "You will not under any circumstances leave your children unattended. And we don't mean only Leo, Marcie. You can't leave J.J. or Hallie alone in the house either."

"Who said I did that? I want to know who said I did that. Whoever it was, they are lying!"

"We're just making sure we all understand what's expected of you, Marcie," Leslie said.

"Last one." Rachael looked up from the paper. "You will move Leo's crib out of the living room and into one of your bedrooms. Yours or J.J. and Hallie's. You decide. And you must notify the police immediately if you suspect Leo is in any kind of danger."

"I already moved the crib."

Rachael ignored her. "If you agree to these conditions, you sign your name and we'll get this to the judge and the case will be dismissed."

"And I'll get Leo back today?"

"Yes."

"I don't have a pen."

Rachael reached across the table and handed Marcie the pen her father had given her when she graduated from law school. Marcie bent over the page and slowly scrawled her name across the bottom. Then she stood, handing the pen back to Rachael as her chair scooted backward. Ivy stood, too.

"Are you going to bring him to me? Is he here?" Marcie looked hopeful.

"I'll bring him to the apartment this afternoon," Leslie replied.

Rachael stood as well. "Good luck to you, Marcie." She wanted to say *God's blessings* but knew she couldn't. She thought it instead. If anyone needed special attention from God it was Marcie and her children.

"Yeah. Thanks." Marcie turned to go and then swung back around. "So the police haven't caught the guy?"

Rachael hesitated. "What guy?"

"The guy who took Leo, of course."

"No. No, they haven't."

"Are they still looking?"

"Yes."

"Well, they better catch him."

Marcie swung open the door and she and Ivy stepped out into the hall. Ivy slipped her arm around Marcie and Rachael heard her say, "There. That wasn't so bad."

She watched as the women walked the length of the hall before turning into the reception area, Ivy patting Marcie caringly on the back with every step.

TWENTY

Rachael wanted to be there when Leslie handed Leo Shipley over to his mother. She wanted to see Marcie's face when Leo was placed back in her arms. If Marcie had been telling the truth, if Leo had indeed been kidnapped and left for dead, she expected to see extreme relief and mother-love splashed across Marcie's face. Tears of joy, perhaps. Laughter. Rivers of maternal sentiment. Even an emotionally sedate mother would ooze visible enthusiasm at being reunited with her lost child. Rachael was sure of it. And she wanted to see it.

But it wasn't customary. County attorneys did not accompany county social workers when they returned children from foster placement to their custodial parents.

"You should just come," Leslie told Rachael after the meeting with Marcie and Ivy broke up.

Rachael shook her head. "I don't want to do anything that will come back to haunt me or the prosecutor's office."

"I suppose."

Leslie hesitated a moment.

"Hey, want to come in the car with me?" she said. "You could see Leo then, if that's who you're interested in."

"Actually I'm more interested in Marcie's reaction to his homecoming. For some reason I want to see her face when you give Leo back to her."

Leslie studied her for a moment. "You already having second thoughts about sending him back?"

"No. Not second thoughts. I don't know. Something just doesn't feel quite right."

"What? What doesn't feel quite right?"

Rachael hastily shuffled the papers on the table in front of her, shoving them into her file folder. "I...I don't know. Maybe it's just that we still don't know who took Leo in the first place. We don't know why. Usually we know more when we send a child back home, not less. This just seems a little...foggy."

A second or two of silence passed between them.

"So you want to come?" Leslie asked.

Rachael considered the idea for another several seconds. "I'll come. And I'll stay in the car. But I want you to pay attention to everything she does and says."

"Okay. I'll pick you up at three."

The drive to the foster parents' home in White Bear Lake was uneventful. Rachael waited in the car while Leslie went inside to fetch Leo. The social worker emerged from the modest but well-cared-for home with a baby carrier in one hand and a diaper bag in the other. A fortyish woman stood at the doorway and watched as Leslie walked out to the car. The woman looked a little sad.

Rachael stepped out of the car and opened the backseat door. When Leslie leaned in with the carrier, Rachael could see that Leo was asleep. Dark hair covered his perfectly round head. His petite nose and lips reminded her of two tiny flowers. A mint green sleeper was barely visible under a downy blue blanket spotted with tiny elephants and giraffes.

Images of McKenna at the same age tugged at her, wrapped themselves around her brain.

How could anyone toss a baby into a trash bin?

How could anyone do it?

"He's a cutie, isn't he?" Leslie said. Her voice was chipper. Completely composed. Leslie was not yet a mother. Perhaps that was why she hadn't the depth of feeling Rachael had at that solitary moment. Rachael didn't know how else to explain the sudden appearance of tears on her cheeks.

Rachael hoped Leslie wouldn't notice.

She did.

"You okay there?" Leslie asked as she stepped back from stretching the seat belt across the car seat.

"Yeah. Pay no attention to me. Long day. Missing McKenna. That's all."

Leslie looked unconvinced.

"Come on." Rachael closed the car door. "Let's go."

She could feel Leslie's eyes on her as she walked around the back of the car to the front passenger door. Then Leslie turned and waved back to the woman in the doorway.

"Bye, Collette!" Leslie called out. The woman waved and blew a kiss toward the backseat. Leslie got into the driver's side, closed the door, and started the engine. "She's a gem, that one. She and her husband have had thirty-some kids in and out of their house over the years. And they have three children of their own. If every kid had parents like Collette and Jim, you and I would be out of a job."

"I don't think I'd mind that too much," Rachael murmured.

Leslie pulled away from the curb, leaving the serene neighborhood behind them.

Twenty minutes later, Leslie was pulling into the parking lot of a decaying two-story apartment complex in south St. Paul. The building was three-sided. Front doors faced each other on two of the sides. The third side, attached at both ends to the other two, faced the entrance and the parking lot, which was pocked with an assortment of saucer-sized divots. Tattered curtains fluttered out of screenless, half-open windows. Clothes were slung haphazardly on the second floor railings, either to dry or to be forgotten. Multicolored graffiti, partially blackened by cover-up paint, decorated one long wall of the complex. A trio of adolescents leaning against a stabilizing pillar eyed the car as Leslie parked in one of just three visitor spaces.

"You might want to keep the car locked," Leslie said as she cut the engine.

"All right," Rachael said softly.

Leslie got out of the car, opened the back door, and reached in for Leo, who was still asleep and quite unaware he was back home.

"I don't think this will take very long." Leslie grabbed the diaper bag.

"Which unit is Marcie in?"

Leslie inclined her head toward the bank of doors and windows on the units that faced the street. "Second floor. Third from the end."

"Tell me she has screens on her windows."

Leslie grinned. "She does. Okay. Be back in a few. And I promise to take good mental notes." She closed the door, walked to the entrance to the enclosed stairs, and disappeared inside. Rachael pressed the power lock. A few moments later, Leslie appeared on the second floor, clearly visible under the overhang that presumably kept most of the snow off the cement walkway in the winter. Leslie arrived at Marcie's door and knocked. The door opened and Leslie disappeared from view. Rachael couldn't see who had opened the door.

She sat back in her seat and studied the units directly across from Marcie, wondering who saw the figure outside Marcie's apartment the night Leo was taken, and which window they had been looking out of. The awning certainly would've made it difficult to distinguish if it had been a man or a woman. Plus it had been dark. Rachael craned her neck around to see if there were light poles in the parking lot. She saw only two, at the entrance to the complex.

As she looked, she saw that the three young teenagers were staring at her.

She willed herself to look back at them. They didn't look away.

On impulse, Rachael unlocked the car, stepped out, and walked toward the trio. They stayed where they were, watching her as she walked toward them. The group consisted of two girls and a boy. Rachael guessed they were thirteen or fourteen.

She plastered a smile on her face. "Hey. Mind if I ask you something?"

"Are you some kinda cop?" one of the girls said.

"No."

When no one said anything else, Rachael assumed she was free to ask. "Do you know all the people who live in this building?"

"Why?" the second girl said.

"I was just wondering if you've ever seen anyone near that apartment up there." Rachael pointed to Marcie's closed apartment door. "Someone who looked like they shouldn't be there."

Three sets of eyes traveled to the door.

"Is that the apartment where that baby got stole?" the first girl said.

"Yes."

The girls shrugged. The boy looked bored out of his mind.

"So you haven't seen anyone lingering around who doesn't live here?"

Again the girls shrugged. Then the first one spoke. "So you're not a cop? You sound like a cop."

"I work for the county. But I'm not a cop."

"She leaves her front door open," the boy said, yawning. "Anybody coulda gone in and taken anything they want."

"She leaves her front door open?" Rachael asked.

"In the winter she don't." The boy blinked lazily.

"Do you know the woman who lives there?"

The boy lifted and lowered his shoulders. "My mom knows her. We live on the same floor."

"But you don't really know her?"

The boy took a drink from the Pepsi he held in his hand. "They all the same to me. This place is full of people like her."

Full of people like her. Like her. The words tumbled around in Rachael's head. *Full of people like Marcie.*

Rachael heard footsteps. She turned. Leslie was walking toward her, surprise evident on her face.

"Thanks," Rachael said to the teenagers, turning her head back around. Then she began to walk back to the car. Back to Leslie.

"What were you doing?" Leslie whispered.

"Just chatting."

They closed the distance to the car and got in. Leslie started the engine. "You were asking those kids about Marcie?"

"Kind of."

"Kind of?"

"They didn't tell me anything we don't already know." Rachael reached behind her head and pulled the seat belt down across her body. "Not really. So what happened inside?"

Leslie backed out of the parking space, put the car in drive, and eased forward. The three teenagers watched as if they'd been paid to. "Believe it or not, Joyce Shipley was there. Sitting on the sofa smoking a cigarette. Couldn't believe it."

"Joyce? Joyce was there?"

"Yes. So I come in and the first thing I have to do is get after Marcie for letting someone smoke in the apartment. She said her mother knew when Leo got there she'd have to put it out. Joyce stubbed it out in a cereal bowl and glared at me like I was an IRS agent." Leslie swung her car into the late-afternoon traffic.

"Well, what about Marcie? What did she do when you brought Leo in?" Rachael asked.

"She reached for the carrier as soon as I was inside. I'd say she was anxious to see him. She took the blanket off him right away and started to lift him out. Joyce said something like, 'For crying out loud, Marcie. He's asleep. You don't wake a sleeping baby.' Marcie just ignored her and took him out, turning him this way and that, like she was making sure he hadn't been tattooed while at Collette's."

"So she seemed happy?"

"Yeah, I guess *happy* works. Actually, it was more like she was satisfied. Like she was glad she got her way."

"She didn't tear up?"

"No. She held him close and kissed his head. She asked where the sleeper had come from. I told her it was paid for with money the county had given the foster parents for stuff like that. She asked if she had to give it back and I couldn't tell if she was pleased or annoyed when I told her she didn't."

"And the other kids were there, too?"

"Hallie and J.J. came running up to Marcie from the back of the apartment as soon as I came in. J.J. wanted to hold Leo right away. Hallie's too young to understand what was going on. Well, then Leo woke up and started howling. Joyce said, 'I told you so.' Hallie started crying, too. And J.J. was jumping up and down the whole time, begging to hold 'Weo.' It was fairly chaotic when I left."

"And you reminded her to lock her door?"

"I did. I reminded her of the other terms in her agreement, too."

Rachael exhaled and sat back in her seat.

It was done.

Leo was home.

The case was closed.

But it felt open. Untied. Undone.

Leslie looked over at her. "You look perplexed."

"Mmm." Rachael said, brows furrowed.

Leslie paused for a minute. "Say, doesn't Ivy live around here?"

"Half a mile away."

"Mind if we go by there? I want to see her place."

Rachael sensed a sudden twinge of expectancy—or was it urgency—rise up within her. If her annoying inkling was to be trusted, if this truly wasn't over, Ivy was someone she wanted on her side.

"I don't mind," she said. "Take a left at the light."

TWENTY-ONE

Cars lined the street in both directions on Ivy's street, their windshields glossy in the late-afternoon sun. Leslie and Rachael parked two blocks away and began walking to the salmon-hued duplex.

"So, what's your impression of Ivy, if I may ask?" Leslie said.

Rachael wordlessly considered the amount of time she'd spent with Ivy Judson as they crossed the street. Mere minutes, really. A few minutes at her office with Marcie, a few more without, perhaps ten minutes at Ivy's house, and then this morning's meeting. Not a whole lot of time. Still, the picture she had in her mind was clear: The woman came across as genuinely empathetic toward the disadvantaged. And somewhat prejudiced against the system. The young women she had invited into her home surely felt a kinship with her just based on those two qualities alone.

"She obviously has a heart for young single mothers and their kids. And she doesn't seem to mind coming to their rescue when they need a hand," Rachael replied. "She also has a—how should I say it—sweetly veiled distrust for the county. My guess is she thinks we really don't know how to help these girls. We just point fingers and take away children. I'm sure Marcie and the rest like that about her."

"Hmmm."

Rachael turned her head to face Leslie as they walked. "You haven't had complaints about her, have you?"

"None at all. I'm just curious. So are a couple other caseworkers. It's kind of odd what she's doing. Volunteering all on her own like that, without being attached to an outside agency or a church. It's wonderful that she wants to help people, but just a little odd that she's off doing her own thing."

"There's nothing illegal about it."

"I know. It's just that we don't see it very often. Usually humanitarian types go through social service agencies or church organizations."

Ahead of them, a block away, a young woman suddenly emerged from Ivy's duplex. She stopped on Ivy's porch, and then turned as Ivy joined her. The woman was obviously pregnant. Even from several houses away Rachael thought she looked familiar.

Rachael and Leslie simultaneously stopped as ahead the two women embraced. When they parted, the young woman wiped her eyes.

"Do you know who that is?" Leslie asked, straining to make out the woman's features.

Rachael watched the woman lower her head and slowly shake it from side to side. Ivy reached out and took her hand.

"I think her name is Arden," Rachael said. "She goes to Ivy's support group. She was there the morning I stopped by."

Ivy said something to Arden. Her words appeared to be consoling. Arden nodded and again Ivy embraced her. Then Arden turned toward the steps. She took them slowly, holding onto the handrail and awkwardly adjusting her balance for the extra weight she carried. Arden looked up at Ivy when she reached the pavement and Ivy waved to her. Then Arden began to walk slowly down the sidewalk, away from Rachael and Leslie as they stood watching. When Arden was two house lengths away, Leslie touched Rachael's arm.

"Come on," she said.

Rachael's heels on the pavement announced her and Leslie's arrival before they had even reached the duplex, and Ivy turned toward the sound. When her eyes met Rachael's, Ivy's immediate response was to glance back to Arden. Almost to make sure she was safely away.

Apparently satisfied, Ivy stepped out farther on the porch, stopping just at the top step. She smiled broadly. It was genuine, as it always was. But out of place, Rachael thought. A surprise visit from two county employees who worked in child protection didn't usually elicit a smile as wide as that.

"Well, hello there." Ivy sounded confident, hospitable. "I didn't expect to see you two again today."

"Hello, Ivy," Rachael said warmly. "Hope you don't mind that we've come by. Leslie and I were in the neighborhood. Leslie just brought Leo back home."

"Of course. And no, I don't mind." Again, Ivy's eyes wandered to the retreating form of Arden, now more than a block away. The young mother was getting into the driver's side of an aging brown sedan. Ivy turned her gaze back to Leslie and Rachael. "Is there something I can help you with?"

Rachael decided to make a bold move, one that she hoped would show Ivy that she wasn't the only one who cared about troubled mothers. "Is Arden okay?"

Ivy's eyes widened slightly and only momentarily, like she wanted to disguise her surprise that Rachael had remembered the name and had seen Arden walking away. She quickly replaced her astonishment with a thin layer of indignation accompanied by the ever-present smile. "You don't need to go bothering Arden about anything."

Rachael took a step forward. Ivy had mistaken her interest. "That's not what I meant, Ivy. I wasn't suggesting Arden needed intervention from the county. She just looked so sad."

"Well, not that it's truly any of your business, but Arden has decided to give her baby up for adoption." Ivy crossed her arms in front of her ample chest. "Of course she's sad. She loves her baby. But she knows she can't be a mother to her child. I think she's being incredibly selfless. And brave. She's making the supreme sacrifice. And I, for one, am quite proud of her. I'm sure if you considered what she has decided to do, at such a young age, and with so much garbage in her past, you'd be proud of her, too. Not looking for ways to condemn her."

Rachael felt as though she'd been slapped. "I assure you I am not looking for ways to condemn her."

Ivy grinned down on her from two steps up. "How can you not be? That's your job."

Rachael decided to smile back. "No, actually it's not. It's to make sure kids are protected from harm and neglect. You know as well as I do there are a lot of people out there who shouldn't be parents."

"There are a lot of people who've never been shown how."

Rachael felt the easy affinity that she had felt from Ivy disappearing. She tried a different tack. "What you are doing is wonderful for these women, Ivy. It truly is. Leslie and I were just saying how amazing it is that you've taken on this support role all on your own, knowing you won't get any kind of payment for it. It's quite remarkable."

"I wouldn't take money even if it was offered to me." Ivy's tone had softened somewhat. The compliment had relaxed her, as Rachael hoped it would.

"It would be great if there were more people like you who invested themselves into the lives of needy people," Rachael said.

Ivy looked thoughtful. "It would be a different world, then, wouldn't it?"

"It certainly would."

Ivy tilted her head. "Would you two like to come in? I'd like to tell you something."

Rachael looked over at Leslie. Leslie took a step forward. "Sure."

They went inside.

The circle of kitchen chairs from the last time Rachael was there were gone. The room resembled a more typical living room. Afghan over the back of the couch. An armchair, two end tables, a pole lamp. Issues of *Better Homes and Gardens* were fanned on the coffee table. A box of tissues sat next to the magazines with several crumpled wads scattered about. A wicker laundry basket full of baby toys rested at one end of the couch. Ivy grabbed the used tissues and invited Leslie and Rachael to sit down. Ivy sat in the armchair.

"Toys for the grandkids?" Leslie said, nodding toward the basket.

Ivy looked startled. "How did you know I had grandkids?"

Leslie hesitated for a second. "I didn't. I just guessed. You seem like the grandmotherly type."

The startled expression dissipated and Ivy smiled. "My grandkids don't come by that often. They live an hour away, by the Wisconsin border. And they're too old for toys like that. Those toys are for the children of the moms who visit me."

"How many grandchildren do you have?" Rachael asked.

"Two. They're my son Dallas's kids. A boy and a girl. Nine and seven. My daughter's not married." Ivy pointed to a bookshelf behind her and two framed five by seven portraits. One of a boy who looked younger than nine and the other, a girl who was surely no older than a toddler. "That's Ryan. And that's Anna," she said.

"They're nine and seven?" Leslie asked.

Ivy looked at the pictures and then waved her hand, as if to dismiss them. "These pictures are a little old. But I keep them up. I just like them."

She hesitated for a second before turning her attention back to Rachael and Leslie.

"Your son's name is Dallas? That's a nice name." Rachael leaned back on the cushions.

"I think so. My ex-husband had to be talked into it. He didn't like the name Amber for our daughter, either. Had to sell him on both."

"May I ask how long your ex-husband has been out of the picture?" Leslie asked.

"He left me when Dallas was two and Amber was ten months old. Just up and left one day. I didn't hear from him for four years."

"Four years?"

A look of sad accomplishment fell over Ivy. Rachael got the distinct impression Ivy was both proud and surprised that she had survived.

"Four years. Not word. Not a call. Not until he wanted a divorce. I tried to get all those back years of child support from him but it was like squeezing blood out of a turnip. I don't even like turnips. Or blood. I finally just decided the heck with him. I didn't need his money. And my kids didn't need a deadbeat like him in their lives. I haven't had contact with him for, let's see, going on twenty years."

"Must've been tough," Leslie said.

"It was hell. I had to work two jobs. I ruined my back standing all day long in an assembly line. And I had no one to lean on. My parents were dead, my sister wanted nothing to do with me. I was truly on my own.

All I had were my babies, my determination, and whatever mercy God wanted to show me. That's it. Sometimes it wasn't enough."

Ivy looked away. Her ever-present smile had slipped. When she looked back up a moment later, it was back. "But those days are far behind me. And I wouldn't wish them on anyone, but I wouldn't know how to help these girls if I hadn't gone through them. That's the thing. I understand where these girls are at. No offense, but I don't think you do."

Rachael didn't want to get into a debate with Ivy. And she didn't want to spoil the mood. Ivy's transparency was something Rachael hadn't realized she had wanted until just that moment. She decided not to rise to Ivy's challenge. Beside her, Leslie was silent. The social worker had probably had this conversation before and knew better than to argue the point.

"You said there was something you wanted to tell us?" Rachael said, tilting her head, hoping she conveyed interest in whatever Ivy had to say.

The woman hesitated for a moment, as if pulling herself out of her old, forgotten world. "Yes," she said a moment later. "Yes, I do. I just want to tell you that I think you county people too often do everything backwards. That's why nothing ever seems to get any better. That's why you have the same people in and out of your offices all the time. And why some of them never leave."

"Backwards?" Leslie asked.

"What I mean is, you focus on the child, which of course you must, but the child is not the problem. You *make* the child the problem by taking him out of the home and making him the one that has to suffer, see? It's the parents who are the problem. They either don't know how to parent, like I told you already, or they are so addicted to drugs or alcohol or their own destructive past that they just can't parent. The parents are the problem, not the child. They are the ones who should be sent away to get their act together. Not the kid. And the parents who need help parenting, well, you should send in a mentor to live with them and show them how it's done. But what do you do? You take the child out of his home and away from his terrible parents, who, God love him, he adores anyway, and that's supposed to make for better parents? How can it? It's all backwards."

Rachael and Leslie sat wordless on the couch. Finally Leslie spoke up.

"That's a very interesting notion, Ivy, letting the children stay and fostering out the parents."

"Or bringing in a court-ordered mentor," Ivy quickly added. "Someone to live with them. Help them. Teach them. These parents you're working with, they're clueless. Some of them can be redeemed, but honestly some of them can't. Because you've been doing it backwards for so long, they can never find their way out. And who has to bear the full weight of your mistakes and theirs? The children. It's just not right. I can only help the few women who come to my group. Who is going to help all the other thousands of mothers and fathers in the system? Who is going to help them?"

"And do you think you are helping them, Ivy?" Rachael asked. "I don't mean to sound skeptical at all. I really want to know. Have you seen a difference through what you're doing? For Marcie? For Sharell? For Liza?"

Ivy stiffened. "You don't erase years of mistakes overnight. Marcie has huge obstacles to overcome. So does Sharell. And Liza is mentally ill as anyone can tell. But that doesn't mean she can't be a mother to her child. She could live with a mentor and be a splendid mother if there was someone there to help her. And yes, I've seen change in my girls. I saw one today. In Arden. She made a difficult choice, the most difficult kind of choice for a mother. She was incredibly brave. And her child was the only person she was thinking about. If you knew her like I do, you'd know there's been a difference in her life."

A long pause followed.

Leslie stood up. "Well, you've been more than generous with your time, Ivy. And it's been great to hear your insights, but we need to be getting back."

Rachael and Ivy stood as well.

"Well, it was nice to have you stop by." Ivy sounded sincere.

"You seem to care a great deal about these women and their children." Leslie slung her purse over her shoulder.

"I do," Ivy replied. "They are precious. Each and every one of them. And my girls are learning to care by watching *me* care. That's how people learn, you know. The group is having a little party here for Marcie and Leo tomorrow afternoon. I'd invite you to come, but I don't think the girls would feel free to be themselves if you were here."

"That's understandable, Ivy," Leslie said. "Well, thanks again. Goodbye."

"Goodbye, Ivy," Rachael echoed.

"Bye."

The women moved to the door and Ivy opened it wide. Leslie and Rachael stepped out into the first throes of the setting sun. Ivy called out another farewell and waved.

They walked back to the car with Leslie doing most of the talking.

Rachael was contemplative.

The encounter with Ivy had been intriguing. What the woman had said kept spinning around in her head as they made their way to Leslie's car. Rachael couldn't get past the notion that Ivy had revealed quite a bit about herself and the women in her group. She felt a compulsion to remember everything Ivy had said.

Rachael began to sort through the snippets of the conversation, mentally filing away phrases like, *Some of them can be redeemed, but honestly some of them can't* and *Who has to bear the full weight of your mistakes and theirs? The children.* And *It's all backwards.*

It's all backwards.

She barely heard Leslie comment that Leo was probably at that moment lying half on and half off J.J's wiggly lap while Hallie put carpet fuzz in her mouth, Marcie flipped through channels on the remote, and Joyce tugged on a cigarette.

TWENTY-TWO

The loft was dark and quiet. The extra time Rachael had spent out with Leslie had put her behind in getting ready for her two days off, and late getting home. Trace and McKenna were usually waiting for her at the loft by six o'clock, but there was no sign of them when she walked inside. And Trace didn't leave the creative notes that Fig did. Wherever Trace and McKenna were, Fig wasn't with them. If he was with Trace and McKenna, there'd be a drawing showing where they were plastered to the fridge or the bathroom mirror or taped to the ceiling in the entry.

Rachael threw the day's mail on the island countertop and opened the fridge to study its contents. Fig would be appalled. A few containers of yogurt, half a bag of baby carrots, a container of feta cheese, and a carton of eggs. Not much else. She closed the fridge door, and then turned and slid open a cabinet drawer. She fished out a menu from her favorite Chinese restaurant down the street. Beef and broccoli, and shrimp in oyster sauce—delivered—would be just fine. She grabbed her cell phone out of her purse, made the call, and then took a Diet Coke from the fridge. Just as she opened the can, the front door opened and Trace walked in.

"Hey," Rachael said, looking past her husband to see if Fig was coming in behind him with McKenna in his arms. But Trace was alone. "Where's McKenna?"

Trace stopped. "I thought you had her." But then he winked. The panic inside her had lasted less than a second. "She's at your mom and dad's," he said.

Her parents lived in St. Cloud. An hour away. "She's at Mom and Dad's?"

"Yep." Trace brushed past her and kissed her right temple. He opened the fridge and stared. "Wow. We have, like, no food."

"Why is she at Mom and Dad's?"

Trace turned to face Rachael. "Because I suddenly had to be at a meeting this afternoon. I couldn't take McKenna with me. I needed to take her somewhere, Rach. I knew your mom would take her. She asked if McKenna could spend the night. I said yes."

He turned back toward the fridge.

McKenna spending the night at her parents' house? Just like that?

"Why didn't you call me?" Rachael sought his gaze.

He swung his head back around. "You were at work, love. What could you have done? Honestly. Could you have taken off early? You know you couldn't have."

Rachael felt her mother-heart flip-flopping. "But you could've called me and told me what you were doing."

"Yeah. I guess I could have. But what difference would it have made? Besides, on Wednesdays McKenna's my responsibility. I made the most responsible decision I could. And I knew you'd want to go get her tonight, but your mom begged to let her stay over. I said okay. I thought we owed her. She came home early from the library to take McKenna. You have tomorrow off. You can go get her whenever you want. Is this really all we have to eat?"

"Did you bring her yellow blanket? Did you take the diaper bag? Does she have clean clothes for tomorrow?" Rachael felt alarm rising within her. It was senseless, and she knew it. McKenna loved going over to her grandparents' house. But she had never stayed overnight there. McKenna hadn't slept anywhere else but with her and Trace.

"Rach. I know how to pack for an overnight. Really, I do. Want to go out? Hey, we could actually go out."

"I just ordered take-out from Wang's. It'll be here in ten minutes."

"Oh. Okay. That's cool." Trace started to walk away.

Rachael took a step to follow him. "Are you mad at me?"

He turned around. "Why should I be mad at you?"

"Well, you shouldn't, actually." She was thinking she was the one who should be a bit peeved.

"So, why'd you ask?"

"Trace, I know we need to decide what to do with McKenna. I'm not ignoring it."

"I didn't say you were."

"So you whisking McKenna off to my mom's to stay the night isn't to show me how bad the situation is?"

"There was no whisking away, Rach," Trace said evenly. "I had to be at a meeting in Bloomington at four. I needed a baby-sitter. I trust your mother. So do you. I drove two hours because I thought it was an arrangement you'd be okay with. Fig had appointments, so I couldn't leave McKenna with him. If you're ticked that McKenna is staying the night, take it up with your mom. You know, I thought it might be nice for the two of us to have an evening alone together."

He turned back around and headed for the stairs to the bedrooms.

Rachael wanted to go after him, but she hung back, wounded and unsure. She rubbed her forehead absently and sauntered to the dining room, sliding into a chair. Her thoughts were a tangle. She knew they had to hire a nanny. Or she had to find a different job. Something with less hours, less stress, fewer rush-hour commutes. The truth was, she didn't want to hand over thirty hours of McKenna's week, the best part of her daughter's days, to someone else. If Trace couldn't have those hours, then she wanted them. No one loved McKenna like she and Trace did. No one could care for her like they did.

She raised her head and stared at the wall ahead of her, where Elizabeth McKenna Flynn's drawing of the sparrow hung. Her eyes fell upon the shaft of light, the watchful eye of God, as the mother bird braved the storm and wind.

The watchful eye of God.

The watchful eye of God.

Time seemed to stand still as she continued to stare at it.

Rachael didn't know how long she was held in a trancelike state, staring at the drawing. She was just suddenly aware that Trace was standing next to her, looking at her with a perplexed look on his face and holding a white paper bag that smelled of the Orient.

"What are you doing?" he said.

"I…I was just…" she stammered. "What's that?" She nodded toward the bag in his hand.

"Didn't you tell me you ordered takeout? It's here. They rang the buzzer three times. You didn't hear it?"

"No…No, I didn't."

Trace set the bag down on the table and looked at his mother's drawing. "Why were you staring at that?"

"I don't know, Trace. Something just kind of fell over me. And I lost track of time. I…"

"Something fell over you." It was not exactly a question.

She let her eyes drift back to the drawing. "That little slash of light, the part where God is looking down on the sparrow, I just…I don't know. I don't want to talk about it anymore."

Rachael stood up, walked back to the kitchen, and grabbed two plates and two forks from the wooden dish drainer by the sink. When she brought them back to the dining room, Trace was still standing there with the bag in his hands, looking at his mother's picture.

The alley was half-lit. A slit of a moon peered down on the cramped and narrow passage, mixing its pale light with the hazy wash of a flickering streetlight several yards away. Rachael shivered and tried to pull her coat around her, but she looked down and saw that she had no coat. She was in her pajamas. She heard movement behind her and she turned, knocking over a rotting crate of rusted tin cans. Whatever had been behind her skittered away. Something warm and wet was on her arm. She looked at it. Blood. The crate had scratched her.

No, it wasn't the crate.

The cat. The cat had scratched her.

Fig's cat. The one in the drawing.

There it was now, perched behind a pile of cardboard boxes. Watching her. Flicking its tail. It meowed. And Rachael realized the cat hadn't meant to hurt her. He had been sitting on the crate when it fell.

She was reaching out to pet the cat when she heard the first cry. It was soft at first. Then it got louder. An infant's high-pitched wail. Rachael looked about. There was no Dumpster. Just boxes and crates and dark corners and eerie light. The cries intensified and then suddenly stopped. For a moment there was no sound. Rachael could hear her own breath and nothing else. Then a blast of noise pierced the dank hush of the alley. A woman was screaming. The baby's mother, screaming for her child. Marcie. Rachael tried to push the boxes and crates out of her way; they were everywhere. They fell about her and blocked her path. She reached out her hands and felt wood. Was it a box? Was the baby inside?

The screams intensified, filling the alley, her ears, her brain. But she couldn't find him. She couldn't see where he was. She couldn't find the baby.

Louder and louder the screams grew until it seemed sound had the ability to suffocate. She squeezed her eyes shut, intent now on only finding air for her lungs. Then she felt a tremendous pull, like she was being yanked through a tight opening. She opened her eyes.

Rachael was standing at the wood railing of the loft stairs, drenched in sweat and inches away from the first step. Trace had his arms tight around her.

She knew as soon as she awoke that the screams had been her own.

Trace handed Rachael a cup of coffee with one hand and rubbed her shoulder with the other as she sat at the loft's island counter. Morning sunlight stretched across the two of them from overhead skylights.

"Did you ever get back to sleep?" he asked.

She shook her head. "I don't think so."

"Why don't you just go back to bed, love? I can go get McKenna."

She sipped the coffee and then set it down slowly. "Maybe we could just go together?"

"Sure."

A few seconds of uncomfortable silence hung between them.

"Rachael, maybe you should just let the job go for a while. It's too much. It's affecting your sleep."

"It's not the job, Trace!" She didn't mean to snap. He stopped rubbing her shoulder.

"Well then what is it?"

She didn't know.

"This isn't normal, Rach," Trace said. "You walking the loft like that, screaming. It's not normal. What if I had been out of town? What if you had fallen down the stairs?"

"I know it's not normal." Rachael laced her fingers around the mug, absorbing its warmth into her body.

"So if it's not the job, then what is it?"

"I don't know!"

Trace turned to the counter and grabbed his own coffee mug but he didn't drink. He just stood there.

Two hot tears slid down Rachael's face. "I'm sorry, Trace."

He reached back and stroked her head. "Knock it off. You don't apologize for having nightmares."

She wanted to say that what she had was no nightmare. It was something else. More like a bizarre vision.

Which sounded absolutely absurd.

But it wasn't an ordinary bad dream. She had the distinct impression she was being let in on something. Like God was clueing her in. She didn't think for a moment that God had led her out of her bed and sent her shrieking down the hall. That surely was her own response to the dream's vividness. But everything else about the dream seemed too otherworldly to be the stuff of nonsensical nightmares. Too stunning. Too real.

Trace turned around as if about to say something else, but Rachael's cell phone resting on the counter where he stood began to trill.

He picked it up. "Want to let it go to voice mail?"

Rachael turned her head toward him. "Who is it?"

Trace looked at the tiny screen. "Will," he said.

Will.

Rachael held out her hand and Trace handed her the phone.

"Will?"

"So, you're up."

"I'm up. I've *been* up. Is everything all right?"

"Well, for me, yes; for you, kind of; but for Marcie Shipley, not at all."

Oh, God, Rachael breathed a prayer heavenward as images of the dream fell over her. "What is it, Will?"

"Marcie Shipley is under arrest."

TWENTY-THREE

An image of Marcie Shipley being led away in handcuffs filled Rachael's brain as she held the phone to her ear. She knew without Will even telling her that whatever Marcie had done, it had something to do with Leo.

Something terrible.

"Is Leo all right?" Rachael said, as Trace took the stool next to her. She turned to look at her husband. His eyes were full of apprehension.

"He's missing, Rachael," Will replied. "No one knows where he is. Marcie called the police at seven this morning to report he had been kidnapped. Again. A unit was over there in less than five minutes. They found no sign of forced entry. None. The crime scene team is still at her apartment, but they've found nothing to indicate an intruder. The baby is just gone. And Marcie claims to know nothing about where he is."

Oh God, oh God! Marcie! The dream from the night before enveloped her. The screaming woman. Marcie. Why was Marcie screaming? Why would she dream that Marcie had been screaming? Nothing made any sense.

"But you think she does know," she finally said aloud to Will. "Is that why you arrested her?"

"The first officer on the scene found a small amount of crack in the bathroom. Marcie claims she has no idea how it got there and that she didn't use it, but she freely admitted she doesn't remember getting up to feed the baby. Doesn't remember much of anything after nine o'clock. She can't account for anything she did after nine. We've already charged her with reckless child endangerment and the narcotics charge. We're running a tox screen to see if she's telling the truth about the crack. There will be more charges later in the day, I'm sure. Especially if anything bad happens to that kid."

Leo! Rachael glanced up at the wall clock above the kitchen sink. It was a few minutes before eight. Leo had been missing for an hour already. Longer, if he had been taken in the middle of the night.

"Joyce Shipley doesn't have him?" Rachael said. "She was at the apartment yesterday when Leslie brought Leo home. Are you sure she doesn't have him?"

"We've talked with her mom. Joyce left the apartment a little before six yesterday evening. She doesn't have Leo. We called the sister, too. She doesn't have him either."

An unbidden image of a sneering Koko wagging a finger and yelling, "I told you so!" arose in Rachael's mind. She willed it away.

"Did you go back to the alley? The one where he was found the first time?" she said.

"We've got units looking in every alley in south St. Paul."

Rachael's pulse began to pound as she pictured Leo's tiny body lying somewhere in the cool morning air. It was late September. The spell of Indian summer days was over. Exposure alone could kill him.

"Have you talked to Sharell? To Liza? Did you try Booth?" Her voice sounded agitated in her ears.

"I know you have your ideas about those three, but we've got nothing on any of them. We've far more reason to suspect Marcie. The drugs in the bathroom are a big red flag. So is the fact that she has a new lock and there was no forced entry."

Rachael dismissed the drugs for the moment. "But did she *use* the lock!"

"What?"

"Does she remember locking the door last night?"

"Yeah. She said she locked the door."

"If she had done something to Leo, wouldn't she have told you she forgot to lock the door so it would appear someone else had taken him?"

"If she had doped herself up there's a pretty good chance she has no idea what she did last night."

"You don't have the drug test back yet?"

"No."

Rachael rubbed her forehead with her free hand. Something wasn't right about any of this. "Can you call me the minute you hear?"

Will paused for a moment. "Rachael, I didn't call you about this so you'd jump into the investigation. I called you because you were on the Chips for Leo. You needed to know."

"I'm not jumping into the investigation. And of course I need to know. When is she being arraigned?"

"Probably later today."

"I want to come."

"It's your day off."

"I want to come."

Will sighed. "All right. I'll let you know when it is."

"And you'll call me about the drug test? And if you find Leo?"

"Yeah. I'll call you."

There was a moment of silence. "Still think Marcie had nothing to do with any of this?" Will asked.

Rachael paused before answering. She didn't know what to think. If the dreams were really more than dreams, then she was fairly certain Marcie was innocent. She was convinced the woman screaming in her nightmare had been Marcie. But how in the world could she know if the dreams were meant to reveal something to her? She had no idea what they meant. Whatever she was supposed to *get*, she wasn't getting.

"I don't know anything for sure, Will," she finally said. "But you know as well as I do that anyone who commits a crime is motivated by something. Marcie has no reason to do this. None."

"And you think someone else does?"

"Someone else has to."

Will was silent for a couple seconds. "You wouldn't have arrested her, would you?" he finally said.

"No."

"You think it was someone else."

"Yes."

"Cops can't operate on hunches, you know," Will said. "We have to go by the evidence."

"So do prosecuting attorneys. And you guys *are* going by your hunches on this one, Will. You have a missing baby, an unforced entry, a teaspoon of a street drug, and a troubled mother, and your hunch is she kidnapped and abandoned her own child."

"Who else could have done it, Rachael? And how? How did they get in?"

Rachael thought for a moment. There was only one other way the offender could've gotten inside. "They had a key."

"Marcie told us she has the only key. She didn't make any copies."

"Then she forgot to lock her door. I know she said she did, but what if what she really did wasn't what she thought she did?"

"Rachael."

"You asked me, Will. You asked me if I would've arrested her and I told you."

"Do you have anything concrete for me that points to anyone else besides Marcie? 'Cause I really do want you to be right about this."

All she had were three inconclusive nightmares. "No, I don't. Not at the moment. But I do have my absurd little hunches. If anything comes of them, you can be sure I'll let you know."

"I never said your hunches were absurd." Will sounded a little wounded.

"Sorry, Will. That wasn't meant for you. They just seem a little absurd to me this time."

"Well, don't dwell on them too much today. It's your day off, remember? And figuring this out is what I actually get paid to do. Hey, I've got to run."

"But you'll call me when the tox report comes back? And the initial hearing is scheduled? And call me the minute you find Leo."

"Yeah. I'll call you."

"Bye, Will."

"Bye."

Rachael hung up and turned to face Trace. He had his cheek resting in the palm of his hand, propped up by one elbow. "That baby's been kidnapped again, hasn't he?" he said quietly.

"Yes," she murmured.

"So what do you want to do?"

Rachael thought of Leo lying somewhere—dead or alive, no one knew—and she answered him quickly.

"I want to go get our daughter."

TWENTY-FOUR

By the time Rachael and Trace set out for St. Cloud at eight thirty, the bulk of the morning commute was over. As Trace merged onto I-94 west, Rachael pulled her cell phone out of her purse. She had already called Leslie before leaving the loft, to make sure she knew what had happened during the night. And she had checked the phone book to see if Ivy Judson's phone number was listed. It was. She had entered the number into her cell phone and now pressed the call button as the skyline of Minneapolis fell away behind them.

The line on the other end rang four times before being picked up.

"Hello?" The voice was Ivy's, but it was breathless, higher in pitch than normal, and inches away from being a sob.

Ivy knew. Someone had called her. Rachael wondered who.

"Ivy, it's Rachael Flynn."

"Oh, sweet Jesus, Ms. Flynn, that poor little baby. Have they found him? Is he okay?" Ivy was distraught. "Please tell me he's all right!"

"Ivy, you know about Leo?"

"Yes, yes! Marcie called me when she woke up this morning and Leo was missing. I told her to call the police. I tried to get over to her apartment to see her, but they were putting her in the squad car when I got there. She was yelling terrible things. It was just awful. Oh, Ms. Flynn, is he all right? Is Leo all right?"

"The police haven't found him, Ivy. I don't know if he's all right."

"Oh!" The woman broke off in a sob followed by a whisper. "He *has* to be all right. He just has to."

"Ivy, did you talk to Marcie? Did she say anything to you?"

"They wouldn't let me talk to her! She saw me through the window of the police car and she yelled for me, but they wouldn't let me go to her."

"The police think Marcie did this."

"Yes, yes, I know they do!"

"Do you?"

Ivy didn't answer.

"Ivy, do you think Marcie abandoned Leo somewhere?"

"I…I just can't think that way about my girls!"

Her girls.

Her *girls*.

"What was that?" Rachael wanted to make sure she had heard her correctly. Ivy might've just unknowingly revealed something huge. That perhaps it wasn't Marcie the two of them were talking about.

"What?" The woman sounded distracted by the question.

Rachael decided to be blunt. "Ivy, do you think one of the girls in your group did this?"

"Oh, sweet Jesus, help us…"

"Ivy, if you know who did this or if you think you know, you have to tell me! Do you want something terrible to happen to Leo?"

"No, no, no…"

"Then tell me what you know. Or what you think you know."

"My girls trust me!"

"And what about that baby? Don't you care about him?"

"Of course I do." The woman sobbed on the other end.

"Ivy, what do you know?"

Rachael could hear Ivy fiddling with a tissue and taking a deep breath. "You shouldn't assume I *know* anything. I have my suspicions, just like you do."

"And who do you suspect?"

"It's not *who* I suspect! It's what I suspect people in crisis are capable of doing! You always point fingers at the person! It's not about the person!"

Yes, it is, Rachael said inwardly. But she didn't say it. "And what are people in crisis capable of doing?" she said instead.

"You don't have to ask me that, Ms. Flynn. They are capable of doing anything. You know that."

"Is one of your girls capable of harming Leo Shipley?"

Ivy sniffed and made little noises in her throat. "People in crisis are capable of doing anything," she finally murmured.

For a long moment, neither one said anything else.

"Is that all you're going to tell me?" Rachael asked.

"It's all I can."

"You do know a baby's life could be at stake."

"Of course I know that! You think I don't know that?" More sobs. More tears.

"Do you think it was Liza? Sharell?"

"Do you honestly think I would keep that from you if I knew?"

"I didn't ask you if you knew if it was one of them. I said, 'Do you think?'"

"I have to go."

"Ivy, listen to me. I want you to promise me something. Will you promise to call me if you learn anything about where Leo is or who took him?"

Ivy was silent.

"Ivy?"

"I promise."

"Call me at this number. Do you have caller ID?"

"Yes."

"Then call me at this number. I don't care what time of day or night. Okay?"

"Yes. And Ms. Flynn, would you please call *me* the moment you hear Leo is all right? Please?" Again her voice broke away in a sob. "Please, will you promise?"

"I promise."

"All right."

"Goodbye, Ivy."

"Yes. Goodbye."

Rachael pressed the disconnect button and sat back in her seat. She was certain Ivy thought it was someone in the group who took Leo. Perhaps even Marcie herself, though Rachael still couldn't bring herself to believe Marcie was the guilty party. Too much didn't add up. The dream was confirmation that her instincts about Marcie were right.

"So?" Trace glanced over at her.

"I think she knows something."

"Like who took the baby?"

"Like who might be desperate enough to take the baby."

Trace turned his gaze back to the road ahead. "And I suppose you've got a pretty good idea who that might be."

Sharell. Or Liza.

Or maybe someone she hadn't considered before at all.

Arden.

Or one of the other girls whose names she hadn't committed to memory. Was there someone named Rose? Anita? She would have to look back through her notes. She couldn't remember the other girls' names.

"Actually, I don't have a pretty good idea," she replied. "But I'm sure it's someone in Ivy's support group."

"Yeah, but the kid just went home yesterday, right? How would someone in the group know he was home?"

Rachael thought for a moment. How indeed? She was about to comment that she didn't know when she suddenly remembered Ivy telling her and Leslie the support group was planning a little welcome-home party for Leo. It was supposed to be today. Ivy had probably contacted all of the girls. She wondered for a moment if Ivy had considered as she made those calls that it was highly likely one of the girls had taken Leo the first time. Did she think that young woman had just snapped that one instance and wouldn't try something so terrible again? Did Ivy think by reuniting the offender with the baby she stole—in the gentle atmosphere of a party—that she would be providing a therapeutic way for the guilty to deal with her misdeed?

"Rachael?" Trace was still waiting for an answer to his question.

"All the girls in the group knew Leo was coming home yesterday, Trace.

Ivy said she and the girls were going to be throwing a party today for Leo and Marcie. They all knew."

"So why exactly do you think it was one of the gals in the group? Why couldn't it have been someone else?"

"If it had been a random act by a stranger, then I don't think it would've happened twice. It has to be someone who knows Marcie and who wants to harm Marcie's child. And I just don't see her sister or her mother wanting that. Neither would the guy that Marcie thinks might be the father, especially now that he knows *we* know who he is."

"And it can't be anyone else Marcie knows?"

"Well, I suppose it could be."

"But you don't think it is."

Rachael shook her head. "I think it's someone in the group."

"How come?"

"Because *Ivy* thinks it's someone in the group."

They rode the next half hour in silence, Rachael sending up frantic prayers that Leo would be found alive, and Trace searching the radio for songs that weren't too peppy.

The trill of her cell phone in her lap a few minutes after nine startled her. Rachael nearly dropped the phone as she fumbled to open and answer it. She could see on the phone's tiny screen that Will was calling.

"Will! Have you found Leo?"

"Yeah. We found him."

Will's voice sounded sad.

Oh, Jesus...

"Is he all right?"

"He's at Children's. I don't think he's all right. But he's not dead."

Leo...

"Where was he? What happened to him?" A tear swelled in Rachael's left eye.

"He was found by a jogger in Riley Park down by the river. He had been dragged and bitten. His blanket was found by a trash can near the path, but he was found several yards away. The wounds look like dog bites."

"Dog bites? Will!"

"I know. It sounds bizarre. We're thinking he was left in the trash can next to where his blanket was found. Looks like a dog heard him or was digging through the trash, pulled him out, and dragged him several feet away. I haven't been to the hospital yet. I don't know how many bites there are or if the dog was playing, fighting, or tasting. Whatever he was doing, he lost interest, thank God. When the jogger came upon Leo's body, he said he saw no dog. Just the baby and the blood. Leo was unconscious when he found him. We're all hoping the fall from the trash can knocked him out before he felt the first bite."

"Oh, dear God, Will! Will he be all right?"

"I dunno. Probably. The EMT on the scene said he'll have scars, that's for sure. Lots of them."

Pictures of Leo being dragged and chewed flew past her brain and Rachael felt physical pain in her chest.

"I can't believe this has happened, Will," she whispered.

"No kidding. And this jogger, he said if he had been running at his normal time, he would've run right past that trash can. He thinks he might've seen the dog and been able to stop him. He's feeling kind of bummed."

"Surely he must know it's not his fault."

"I'm sure he does. But everybody plays the 'what if' game when they come across something horrific."

"Does Marcie know?"

"I'm going over to the jail to talk to her now."

"You are?"

"This baby could've easily been killed. That's my department. Yeah, I'm going over."

Rachael flicked the tears away. "You are charging her with attempted murder?"

"Not yet."

"You're sure she left him there, Will?"

"Her drug screen came back, Rachael. She tested positive for ketamine."

Ketamine was a heavy-duty analgesic used in the past by veterinarians, and lately by users at parties and raves. Thefts of the drug were routinely being reported by animal clinic owners. It was cheaper than rohypnol and legal.

Marcie, what were you thinking?

"And that makes you sure?" Rachael shook her head, thinking *stupid, stupid girl.*

"That makes for convincing evidence."

Rachael's head was beginning to ache with the weight of too many troubling thoughts. "Do you know when she's being arraigned?"

"Three o'clock today."

"I'm going to come."

"I figured you would."

"Call me if you hear any updates on Leo?"

"Will do."

"Thanks, Will."

"Catch you later."

She pressed the off button, sat back in her seat, and closed her eyes. What had happened to Leo was too gruesome to contemplate.

"Did I hear you say 'dog bites'?" Trace turned to look at her.

Rachael began to cry then. Not just a welling tear in both eyes, but a steady flow that trickled down both cheeks and had her shaking in her seat. A terrible thought had suddenly occurred to her.

She had sent Leo home. She had sent him home to this.

With dread and misgiving she had sent him home.

"Rachael?"

"Just get me to McKenna," she whispered.

TWENTY-FIVE

Eva Harper watched silently as her daughter Rachael enveloped McKenna in an embrace that lasted several long moments, longer than one would expect for a mother-child separation that had only lasted twenty-four hours. Rachael stroked her daughter's silky, thin curls and inhaled her sweet fragrance. It seemed to her that she could not hold McKenna tight enough against her. She knew her mother was watching her, wondering. She knew fresh tears had sprung in her eyes, though for the last few miles to St. Cloud she'd been able to calm her emotions.

"What's the matter?" Eva whispered to Trace, though Rachael heard her.

"A case at work. Bad one." Trace didn't elaborate. Rachael was glad he didn't.

Rachael could sense her mother's gaze on her. "I'll be all right, Mom."

"Mum-Mum," McKenna cooed, patting Rachael's back with her little hand while Rachael stroked hers.

"She slept okay last night?" Rachael flicked the tears away.

"Like an angel."

"Thanks for taking her on such short notice, Mom. I'm sorry you had to leave work early yesterday."

"It's not that big of a deal, Rachael. You know that. I'm thinking of retiring anyway."

Rachael smiled. "No, you're not."

Eva smiled back. "Thinking is not the same as doing."

McKenna squirmed to get down and Rachael set her gently onto her feet. "I'm thinking of retiring, too," Rachael said, watching as McKenna toddled over to the family cocker spaniel.

"You are not!" Eva continued to smile, but her eyes were wide.

"Well, not really retire, retire. Trace and I are just thinking about me making a career change for a little while. Like maybe some consulting work or a few hours a week for Legal Aid or some other organization like that. Something with less hours. I either do that or we hire a nanny. And I really don't want to give all those McKenna hours to someone else. I don't. Does that sound crazy?"

"You're asking *me* if that sounds crazy?" Eva grinned.

"It doesn't, does it?"

"No. It's not crazy to want to soak up these first years with McKenna. They fly, these years do. She'll be starting kindergarten before you know it. Then high school. Then college."

Rachael looked up from watching her daughter. "So you've told me."

"It's true. You know it's true!"

"Dah dune!" McKenna said, picking the dog's rattle toy and handing it to Trace.

"So when will all this happen?" Eva said.

"I don't know yet, Mom. I need to pray about it. I need to think about how my life will change. I need to make sure it's the right thing."

Eva looked down on McKenna. "How can it not be the right thing?"

"Dad won't flip, will he?" Rachael said. Cliff Harper, Rachael's father, had paid generously for Rachael to attend law school.

"He won't flip. Just because you're not in a practice doesn't mean you're not a lawyer anymore. Even I know that. Besides, you will make a fabulous consultant. You have a gift, Rachael. You see things other people don't. You have tremendous insight. That won't change just because you're out of the courtroom. And I can see you going back to it when McKenna is a little older. So will he."

Rachael turned to her mother and wrapped her arms around her. "Thanks, Mom."

Eva hugged her back. "Do you have to rush off? Want to stay for some French toast? McKenna and I just had some. You look tired, Rachael. Are you not sleeping well?"

Rachael released her mother. "Thanks for the offer, Mom. But we have to get back to the city. I've got some…some things going on." Rachael didn't address the question of the quality of her sleep.

"But it's your day off."

Rachael looked over at Trace as she answered her mother. "Something's come up and I need to take care of a few things."

Trace held her gaze for a second and then winked. He and Fig would take McKenna.

Rachael decided not to tell Ivy by phone the news of Leo's injuries. Instead, when she and Trace arrived back in Minneapolis, and after McKenna and Trace were on their way to Fig's and the studio, she got back in the car and headed to St. Paul.

She had an agenda for her so-called day off.

First, stop at Children's Hospital and see for herself how Leo was.

Second, pay a visit to Ivy and not only tell her the extent of Leo's wounds, but pump her for information about the girls in her group.

Third, attend Marcie's arraignment.

A niggling voice inside her—one that sounded a lot like Will's—told her she was involving herself in a police investigation concerning a client. She hushed the voice by mentally arguing that the police weren't investigating Ivy or the girls in the group. She couldn't mess with an investigation when there wasn't one. As far as the police were concerned, they had their suspect.

The fact was, she wanted to talk with Sharell herself.

And Liza.

And any of the others, if she could get the information as to who they were. She had looked at her notes in the loft before getting back in the car. She had first names: Arden, Danitra, Rose, and Toni. But no last names. She wouldn't get far without them. And she wasn't entirely sure Ivy would provide the last names. Her gut told her she wouldn't. But she had to ask.

Rachael pulled into the visitor's lot at Children's Hospital, found one of only a few open spaces, and parked. She walked briskly inside and inquired where she would find one Leo Shipley, a two-week-old infant brought in that morning.

Minutes later Rachael was standing in front of a nurse's station on the pediatric floor, defending her need to see him. She was getting nowhere.

"The patient is not allowed any visitors, ma'am," the nurse was saying.

"But I'm with the county! I am the attorney who handled his case!"

The nurse shrugged. "I'm sorry, ma'am. Your name isn't on the list."

She turned in frustration to find a quiet place to call Will and almost ran into him. The detective had silently walked up behind her. "Will!"

Will tipped his head toward the nurse. "It's okay. She's with me."

Rachael stepped away from the desk. "You're here."

"So are you."

"You've already been to the jail?"

"I wanted to see the baby first. Apparently, so do you."

Will began to walk toward a long hallway. Rachael fell in step beside him.

"So you've seen him?"

"Yep."

"How bad is he?" she said.

"He'll survive. He'll lose most of his ear. They were able to save his foot. But he'll have scars on his face, arm, and legs. How bad would you say that is?"

"I still can't believe this has happened. I just saw Leo yesterday."

"Did you?"

"When Leslie took him home. I rode in the car."

"Yeah, well, it happened."

"Have you ever heard of a dog attacking a baby like this?"

"Well, the thing is, the baby had been left atop an overflowing trash can. The dog—which, by the way, we believe we have found—was expecting to find discarded food there." Will sounded angry. "The really sick part is, his tiny arms show defensive wounds. He was moving them while he was being bit."

Rachael closed her eyes and steadied herself against the wall behind her. "You said he was knocked unconscious when he was pulled out and dropped," she whispered.

"I said that's what we hoped. He was found unconscious because of blood loss, not a concussion. I'm sorry to have to tell you that, Rachael. But you were going to find out sooner or later. Leo was abandoned where anybody or anything could've done whatever they wanted with him. And that's exactly what happened. A hungry stray came upon Leo, maybe smelled the contents of his diaper, decided he had found some tasty food, and away he went. As Leo cried and resisted, it's likely he just made matters worse. It was probably an act of God that the dog decided Leo was too much trouble."

Bile rose up within her and Rachael fought it back down. *Concentrate on building the case, concentrate on gathering the facts,* she told herself. She took a deep breath. "You said you found the dog?"

"We think we've found the dog. We found a mean stray with a nasty bite radius loitering in another part of the park. Could be that dog. Probably is. But since no one knows for sure at the moment, Leo's being subjected to rabies treatment. Not a pleasant experience by any stretch of the imagination."

Rachael licked her lips. They felt dry and cold. "Do you have any good news to tell me, Will?" Her voice sounded like a car crunching on gravel. She cleared her throat and looked up at him.

The corners of Will's mouth rose slightly. "He still has his beautiful blue eyes."

Rachael let a tiny smile escape as well.

"Ready to go in?" he said.

Will opened the door. A nurse in scrubs looked up from the chart she held as they came in. "We'll only be a moment," Will said to her.

The nurse tipped her head and then bent down over the chart again.

Will led Rachael past two open cribs to where baby Leo lay in a sea of white. His head was covered with a gauzy helmet of bandages, leaving just his face exposed. A swath of gauze was taped from just below the bridge of his nose to the corner of his mouth. His left arm was wrapped in dressings from shoulder to fingertips. Both legs were covered in bandages, too. There wasn't a millimeter of red to be seen anywhere and Rachael thanked God for it. The bandages were still fresh. Nothing had yet soaked through.

Wires attached to places where his skin was still visible snaked around Leo's tiny body to beeping machines at the side of the crib. A steady beat played out. Leo didn't make a sound.

"He is all right, isn't he?" she whispered. "He's so still."

"He's sedated. He's going to have surgery later today on his left ear. Or what's left of it."

Rachael couldn't keep her voice from cracking. "Please, Will! Don't tell me any more! Just tell me he's going to be all right!"

Will hesitated a moment. "He'll live, Rachael. And he won't remember what happened to him today. But who can really say if he'll be all right?"

Will turned, nodded to the nurse, and left.

Rachael reached out her hand to touch a bit of Leo's creamy skin on his torso, the only part of him not covered by bandages. She closed her eyes. *Watch over him. Keep him safe, Lord Jesus,* she silently prayed. *Be close to him always. May he never feel like he's unwanted. May he never know pain and fear the likes of this again.*

She kept her hand there a minute longer, willing a blessing to radiate from it.

Then she stepped away from the crib, turned, and followed Will out of the room.

TWENTY-SIX

Rachael and Will stepped out of Children's Hospital into a light rain.

"I'll let you observe, if you want," Will said, as he pulled up the collar of his jacket.

Rachael knew what he meant. He was telling her if she wanted to watch him question Marcie, he would allow it.

"Behind the glass?"

"Behind the glass."

Rachael could already envision how difficult the interview was going to be to watch. If Will explained to Marcie what had happened to Leo the same way he explained it to her, there was going to be some heat. But she wasn't going to pass up the opportunity to hear Marcie's response, as agonized as it might be.

"I'll come," she said.

"I'm headed there now."

The two of them started to dash across the parking lot. Rachael reached her car first. Will waved as he kept running past her.

"Will?" Rachael called out.

The detective turned, his eyes squinting against the falling rain.

"How come you're letting me come?" she shouted.

"Because you think she didn't do it!" he yelled back.

Rachael had been in the interrogation room before. She had stood before the thick, smoky-hued window that bore a mirror on its other side. But she still felt conspicuous as Marcie was led into the room on the other side of the glass. Will was already seated at the table in the middle of the room, sipping a cup of steaming coffee.

The young mother looked dazed and unsure as her police escort ushered her in. Marcie wore the typical crayon-orange jumpsuit that was standard issue for inmates of Ramsey County Jail. Her mousy brown hair was pulled back into a ponytail except for a few wispy, long bangs that had sprung free.

"We have a few things to talk about, Ms. Shipley." Will's voice sounded thin over the speaker behind Rachael.

"I didn't do anything." Marcie's dazed expression had quickly morphed into a pout.

"Let's start with your drug test, shall we?" Will lifted a piece of paper in front of him. "You tested positive for ketamine."

Marcie whipped her head up. "What?"

"Ketamine. Special K. Jet. A popular club drug. I'm sure you've heard of it. You took it last night."

Marcie's nostrils flared. "That's a lie! You're framing me! I don't do drugs anymore!"

"And officers found some crack in your apartment this morning."

"That's not mine! I don't know how it got there! It's not mine!"

"So you're saying you didn't shoot up or snort or swallow anything last night. Nothing."

"That's right. I didn't! I took a Tylenol for a headache and I drank it with milk. *Milk.* Did you check my pee for Tylenol and milk?"

"Tylenol."

"That's right."

"Where'd you get the Tylenol?"

"From my bathroom medicine cabinet! You go see for yourself!"

"Okay, we will."

"I want to know why you haven't found Leo! I'm not peeing into any more cups until you find him."

Will took a sip of his coffee and then calmly set his cup back down.

"We did find your son, Ms. Shipley."

"Well, where is he?" Marcie was mad, not relieved. "I want to know where he is!"

"He's at a hospital."

"Again? What for? Which one?"

"He's at a hospital because he has injuries."

Marcie's mouth, which had been open, now shut. For the first time, a sliver of fear seemed to move across her. Then she opened it again. "You sayin' someone hurt my baby?"

Rachael involuntarily moved toward the glass, though the audio from the room was being fed into the speakers behind her. She knew the next words out of Will's mouth would reveal to Marcie how much Leo had suffered, how close he had come to dying.

"Your baby was found on the ground near a trash can in Riley Park, seven blocks from where you live." Will's voice was calm and measured. "He was attacked by a stray dog and bitten over fifty percent of his body. He may lose his left ear. He's lucky he will keep his left foot. He will have scars for the rest of his life. But at least he still *has* his life."

Marcie seemed not to have heard what Will said. She didn't blink, didn't move a muscle. When she opened her mouth to speak, her voice was low and even. "You're lying," she murmured.

"I assure you, I am not. Your son was almost killed this morning."

Again, Marcie didn't blink, nor did her face register that she had understood what she had just been told. Then a deep and guttural cry erupted from her and she sprang from her chair, lunging for Will. The coffee cup went flying and Will bolted from his seat catching Marcie around her middle as she crashed into him. The second cop in the room dashed toward them, pulling Marcie off Will. All the while, Marcie was screaming at banshee-like decibels, damning everyone in the room, her life, her world.

Several tense seconds passed before she was subdued and handcuffs placed back on her wrists. Two additional police officers entered the room to drag Marcie back to her cell as she screamed obscenities.

When the door had closed behind her Will looked up at the glass as he shook hot coffee off his sleeves and hands. He motioned with his head for Rachael to join him.

Rachael moved quickly from one room to the other.

"You okay?" she said as she entered the interrogation room.

"It's not the first time I've had hot coffee spilled on me." He blotted at the hot wetness with a handkerchief he pulled from his pants pocket, then looked up at her. "Well?"

"You're going to check out that bottle of Tylenol, right?"

"We'll check it."

"Don't you think it's kind of odd she would have ketamine and crack in the house? Both?"

Will shook out the handkerchief. "I've seen six different kinds of drugs in the same broom closet, Rachael."

"But we're talking a welfare mom with a brand-new baby. She's not a dealer. She doesn't have any money. Where's she going to get this stuff?"

"Where do any of them get it? Where did she get it two years ago when she was a welfare mom on meth?" Will picked up the paperwork he had brought with him into the interview. The documents were spotted with drops of hot coffee. He waved them back and forth to dry them.

"I'd say she was pretty surprised to hear Leo was found at the park," Rachael offered.

"That's because she doesn't remember leaving him there. Why are you so convinced she didn't do this?" He sounded annoyed.

"Because. Because I've had…I've had some weird dreams, Will. You know how I get sometimes. I just don't think she did it. Why are you so annoyed that I don't think she did it?"

Will brushed stray drops off the top of his pants. "Because you're usually right. And I don't see how you can be this time. But you usually are. Figure it out for yourself."

Rachael slipped her purse over her shoulder. "Would you mind calling me if you find out the Tylenol bottle's been tainted?"

"Yeah, yeah." Will had been looking down, but he lifted his head quickly. "Where are you going?"

"I've got some errands to run."

"Rachael, I want to know where you're going."

She turned to leave the room. "No, you don't. See you in the courtroom at three."

It was almost noon when Rachael arrived at Ivy Judson's duplex. She had a phone message from Ivy when she checked her voice mail after leaving the jail. Ivy had wanted to know if Leo was okay, if he had been found. She sounded on the edge of panic. But Rachael didn't call her back. She wanted to tell Ivy in person what had happened to Leo Shipley. She was banking on an outpouring of empathy to get Ivy to talk.

Rachael was able to find a parking place just across from the duplex. The rain had stopped and she dodged little puddles as she crossed the street and climbed the three steps to Ivy's porch. It seemed to take a long time for Ivy to answer the doorbell.

When the door opened, Rachael could see that Ivy was definitely not her usual cheery self. She looked particularly unkempt. Her lightly graying hair was flying in all directions. Her shirt was untucked. Her face was lined with worry. When she saw Rachael on the step, she threw her screen door open to let her in.

"Oh, Ms. Flynn! I tried to call you. Did you get my message?"

Rachael stepped inside. "I did, Ivy. But I didn't want to tell you over the phone."

The color drained from Ivy's face. "Tell me what? Oh, dear God in heaven. Don't tell me he's dead!"

The woman seemed to stagger backward as if she would faint. She covered her mouth with her hands.

"He's not dead, Ivy!" Rachael said quickly. "Okay? He's not dead!"

Ivy's eyes were glistening. She pulled one hand away from her mouth. "He's okay?"

"He's been injured, but he'll recover."

Ivy's eyes widened. "Injured? How? What happened?"

"Can we sit down?"

Ivy motioned to the couch and Rachael took a seat on the end. Ivy took the same armchair as the day before.

"Injured how?" Ivy said. Her eyes shone with anxiety.

"He was found by a jogger this morning in Riley Park. He had been in a trash can. A dog had attacked him, Ivy. By the time the jogger found him, the dog had already bit him several times. He has many wounds, some of them severe, but his doctors are pretty sure he will survive."

For the second time in the span of a minute, Ivy's face went ashen. Again her hands flew up to her mouth.

"No," the woman said from behind her fingers. "This can't be true."

"I'm afraid it is, Ivy. That's why I came over. We need to talk. I think maybe someone from your group might be involved with this."

"No, no, no, no, no," Ivy murmured, shaking her head back and forth. Then she pulled her hands away from her face and screamed it. "NO!!"

Rachael flinched as Ivy screamed it again, louder and longer. "NOOOO!!"

Ivy jumped up from her chair and ran down the hall to her bathroom. Rachael heard the toilet lid hit the tank as Ivy swung it back on its hinges.

Ivy began retching into her toilet. Again and again and again.

TWENTY-SEVEN

Rachael stood at the doorway to Ivy's bathroom with a glass of water she'd brought with her from the kitchen. Ivy had stopped vomiting and now sat leaning against her toilet, panting. Her reaction to the attack on Leo went far beyond what Rachael had expected. And confirmed for Rachael what she had just lately come to believe: Ivy knew something that she wasn't telling. Ivy either knew or had a fairly good idea of who had taken Leo, and she apparently thought her silence had allowed Leo Shipley to be mauled.

"Here, Ivy." Rachael took a step forward and held out the glass of water. Ivy made no move to take it. "Ivy?"

"I want you to go now." Ivy's voice was hushed yet unyielding.

Rachael took another step and knelt down by Ivy. She bent her head, trying to make eye contact. Ivy wouldn't look at her. "We need to talk," Rachael said.

"I want you to go."

"Ivy, the police think Marcie did this. Drugs were found in her home and in her urine. She has no memory of what happened last night. I think those drugs were planted."

Ivy looked up at her. "What do you mean?"

"I think someone is trying to bring Marcie down. They are using Leo to do it. And they don't care if Leo is harmed in the process. I think it might be someone in the group."

Ivy's gaze darted away and Rachael could almost see the wheels turning in the woman's panicked brain. "Marcie told me she was off the drugs," Ivy said, clearly in frenzied, flustered thought.

"Yes, she told the police that, too."

"Sometimes the girls aren't truthful." Ivy stared at the water in the toilet. "Sometimes they just can't leave their old life behind, and they do things they thought they would never do."

Was Ivy talking about Marcie? Or someone else? Was she protecting one of the other girls? Why would Ivy protect one girl over another? Especially someone who had put Leo's life in such danger?

Rachael set the glass of water down on the floor. She reached out to touch Ivy on the shoulder. "Ivy, it's time for all of us to start telling the truth. A baby nearly died this morning."

Ivy closed her eyes. Her lids were rimmed with glistening tears. "I've not lied to you."

"But you know who did this, don't you? Do you think by protecting this person you're helping her? You aren't, Ivy. And Marcie will go to prison for this if she's found guilty. Have you thought about what that will mean for her and her children?"

Ivy said nothing. Tears slid down her cheeks from her closed eyes.

"Ivy, please help me."

"I can't help you." Ivy opened her eyes but continued to stare at the toilet.

"Can't or won't?"

"What difference does it make?" Her voice sounded lifeless.

"It would've made a huge difference for Leo earlier today."

Ivy blinked slowly but said nothing.

"Is it Sharell?" Rachael said. "Is it Liza? Is it one of the others?"

Silence.

"Ivy, please."

"You'll come to your own conclusions. You county people always do. I want to be alone."

"Ivy."

"I want you to go."

Rachael waited for several seconds but Ivy said nothing else. Rachael stood, grabbing the glass of water. "Call me if you change your mind and want to talk."

No response.

Rachael walked out of the bathroom and carried the glass back to the kitchen. When she set it on Ivy's kitchen table she noticed a stack of party plates and napkins, still wrapped in plastic and bearing the words Welcome Home! in bright blue.

Leo's homecoming party would've been that afternoon.

Rachael paused for a moment at the front door, waiting to hear movement from the back of the duplex.

There was no sound. She opened the front door and reached into her purse as she took the three steps to the sidewalk, fishing for her cell phone. As she walked across the street she pressed the speed dial for Leslie.

No answer. She opted not to leave a voice mail.

Rachael unlocked her car, got inside, and thought for a moment. Then she punched in the number for another office at Human Services: records.

Seconds later she was driving away with two addresses scribbled onto a notepad on the seat next to her, one for Sharell Hodge and one for Liza Cooley.

Sharell Hodge lived in a tiny box of a house only five minutes from Ivy's duplex, on a street of broken dreams. Every house on the block was in need of paint and repair and the yards were littered with broken toys, newspaper advertisements never read, and the leavings of people who worked hard for little pay and whose landlords didn't worry too much about aesthetics.

Rachael parked her car in front of Sharell's house and exhaled heavily. She hadn't felt fear until just that moment—not until it dawned on her that she was about to confront an angry woman who'd quite possibly kidnapped a child. Twice.

And nobody knew that's what she was about to do.

"Okay, God," she prayed aloud as she unbuckled her seatbelt, "a little help here would be nice. Really nice. A little voice from heaven, that would be great, too. No weird dreams in the middle of the day, though, please."

She got out of the car and quickly considered calling Trace to let him know where she was. But he would want to know why she was calling him to tell him that. And she'd have to tell him she was a little afraid of what Sharell might do.

And he would tell her to stop pretending to be Will and get the heck out of there.

Maybe he'd be right.

Maybe she should stop pretending to be Will.

What was she doing here?

What was she going to say to Sharell? *Hey, Sharell. Was in the neighborhood. Thought I'd stop by and ask you if you had kidnapped Leo Shipley last night. And the time before. You know, just wondering.*

Rachael leaned up against her car, trying to recall why she thought coming to Sharell's on her own was a good idea. She was deep in thought when Sharell's front door suddenly opened. Rachael looked up. Sharell, frowning and with one hand on her hip, stood framed in the doorway. Rachael stood straight.

"What are you doin' here?" Sharell's voice was under control, but clearly laced with aggravation. "I seen you from my front window. I want to know what you're doin' here."

Rachael opened her mouth, but she didn't have a good answer at the ready. *God, some help, please?*

"I said, what are you *doin'* here?" Sharell said angrily. Her voice carried easily across her postage-stamp lawn to where Rachael stood at the sidewalk.

"Sharell, I just want to talk to you." Rachael's voice sounded feeble to her ears.

"Well, I don't want to talk to you. We got nothing to talk about."

"I think maybe we do."

"Well, you'd be wrong then."

Rachael took a tentative step forward. "I want to talk to you about what happened to Leo Shipley."

"Leo Shipley, in case you haven't noticed, isn't my problem. And I already talked to you people about what happened to that kid."

Rachael watched Sharell's face, studying it to see if the woman was only pretending not to know there were new developments. Rachael couldn't detect anything amiss.

"Can I come inside and talk to you?" Rachael said.

"No."

"Sharell, I want to talk to you about what happened this morning."

"This morning?"

"Yes."

Sharell stared at her. "Girl, I don't know what you talkin' about."

Rachael took several steps toward Sharell, her eyes on the woman's face the whole time. Sharell didn't move. Her expression didn't change. She was either an expert at deception or she truly didn't know what had happened to Leo earlier that day.

Rachael was now only a few feet from Sharell. "Leo was found by a jogger this morning in Riley Park. He had been attacked by a stray dog. He survived, but he was injured pretty bad."

Sharell tipped her head back slightly. The news seemed to surprise her. Rachael couldn't tell if Sharell was surprised to learn Leo had been abandoned a second time or that he'd been attacked.

For a moment, Sharell said nothing. Then she raised her eyebrows and slid her other arm to her hip in the classic posture of defiance. "And why are you telling me this?"

"I was hoping you could help me figure out who is doing this."

Sharell laughed. It was mirthless. "And what makes you think I could help you?"

"Because you're smart, Sharell. You see a lot. You know how things work. You know why some things don't."

Sharell was silent. Rachael's estimation of her had visibly surprised her.

"Why you asking all these questions?" she finally said.

"The cops think Marcie did it."

The woman shrugged. "So?"

"I don't."

Sharell cocked her head, then she narrowed her eyes. "She got you, girl. You fell for her big time. She got you thinking all her problems are everyone else's fault. That's her line. And you a fool for falling for it. That's it! I'm through with you."

Sharell started to let the door close and Rachael took a step forward and reached out to stop it.

"Get your hand off my door," Sharell said, frowning.

"I didn't fall for anything, Sharell. Marcie's got a boatload of problems that are *all* her fault. This just isn't one of them."

"Get your hand off my door." Sharell said each word with controlled force.

Rachael knew she had only seconds to find out anything more from Sharell.

"Sharell, is there anyone in Ivy's support group who could've done this? Please?"

Sharell moved away from the door to go back inside her house. Her back was to Rachael as she stepped inside her entryway.

"Please, Sharell. Do you think anyone in the group could've done this?"

"Take your pick, lady," Sharell said sarcastically as she walked away from Rachael. "We're all actually the worthless, hopeless people you think we are. Just take your pick."

"Sharell!"

"And close my door on your way out." Sharell turned into a room off the entry. A door slammed shut.

Rachael stood for a moment longer but Sharell didn't reappear. Rachael turned and stepped away from the threshold, pulling the door shut behind her.

TWENTY-EIGHT

Rachael pulled away from the curb at Sharell's sure of two things: One, Sharell's hatred ran deeper than just simple disgust for Marcie's blaming everyone but herself for her troubles. Two, Sharell was angry enough to do something about it.

She frowned. If Sharell had lashed out at Marcie by harming Leo, why would Ivy want to protect her? Unless Ivy was afraid. Afraid of turning against Sharell by turning her in? Afraid Sharell knew something about Ivy she didn't want anyone else to know? Afraid Sharell would retaliate somehow? Fear was a powerful motivator. And if Ivy exhibited anything in her duplex earlier that day it was fear.

What was she afraid of?

Rachael wanted to turn the car around, go back to Ivy's, and ask her. But she knew enough about human character to recognize she'd get nothing more from Ivy that day. Tomorrow, perhaps. Especially if Ivy's fear grew. The more afraid Ivy became, the more Rachael believed it would become too much to handle. Ivy would eventually cry out for help and Rachael wanted to be the one she cried out to.

Rachael glanced down at Liza's address on the seat next to her. All the girls lived within a dozen blocks or so of Ivy's duplex. Made sense. Most of them had heard about Ivy's group from the flier she had pinned up at the local Laundromat or from each other.

Liza's address led Rachael to a faded four-story apartment building on a busy side street that perhaps was chic once upon a time. Tattered aqua awnings hung from windows decked with rusted grill work. Twisted junipers that needed a trim snaked their branches every which way. A sign above the lobby entrance said "ea Cove Apts." Sea Cove without its S. Rachael cocked an eyebrow as she stepped out of her car in front of the building. The nearest sea was 1800 miles away. A dreamer had built this building.

A column of metal buttons, tarnished by wear and age, bore under plastic the last names of the occupants. "Cooley" was taped to the right of "Ruiz/Halder" at the bottom, like she hadn't been there very long. The button that corresponded with Ruiz, Halder, and Cooley was missing its plastic cover. Rachael pressed it and it poked into her skin. The speaker next to the buttons squawked.

"Ello?" a woman's voice said.

Rachael spoke into the opening near the speaker. "Hello, is Liza home please?"

"No. She's at work."

Rachael thought for a second. Where did Liza work? Not many of the moms in Ivy's group held down jobs but she remembered that Liza did. Leslie had mentioned it. A tattoo salon.

"At the tattoo place?" Rachael said.

"*Sí*."

"Can you tell me where it is? I need to talk to her."

"She owe you money?"

"No. I just need to ask her something."

"You a friend?"

Rachael hesitated. "I'm not her enemy. Really, I'm not. I just need to talk to her."

"Apollo."

"Apollo?"

"The place is called Apollo something. On Eighth Street."

"Thanks. Thanks so much."

The speaker fell silent.

Rachael turned and headed for her car.

Rachael had actually been in a tattoo parlor once before. Fig had tried to convince Trace to get one like his: a Celtic cross in turquoise blue on his left bicep. It didn't happen, though. The visit to the parlor only served to seal Trace's ardent aversion to needles. Fig got a second one instead. An angelic creature bearing a flaming sword.

Still, Rachael felt completely out of place as she walked into the Apollo Tattoo and Piercing Parlor. The reception area's subdued lighting and dark walls made her squint as the door fell closed behind her. The air smelled heavily of incense, ink, and strong coffee, and heavy-metal music blared from beyond another wall. The woman behind the counter who looked up at her had perhaps twenty piercings. Her ears, lips, nose, eyebrows, and tongue were all studded and glistening. The woman's eyelids were shaded in deep purple which matched the hue of her short, spiked hair. She blew a bubble with the gum in her mouth, popped it, and then winked at Rachael.

"Can I help ya?" she said.

"I'm looking for Liza."

The woman chewed. "You got an appointment with Liza?"

"No, I just need to talk to her."

The woman sized Rachael up, cocking her head.

"Please?" Rachael continued, refusing to look away. "I just need to talk to her for a few minutes."

The woman continued to chew her gum, the little silver stud on her tongue flashing as the minimal overhead lighting fell on it. Then she moved away from the counter, pulled apart a curtain made of beads on an adjoining wall, and stuck her head inside. "Hey, Liza. Someone here to see you." She let the beads fall, taking her place behind the counter again, chewing all the while.

Rachael smiled at her. "Thanks."

"No problem."

The woman continued to stare at her, smiling and chewing. Several seconds later, the beads parted again and Liza appeared. She was wearing a thin, white T-shirt bearing a logo Rachael didn't recognize, a pair of expertly shredded jeans, and a dozen bangle bracelets on her left arm. A white and yellow daisy tattoo, not there when Rachael first met her, decorated her right cheek. Liza looked at Rachael. There wasn't a hint of recognition on her face.

"You looking for me?" she said.

Rachael took a step toward her. "Hi, Liza. We met at Ivy's the other day? Rachael Flynn?"

For a second, Liza just stood there and stared. Then she broke into a wide smile.

"Oh, sure! I remember you." Liza seemed pleased with herself. Then she flinched, as if nudged. "Omigosh! Did you come for a tattoo? That is so totally cool. I only do temporary tattoos, though. I don't use the needles. But I'm really good. See my daisy?"

"Your daisy is beautiful but…"

"Thanks! I do all the flowers. All of them. Well, except I suck at irises. I can do great roses. Mo, he's the owner, he says my roses are better than his. And he's been doing them for years."

"That's really great, Liza, but I actually didn't come for a tattoo. I just wanted to talk to you."

"Oh. Okay. Sure." Liza put her hands in her back pockets. Her bracelets jangled. "What about?"

Rachael hadn't really planned what she was going to say to Liza. She suddenly felt as unprepared as when she had showed up at Sharell's and could think of nothing to do but lean on her car and stare. The purple-headed woman at the counter was obviously waiting to hear the answer, too.

"Um, do you mind if we take a little walk? Is it okay if you take a short break?"

"Yeah. Sure." Liza walked past Rachael, pushed the front door open, and stepped outside. Rachael followed her. Behind her, Rachael could hear the pierced woman popping a bubble.

"Oh, cool. The rain has stopped." Liza was looking up at the sky. "I don't like rain." She turned her head toward Rachael. "So how come you were at Ivy's the other day? Ivy doesn't usually like the county messing around with her. You know. No offense."

"No. I understand. I was there for Marcie, actually. She wanted me to see the group she was involved with. To meet all of you." Rachael started to stroll slowly down the street. Liza fell in step with her.

"How come? How come she wanted you to meet us?"

Rachael chose her words carefully. "She was hoping to get Leo back. She wanted us to see she's trying hard to be a good mom."

"Oh."

"Do you think Marcie's a good mom?"

Liza furrowed her brow and stopped. "Is that why you came? To ask me if Marcie's a good mom? I think you're a little late. She's already got him back. There's a party today for her at Ivy's and everything."

Rachael studied Liza's face, her eyes, her body language. She sensed not a hint of fear or deception. There was nothing to suggest Liza knew Leo had been taken and abandoned a second time. She was about to tell Liza there wasn't going to be a party after all when Rachael felt a strong inward tug not to say too much about Leo just yet. Not until she had asked everything else of Liza. She suddenly knew that once she told Liza what had happened to Leo, the whole backdrop of their conversation would change. If Liza had had a part in Leo's abduction, even subconsciously, then she would certainly learn nothing further from her.

"Ivy's really a great support to you girls, isn't she?" Rachael said, deftly changing the subject without changing the subject.

"Yeah. Ivy's the best."

"Must've been hard for you before you had her as a friend."

"Yeah." A vacant look seemed to creep over Liza.

"Do you have a picture of your little girl?" Rachael said brightly. She didn't want to lose Liza's interest.

"What?"

"Do you have a picture of your daughter?"

Liza shook her head as if to shake water off of it. "Oh. No. I have one at my apartment, though."

"I bet she's really beautiful."

"Yeah." Again, the vacant look.

Rachael started to walk again. Liza hesitated and then joined her.

"Say, Liza, are you pretty good friends with Sharell?"

"No one is pretty good friends with Sharell."

Rachael smiled. "She's a little prickly."

Liza smiled back at her. "That's a great word. Prickly. I like that. Yeah, Sharell's prickly."

"It's kind of funny that she likes coming to the group, you know. Does she get along with anybody in it?"

Liza looked thoughtful. "Well, she likes Danitra okay, I think. I don't know. She comes because of Ivy."

"Because of Ivy?"

"Yeah. Ivy lets her be…prickly. Ivy doesn't ask her to be something else. Ivy doesn't ask any of us to not be who we are, you know?"

"I think I can understand that."

"Actually, Sharell scares me."

"Really?"

"She's got such a hot temper. And she can't stand me or Marcie."

Rachael made a special effort not to appear too interested. "How come?"

"Well, she doesn't like it when I fade. She can't stand it."

"When you fade?" Rachael stopped walking and turned to face Liza.

"Yeah. You know, sometimes I have these moments when I just fade. I get kind of sad or dreamy. I don't know. Sometimes I'll just start crying when I fade. Sometimes I start yelling. Sometimes I get sleepy. She thinks I do it for attention. She is so wrong. I hate it."

"Does your doctor know this?"

Liza smirked. "You mean my psychiatrist? Yeah, she knows." She looked away from Rachael.

"How often does it happen?" Rachael said gently.

Liza shrugged. Embarrassment washed over her face.

"Does it happen at night or in the daytime?" Rachael said.

"Both," Liza muttered.

"Do you remember the times you fade?"

Liza laughed, but it was filled with raw sadness. "Oh, I think I do. But my parents say I don't. The county says I don't. The judge says I don't. That's how I lost Kylie. That's how I lost my little girl."

Rachael could sense Liza drifting away again. She needed to redirect the conversation. "And why doesn't Sharell like Marcie?"

Liza didn't answer.

"Liza?" Rachael touched her lightly on the arm.

"What?" the girl said, turning her head slowly toward Rachael.

"Why doesn't Sharell like Marcie?"

"Because Marcie was going to tell on her."

"Tell what?"

Liza sucked in her bottom lip and said nothing.

"I won't share this with anyone unless we agree it's the right thing to do," Rachael said.

Liza opened her mouth. "Marcie was going to tell that she saw Sharell whip her little boy with a belt."

Rachael let no emotion cross her face. "Did Sharell whip her little boy with a belt?"

"Marcie saw it."

"Did you?"

"No."

"But Marcie told you she did."

"Yes."

"Does Ivy know this?"

A look of regret swept across Liza's face. "No, I promised not to tell."

Rachael fought for the right words. "Liza, why would you and Marcie keep this a secret? You don't want Sharell to keep doing that to her little boy, do you?"

"No! Marcie told me as long as she had this over Sharell, Sharell wouldn't do it anymore. And she'd have to stop treating Marcie like dirt because Marcie would tell on her if she didn't. I didn't want to keep it a secret but Marcie made me."

"How did she make you?"

"She just...did."

"And you didn't think you could go to Ivy with this?"

Liza frowned. She offered no answer.

Rachael waited.

"I got to get back." Liza suddenly turned to walk back to the tattoo parlor.

"Liza, wait. I need to tell you something." Rachael followed her.

The girl stopped and turned back around.

"There isn't going to be a party at Ivy's today," Rachael said.

Liza cocked her head. "Yes, there is."

"No. There isn't. Leo's in the hospital."

"No, he's not. He's at home. With Marcie."

Rachael took a deep breath. "Marcie's in jail, Liza. She was arrested this morning."

Liza stared at her. "Why is she in jail?"

"Because Leo was found abandoned again. This morning. The police think Marcie took drugs and then abandoned Leo in the park. He got hurt there, Liza. So he's in the hospital." Rachael decided not to say anything about how Leo got his wounds. The echo of Ivy's retching still swam in her ears.

Liza looked away, past Rachael, to the busy street beyond them. "So there's not going to be a party."

"No."

Liza said nothing as she continued to stare at the zooming cars.

"Liza?"

The girl slowly turned her head toward her but said nothing.

"Liza, do you have any reason to believe it wasn't Marcie who did this?" Rachael took a step toward her. "Do you think anyone else could have? Someone Marcie knows? Someone who maybe is going through a tough time? Maybe someone else in the group? I understand all about tough times, really I do."

Liza was looking at Rachael but her eyes weren't connecting with Rachael's eyes. It was as if she was seeing past Rachael. Or not seeing at all.

"So there's not going to be a party?" Liza finally said, as if no question hung between them.

"No, Liza. There's not."

Liza tipped her head to the sky, now gathering clouds again. "I'm glad the rain stopped. I don't like rain." She turned and walked briskly back to the tattoo parlor's door. Rachael stood and watched her. When she reached the door, Liza turned and waved. "Bye!" Her voice was cheerful.

Rachael waved back.

A drop of rain fell on her as she walked to her car. And then another.

TWENTY-NINE

Raindrops began to drum on the windshield as Rachael sat in her car and stared at the tattoo parlor across the street.

She wasn't sure what she had hoped to gain from meeting with Liza, but she had certainly expected to gain a little clarity.

Nothing was clear.

Liza appeared to be genuinely surprised by the news that Leo had been abandoned a second time. But she also seemed strangely detached. She didn't even ask how Leo had been hurt. Nor if he was okay. It was like Liza didn't want to know anything in detail about what had happened to him. She was more concerned with there not being a party than the fact that Leo was in the hospital.

And her admission that she sometimes "fades" concerned Rachael. If Liza was truly schizophrenic, it would be probable for her to have periods of lost time—time when she was active, purposeful, and conversant but unable to remember any of it. Leslie had said Liza's previous mental assessments had been inconclusive, which meant no one really knew the true depth of Liza's mental illness. Or what she was capable of doing.

And incapable of remembering.

Rachael wondered if Liza remembered being found by the police under a freeway overpass with her infant daughter in her arms. Did she remember getting there? Did she remember anything at all about that experience?

The day was more than half over and she now had more questions than answers. Meeting with Ivy, and then Sharell, and now Liza had been eye-opening but didn't explain who took Leo and why.

As the rain turned to a downpour, Rachael reached into her purse and pulled out a notepad. She needed to get a handle on what she knew, what her instincts were telling her. She wished she had written down her dreams the moment she'd had them. Rachael was certain something was being revealed to her in them. And she was missing it. She also had a sudden desire to look at the artists' drawings again, as if the key to understanding the dreams was hidden somewhere in the drawings. But the sketches were all back at the loft.

Rachael wrote Sharell's name at the top of the notepad, thought for a moment, and then wrote the words *angry, threatened, alone, bitter, resentful, untrusting, capable* underneath it. She did the same for Liza: *vulnerable, isolated, mentally unstable, hurting, compassionate, weak, afraid.* And though she did not believe Marcie had abandoned Leo on either occasion, she wrote her name down as well, and the descriptions that sprang to mind: *manipulative, irresponsible, selfish, insistent, user, naïve.* It struck Rachael as odd as she held the pen over the paper that she could think of nothing nice to say about Marcie, despite the hunch that Marcie was innocent. She also pondered the two words that started and ended the list of descriptions. Manipulative and naïve. Was it possible to be both? Or was Marcie's apparent naiveté evidence of her scheming nature?

She moved on to Arden. What could she write? All Rachael knew about Arden was that she was young, single, and pregnant and she had decided to give her baby up for adoption. She knew nothing at all about Danitra, Rose, and Toni. Their names hadn't come up at all in the last few weeks as Rachael worked Marcie's case, and that fact alone suggested they probably had nothing to do with what happened to Leo. She wrote their names on the notepad and stared at them, then she crossed the three names out.

Rachael tapped the pad with her pen. Somehow Ivy figured into all of this. Ivy. *Devoted, maternal, protective, empathetic, helpful, fearful. Loves the girls and their children. But knows something.*

Koko and Joyce. A real pair: *indignant, callous, irritated, fed up, but no motive.*

Booth.

She knew next to nothing about Booth Rubian.

Rachael rubbed her forehead, and a tall caramel macchiato beckoned as the rain beat down on the car.

She looked at her watch and gasped.

Rachael had exactly eight minutes to get to Marcie's arraignment.

The courtroom was full when Rachael stepped breathlessly inside. The gallery was brimming with men and woman of all ages: attorneys, family members, police officers, and those being charged who weren't under arrest. Court had been in session for an hour already. The judge was in between cases.

A name was called out, and a man from behind the closed door at the front of the courtroom was ushered in by a uniformed police officer. An inmate in orange.

Rachael saw that Leslie was standing along the back wall. Rachael moved to stand by her.

"You came, too, huh?" Leslie whispered as the man before the judge stated his name.

Rachael nodded.

"Guess who else is here?"

"Who?" Rachael whispered back.

"Booth Rubian and his mother."

Rachael searched the seats. "Where?"

"Third row on our side. He's two in from the center aisle. Black hair. Mama is next to him. Name's Janine."

"Why are they here?"

"Booth finally told his mother he might be Leo's father and his mother has decided he should ask for custody. She wants him. They want to talk to me after the hearing."

"How did he find out so soon? Marcie was only arrested this morning."

"Because Marcie called Booth when she woke up and found Leo gone. Before she called her mother or Ivy."

"She thought he had him?"

"I don't know. I think she was hoping he'd come over and take control of the situation. He didn't, of course. He called his mother. I think he was afraid the cops would want to question him again and he wanted his mama on his side. Well, now Mama wants her grandson."

"Are you thinking of letting Booth take Leo?"

"I won't even consider it until he takes a paternity test. And even then, he's not your model citizen. If his mom is Carol Brady-ish and helps him, maybe."

Rachael let her eyes rove across the crowded seats. Will was near the back, sitting with another plainclothes detective.

Just ahead of them were Koko and Joyce.

As if sensing Rachael's eyes on her, Koko slowly turned her head and caught Rachael's gaze. The woman's expression was all that Rachael had figured it would be: cool, calculating, and condescending. Koko unhurriedly turned her head back to face front.

"Did you talk to Koko and Joyce?" Rachael whispered to Leslie.

"I guess you could say we talked. They talked and I sat there. They blame you and me for this, of course."

Rachael inwardly winced. She blamed herself somewhat, too. "Do they have J.J. and Hallie?"

"No. They're in emergency foster care at the moment. Neither one of them really wants Marcie's kids. But they don't want Booth to have Leo, either. Typical."

The judge had concluded with the man on the stand. He left the way he came in and there were several seconds of busy activity as the court clerks and charging attorneys readied for the next case. Marcie's.

As Marcie's name was called, Rachael saw a public defender she had worked with on a previous case step forward. Marcie may not have requested a public defender but, considering the seriousness of the charges, the court had likely insisted she have one.

The door to the right of the judge opened and Marcie appeared, dressed in orange from neck to ankle, accompanied by a police officer. She looked both dazed and irritated. Marcie searched the courtroom, looking for a familiar face it seemed, as the judge stated the case and then began to ask Marcie the usual questions: her name, if she had been provided a copy of the charges against her, and if she understood them—reckless child endangerment, assault in the third degree, gross negligence, intent to cause bodily harm, and possession of a controlled substance.

Marcie had apparently found her mother and Koko in the gallery. She lifted her chin and her eyes seemed to zero in on Koko and Joyce, who sat motionless.

"Ms. Shipley, do you understand these charges?" the judge said.

Marcie seemed to be waiting for movement from her mother or sister, a nod of the head, perhaps. Anything to let her know they were looking at her.

"Ms. Shipley, do you understand these charges?" The judge was looking at Marcie over his reading glasses. He held her file in his hand.

Marcie swung her head around to face the judge. "I didn't do it!"

"I asked if you understand the charges, Ms. Shipley. Not whether or not you are guilty of them."

"But I didn't do it."

"Counselor?" the judge said in a tired voice.

The public defender cleared his throat. "I spoke with Ms. Shipley about these charges a few moments ago. I explained them in detail. She understands them."

"Well, perhaps you can advise your client to tell the court herself that she understands them."

The public defender looked over at Marcie. "Ms. Shipley?"

"I understand them, but I'm tellin' you I didn't do this. Someone is framing me! You have the wrong person!"

"Counselor?" Again, the tired voice.

"Ms. Shipley, please," the defender said, in a voice nearly as bereft of enthusiasm as the judge's.

"How does your client plead, Counselor?" the judge said.

"I didn't do it!" Marcie yelled.

"Not guilty on all counts, Your Honor."

"Note that the defendant has entered a plea of not guilty to all five charges. The defendant will remain in custody unless bail is posted. Bail has been set at $100,000. Will your client be posting bail, Counselor?"

"Ah, no, Your Honor."

The judge began to sign something. "That's all for today."

"But I didn't *do* it!" Marcie screamed.

"Bailiff?" The judge motioned the police escort at Marcie's side. The bailiff placed a hand on Marcie's arm to lead her back to her cell. She whipped it out of his hand. "I'm innocent! I didn't do this!"

The bailiff began to pull Marcie away from the stand. Marcie's eyes darted to Koko and Joyce, and then to Rachael and Leslie, who were watching wide-eyed at the back of the room.

Marcie's eyes locked on Rachael's. "I didn't do it!" she shouted from across the room.

Without forethought Rachael found herself mouthing the words, "I know."

THIRTY

Rachael followed Leslie out of the courtroom. When the doors hushed closed behind them, Leslie turned to her as the two began to walk down the expansive hallway outside the felony courtroom.

"Well, want to come to the meeting?" Leslie said.

Before Rachael could answer, the doors to the courtroom opened and Koko and Joyce joined them in the corridor. The four women stood silent and staring at each other for a split second.

Then Joyce took a step toward Rachael. "If you had just listened to me, my daughter would not be in jail and that baby wouldn't be in the hospital. But did you listen to me? No. You went ahead and did whatever you wanted and look where it's gotten us. You never should've given that baby back to Marcie. I told you that."

"Mrs. Shipley, I..." Rachael began, but Joyce raised a hand to silence her. "I don't want to hear your lame excuses. That baby got hurt because you people care more about your statutes and regulations and covering your own butts than you do about people."

Rachael opened her mouth to speak but Koko filled the silence.

"You just couldn't take advice from people who know better, could you?" Koko said. "You just did whatever was easiest for *you*."

"Look, I had no proof that Marcie did anything to Leo." Rachael finally got a word in. "The police didn't either. I'm sure you're aware there were no criminal charges filed against her until today. If you had hard evidence that Marcie had abused Leo or her other children, you should've reported it. Because as a matter of fact, I *do* have to follow the statutes."

"Maybe we should continue this in a conference room?" Leslie said.

Joyce ignored Leslie. "Sending that baby home to Marcie was the same as throwing him in the trash yourself."

Rachael felt her pulse quicken. Anger welled up within her. "Let's just get one thing straight. I don't *send* babies home to their parents. I represent the county when allegations of abuse and neglect have been presented to me and I have the evidence to prove they are true. I didn't have it. The county didn't have it. The police didn't have it."

"You telling me throwing your baby in a trash can isn't evidence?"

"Or my office?" Leslie said.

"Obviously throwing a baby in a trash can is evidence of abuse but the police weren't able to provide proof that it was Marcie who did it." Rachael willed her body to calm down. "And she maintained that she didn't."

"Well, who else would have done it?" Joyce retorted, tossing her head.

"Who else, indeed?" Rachael shot back. "Maybe it was someone who has it out for Marcie. Maybe it was a psychotic neighbor. Maybe it was you. Maybe it was Koko."

"Rachael," Leslie said softly.

Joyce glowered at Rachael and Koko narrowed her eyes.

"How dare you say such a thing," Joyce murmured, seething.

Before Rachael could say anything else, the doors behind them opened. Booth and his mother emerged. Rachael could see for the first time that Booth looked a lot like his mother. Both of them had narrow-set eyes, wavy hair, and ample flesh around the middle.

"I want to talk to you," Janine Rubian said to Leslie. Booth shuffled behind her, his hands in his pockets.

Joyce turned to Leslie. "You're not actually thinking of giving that baby to *him,* are you?"

"Who are you?" Mrs. Rubian whipped her head around to face Joyce.

"I'm Leo Shipley's grandmother." Joyce's tone was mocking.

"Well, I'm his other grandmother."

"Okay, we are *not* having this conversation here in the hallway," Leslie said.

Joyce took a step toward Janine. "The heck you are! Your boy isn't even sure it's his!"

"Easy enough to take care of that," Janine said hotly. "Besides, what do you care? You don't want that baby. I know you don't. Booth told me."

"Let's take this back to my office, shall we?" Leslie said brightly.

"I don't want to raise Leo. Not that it's any of your business, but that doesn't mean I want a loser like *him* taking the baby." Joyce pointed to Booth. "The kid deserves a normal home. Your son can't provide what he doesn't have himself."

"Who made *you* judge and jury?" Janine fumed. "Who do you think you are? You don't even know my son. You don't even…"

"Okay, stop!" Leslie commanded. "We are *not* continuing this conversation in the hallway. If the four of you would like to come to my office at Human Services, we will continue it there." Leslie turned to Rachael and raised an eyebrow. It was a silent invitation to join them.

Again the door to the courtroom opened and this time Will and his colleague stepped out. Will was talking to his companion but he nodded to Rachael as their eyes met and he continued walking past.

"I'll catch up with you later, Leslie," she said. "There's someone I want to talk to."

Rachael turned to follow Will.

"Okay, Rachael, what's on your mind?" Will had said goodbye to the other detective and was now walking through the double doors that led outside. Rachael was at his side. They headed for the police station across the parking lot.

"I just want to run something by you." She walked quickly to stay in step with Will's long strides.

"Does this have to do with wherever you went after you left the hospital this morning?"

"Yes."

"So, you're going to confess to me which part of my police investigation you've been meddling with?" He turned his head to look at her. His voice was stern but his eyes were crinkled by a veiled grin.

"It's not meddling when I talk to someone you don't think has anything to do with it," Rachael said.

"It's those girls in that support group. You still think it's one of those girls, don't you?"

"You saw Marcie in the courtroom. She sure didn't come across as particularly guilty. Hers was quite the reaction, don't you think?"

"I've seen it before. So've you."

"But, Will, why would Marcie take a party drug when she was all alone?"

"You don't need to be at a party to take a party drug."

"Okay, but don't you think it's odd that she had crack in the house, and she took the ketamine instead? And to take it the very night Leo had been returned to her? After she had just signed an agreement to abstain? And that whole thing with the door. She vehemently maintains she locked it when she went to bed. If she'd gone to bed with ketamine, wouldn't she want to cover for herself by saying she forgot to lock the door? By insisting she locked it, when she knows there's no sign of forced entry, she's incriminating herself. Doesn't make any sense."

"So she's not very bright."

"Will."

"Yeah, okay. I see where you're going. But it's still a whole lot of conjecture. And it doesn't explain how whoever took the kid got in."

"But don't you think it's worth looking into?"

Will stopped at the entrance to the station. "What've you got, Rachael? You get a vision from the Almighty you haven't told me about?"

Rachael inhaled. What did she have? Three dreams, five sketches, two troubled young mothers with motive, one maternal mentor with something to hide.

"Got ten minutes?" she said.

Will sat across from Rachael at his desk in the homicide department. His ebony-toned fingers were laced together atop his day planner and he wiggled them back and forth as he considered what Rachael had just told him about her three visits that morning. And her dreams.

"I don't know anything about dreams, Rachael, so I'm not even going to go there." Will stopped wiggling his fingers and sat forward. "But I admit I'm curious about why Ivy acted the way she did. I think I'll need to have a little chat with her. And it can't hurt to pay another visit to Sharell Hodge and Liza Cooley, if nothing else than to make certain we have the right person in custody. And since that's what I plan to do—make them a part of my investigation—you will have to consider any future conversations with them about this as meddling. Know what I mean?"

The corners on Rachael's mouth rose. "Thanks, Will."

"So we have an agreement?"

"I shall try very hard not to meddle."

"Rachael."

"I'm not going to lie to you, Will. I promise I'll try."

"Mmm."

"Will you promise to tell me everything you find out? That will help me keep my promise to you."

He paused. "I promise."

"And can you go easy on Liza? She's not well. In fact, maybe you should start with her parents or the therapist she's seeing at mental health services."

"Any other instructions?" Will offered her a crooked smile.

"Sorry, Will. I just don't want Liza to slip off mentally somewhere and not come back. I'll stop telling you how to do your job now." Rachael stood to leave.

"Are you, like, on your way to meddle somewhere?" Will cocked his head, as if anticipating an answer he didn't want to hear.

"I'm just going over to Human Services. I want to talk to Leslie."

"Oh."

"So you'll call me?"

"I'll call you."

Rachael started to head for Will's open door.

"Marcie's awful lucky to have you on her side," Will called out. "I'm surprised you like her. She doesn't seem very…likable."

Rachael stopped and turned as she considered Will's question. "I don't like her or dislike her," she replied. "I just don't think she did it."

Leslie was seated behind a tall stack of case files when Rachael poked her head inside the social worker's office. Her friend looked deep in thought.

"Did I miss the meeting?" Rachael said sweetly.

Leslie jumped in her seat. "For crying out loud, Rachael. Yes, you missed the meeting. It was a three-alarm Excedrin nightmare. I should've videotaped it for you."

Rachael stepped inside the office and sank into one of two chairs opposite Leslie's desk. "So did you get it all worked out?"

"Ha-ha. Very funny. Booth's going to have the paternity test, but it's plain as day his mother wants Leo and that Booth doesn't give a hoot. I think she wants a do-over on motherhood. She's got this hoodlum of a son who doesn't quite measure up and she's thinking she can have another crack at raising a boy with Leo."

Rachael fidgeted in her chair. "Will you let her have him?"

"I can see you squirming in your seat there. No, I won't just let Janine have him. You know, I don't have a whole lot of respect for Joyce Shipley, but I do agree with her that Leo deserves a normal home with a normal family. J.J. and Hallie do, too. I want the three of them growing up in a regular home with a mom and a dad and three square meals and footed pajamas and a minivan and a golden retriever."

"You're not talking foster care, are you." Rachael didn't even phrase it as a question.

"No. I think the best permanency plan for all three of those kids is to terminate Marcie's parental rights and allow them to be adopted while they're still young."

Rachael felt a pang in her chest, a sympathy ache for the mother in Marcie. "All three of them?"

"Rachael, Marcie will go to prison if she's found guilty."

"And you think she will be?"

"Yeah. I do."

"You think she did it."

Leslie paused for a minute. "Yes."

"Can I ask what you think her motive was?"

Leslie shrugged. "There was no motive, Rachael. She was high. She hadn't a clue what she was doing. She's a young, completely unskilled mother who was raised poorly, uses drugs, who never should have had children at the age she did and who, despite all our efforts, still has no idea how to care for three little human beings. If she weren't in the situation she's in right now, we could step in yet again, but the fact is, she's probably headed for prison."

"And you think she was high both times. That she abandoned Leo both times?"

Leslie sighed. "I really don't know what happened the first time. She could've taken something that metabolized fast and didn't show up on the screen or she might've taken a cleansing drug. But she's got five charges against her, Rachael. Five big ones. If they stick it means a TPR. You know it does."

TPR. Termination of Parental Rights.

Rachael sat wordless across from her colleague. Then she stood. "Les, I'm going to ask that another attorney handle the TPR for you. I'm too involved with this. I don't want to be the one to prosecute it. You understand, don't you?"

Leslie hesitated for a second. "Yeah. I guess so. You're not mad at me because I'm going for the TPR, are you?"

Rachael shook her head. "No. You need to do what you need to do."

And so do I, she thought.

Rachael made as if to leave, but then turned back around. "Ann Tremonette is Liza Cooley's caseworker, right?"

"Uh, yeah. She is."

"Is she in today?"

"Yeah. I think she's at her desk. Why?"

"I just need to rule something out. Thanks, Leslie. Catch you later."

Rachael waved, stepped out of Leslie's office, and headed for the last cubicle at the end of the long hallway.

THIRTY-ONE

Ann Tremonette smiled broadly as Rachael tapped on her open office door.

"Hello, Rachael. What brings you here today?"

"Do you have a couple minutes, Ann?" Rachael stepped inside. Ann's fondness for the outdoors and big woods was evident on all four walls of her small office. Prints of pine valleys and woodland wildlife and photographs of canoe trips to the Boundary Waters lined the walls.

"Sure," Ann said. "Have a seat."

Rachael took a chair opposite Ann.

"I thought you had Thursdays and Fridays off." Ann closed a file she had been working on. "Just can't stay away, huh?"

Rachael smiled. "I'd much rather be home with my daughter and husband, that's for sure, but something is bothering me about Marcie Shipley's case and that whole thing with her baby winding up in a trash can again. You did hear it happened again, didn't you?"

"Yes, I heard about it."

"Well, the police have arrested Marcie and I just can't get past the notion that they've got the wrong person."

"Really?" Ann's face registered interest and surprise.

"Yes. Did you know that Marcie and Liza Cooley attend Ivy Judson's support group together?"

"Um, yes I do. Liza's mentioned it. I think it's a great idea."

"Oh, it is. I agree. But what I'm wondering about has to do with Liza. I know a little about Liza's history. I know she's had some inconclusive psychological assessments and that she may be an undiagnosed schizophrenic. I was wondering if you know how often she has episodes of lost time."

Ann sat back in her chair. "What exactly does this have to do with Marcie Shipley?"

"I'm getting to that."

Ann shrugged. "I don't know exactly. I don't think anyone does. I think she needs a complete mental assessment, in residence. Her parents won't pay for it, though, and the court won't order it—not while she's voluntarily granting custody of her daughter to her parents."

"Was she having one of her episodes when she was found under the freeway overpass with Kylie?"

"Yes," Ann said slowly.

"Does she remember being found there?"

"No. She doesn't."

Rachael leaned forward in her chair. "Can I be completely candid with you?"

Ann blinked. "Sure. Of course."

"I have this feeling Liza Cooley knows something about what happened to Leo."

Ann said nothing at first; Rachael had clearly surprised her. "Why do you think that? Have you talked to Liza recently?"

"This morning."

"You talked to Liza this morning? I didn't even know you knew her."

"She and I had met at Ivy Judson's support group. I visited the group at Marcie's request before Leo was given back to her. And I met Liza there."

"And why do you think Liza knows something about what happened to Marcie's baby?" Ann's face was creased in puzzlement.

Rachael sighed. "It's mostly a hunch that I can't really explain. And

I've noticed her mental instability in the few short conversations I've had with her. It's rather obvious she has some issues."

"Well, I'll grant you that. But that still doesn't explain why you think she knows something."

"Because of how she reacted when I told her Leo had been abducted again. I visited her at work today and told her Leo had been hurt this time and she didn't even ask how or how badly. She was only concerned that there wasn't going to be a welcome home party today. And she kept looking like she was going to mentally disappear from me. I think she was on the edge of having an episode right there in front of me."

"You made a special trip to go talk to her at work? On your day off?"

"Like I said, something about this case is troubling me. I don't think Marcie did what she's being charged with doing."

"And you think *Liza* did it?" Ann was clearly stunned.

Rachael shook her head. "I don't know what to think, Ann. But I do think we're missing something. I think Liza knows something. I think Ivy does, too. And Sharell."

"Who's Sharell?"

"Sharell Hodge is another young mother in the group."

Ann exhaled heavily. "I think you need to go to the police with this, Rachael. I don't see how I can help you. If you really think something's going on in Ivy Judson's group, you need to tell the cops."

"I did. But I just wanted to hear from you what your feeling is about Liza. The police have nothing to go on except my hunches. It's not enough. I wanted to give them more."

Ann lifted her open palms into the air in a gesture of emptiness. "I don't know what else I can tell you. I only see Liza once a month. She's taking her mood-stabilizers near as we can tell. She's keeping her appointments at the mental health clinic, and she's voluntarily given her parents custody of Kylie."

"But do you think she could've taken Leo and abandoned him? Could she have been motivated by jealousy and done it during one of her episodes and then not remembered it?"

Ann shrugged. "I'm sure her psychologist could give you a better answer than I could. You don't have a court order that would allow him to tell you anything, do you?"

"No."

"Well, it's just my opinion, then."

"And what is your opinion?"

"Is it probable she did it? Who knows? I don't know who would want to knowingly hurt Marcie Shipley and her child. Is it possible? All I can say is Liza's a sweet girl with a ton of issues—issues she knows she has and issues she doesn't. So, yes, I think so. I think it's possible."

Rachael could hear Fig speaking from behind the studio's slightly ajar front door. She gently pushed on it and the door slowly swung open.

Fig was standing in front of McKenna. The toddler was sitting in a chair holding a little bowl of Pepperidge Farms goldfish and staring at Fig.

"And I promise you that you will never know what it is like to be alone," Fig was saying to McKenna. "You will never be loved by any man like I love you. This love has no parallel. Whether God gives us twenty thousand days together or twenty thousand hours or even just twenty thousand minutes, I will be there for you, Jillian. Always."

Fig lowered his body to one knee. "Marry me."

"Un gaga din!" McKenna said, crunching on goldfish.

"I'll take that as a yes." Fig bent down and swept McKenna into his arms. Several orange fish-shaped crackers scattered to the floor. "And now, my dear. Where would you like to get married? Sorrento? Nepal? The Galapagos?"

"I think she might like Disneyland," Rachael said, stepping all the way into the studio.

"Kumquat!" Fig spun around to face her. "How long were you standing there?" His eyes were bright with equal parts excitement and embarrassment.

"Mum-Mum!" McKenna said, pointing to Rachael.

"I only heard the last line, Fig. I promise." Rachael walked over to Fig and reached for her daughter.

"Well, what do you think? How did I sound? Think she'll say yes?"

Rachael snuggled McKenna close to her. Her daughter giggled. "I think the little bit I heard sounded lovely, Fig. I'm sure she'll say yes."

"I'm going to ask her on Thursday."

"Thursday? Doesn't she get back on Monday?"

"Yes, yes. But I love Thursdays. I want to ask her on a Thursday."

"Sounds like a plan."

"And I want you and Trace and McKenna to be there. Brick and Sidney, too."

Rachael set McKenna down on the floor. The little girl began picking up the fallen crackers. "I don't think that's a very good idea, Fig."

"It's a splendid idea. You must be there. It's essential."

"Most people like to propose in private."

Fig laughed heartily. "Silly Kumquat, I'm not like most people."

"Okay, true, but Jillian might like a little privacy."

"This isn't about privacy. It's about a marriage. Marriage isn't private. It's a very public thing. When you're married, everyone knows it. And you and Trace and the Princess are my family. Trace is like my brother. When Jillian marries me, she marries my family. That's you and the Princess and Tracer. She gets all of us, not just me."

"Well, Fig, still you might want to…" Rachael began.

"No, this is the way it has to be, Rachael. Family is everything. You must be there. You all must be there."

"Okay, but can you let Jillian answer you in private if she wants to?"

"Why would she want to do that?"

"Because she just might."

Fig inclined his head, deep in thought. "Nope. If it's yes, she will want you all there. If it's no, I will want you all there. I win." Fig bent down and said something to McKenna in another language in his falsetto.

Rachael laughed lightly. "What did you just tell her?"

Fig stood back up. "That she'll make a lovely bridesmaid."

The door opened and Trace walked in with two tall Caribou Coffees in his hands.

"Rach! You're home. I should've gotten three."

She smiled at her husband. "I'll share with you."

Half an hour later, Rachael and Trace were back in their own loft. Trace had gone to the grocery store earlier in the day and now Rachael pulled an assortment of vegetables out of the fridge to cut up for stir-fry.

Trace hoisted McKenna onto the countertop near Rachael and gave the little girl a wooden spoon to play with as he held her steady.

"So what do you think about Fig wanting us to be in the room when he proposes to Jillian?" Rachael said.

"Well, if you're asking me if I was surprised that he asked, I'd have to say no. Fig stopped surprising me years ago. But I am honored that he wants us there. I think family is more important to Fig than any of us realize. And I think it's because we're *it*. We're his family."

"I sure hope Jillian doesn't mind us standing at attention while he's on one knee, proposing," Rachael said as she began to slice a carrot on the bias.

"I think Jillian has come to expect the extraordinary from Fig, just like the rest of us," Trace said, stealing a slice of carrot. "I don't think she'll mind too much."

There was a momentary pause.

"So." Trace stole another carrot slice. "Did you get done what you needed to get done today?" McKenna began to tap the countertop with the spoon.

"Well, yes and no," Rachael replied. "I think I persuaded Will to take another look at the girls in Ivy's group. And to talk to Ivy, too. She's hiding something, Trace. I'm sure of it."

"But you talked to Will about all this? About all of it?"

"Yes."

"So it's all in Will's hands now, right?"

Rachael carefully sliced the top off of a bell pepper. Her answer was slow in coming.

"Right," she said.

"Tomorrow's your day off, Rach."

"I know it is."

"Want to come with me to Rochester? I'll drop off some artwork at Mayo and then McKenna and I can take you out to lunch."

Rachael let the inviting words promising an ordinary day fall about her. It sounded pretty wonderful. Besides, what more could she do? Who else was there to go and talk to? She had done all she could. And the dreams told her nothing more than what she already knew. Everything really was in Will's hands now.

"Sounds great," she said.

THIRTY-TWO

Rachael awoke Monday morning after a long, restful weekend to a sudden chill. Her first waking thought was that she had begun to spin another strange dream at the moment of waking, but actually the loft itself was cold. The summer days were slipping away. The first autumn chill had fallen over the Twin Cities.

"I'm going to turn the heat on," she said to Trace.

He mumbled a wordless comment and fell back asleep.

Though it was still early she made coffee and then showered. She felt a compulsion to get to work ahead of schedule, like it was going to be a busy day and she would later be glad she had awakened early.

By a little after seven, she was ready to leave, and neither McKenna nor Trace were awake yet. She opened McKenna's door so that Trace would hear her, and drew a heart on a yellow sticky note and stuck it on the bathroom mirror.

Traffic was only slightly lighter than her normal drive time. She pulled into the courthouse parking lot at seven-thirty, an hour earlier than usual.

The county attorneys' offices were numbly quiet. Rachael walked past

Kate's empty reception area and unlocked her office door. Mail from Thursday and Friday lay on her desk as well as a fan of newly filed petitions. She spent fifteen minutes studying the new petitions before noticing her phone was blinking with phone messages. She pressed the button to play them.

The first one was from an attorney in neighboring Anoka County about an upcoming training session. The second one was from Will. She put down the petitions and listened.

"Yeah, Rachael, it's Will. Friday five-ish. You wanted me to call if I found out anything. I suppose you also wanted me to call if I didn't. We're coming up with zilch over here. Call me Monday if you want to know more."

Rachael set the petitions down and pressed the speed dial for Will's office. He answered on the second ring.

"Will, it's Rachael. I got your message."

"Hey. We gave it all Friday afternoon, Rachael. We didn't come up with any hot new leads, I'm afraid."

Rachael frowned. "Who'd you talk to?"

"Well, Ivy first off. She wasn't too happy to divulge the last names of those other girls, but she did. I sent a couple other detectives out to ask some basic questions. They've all got alibis, Rachael. One was working the night shift when Leo was taken, one still lives at home and doesn't have a car, and one was baby-sitting her sister's kids overnight. None of them have any beef with Marcie, so no obvious motive either. I spoke with Sharell myself and she was as cordial as ever. Said she was at home with her children both of the blankety-blank nights Leo was abducted. She had some nice adjectives for Marcie, too. But not liking someone isn't a crime."

"Did you talk to Liza?"

"I went to her parents. They were pretty much ready to throw me out of the house after the first five minutes. I don't know if they think it's impossible their daughter had something to do with Leo's abductions or if they just don't want to consider it. I sent someone else out to question her psychologist. He flat out said Liza's a bit of a walking time bomb. He couldn't rule out that in her current mental state she couldn't have done it, which is the same as saying she might have. We can't ask a judge for a month-long stay to get the testing this gal needs until there's more to go on. I'm not saying I'm giving up, just telling you where things are at."

Rachael toyed with the cord on her phone. "All right," she sighed. "Thanks, Will."

"Rachael."

"What?"

"It's not your problem."

She thanked him again and hung up but in her mind she was saying, *Yes, it is.*

Rachael slipped her head into her hands and massaged her temples. *God, I don't know what else to do. I don't want Marcie going to prison. I don't want her to lose her kids forever. I'm missing something. What is it?*

She dug the fleshy pads of her thumbs into the sides of her head, as if to rub the fog away.

The dreams.

She stilled her hands.

Something in those terrible dreams was a clue. But what?

Rachael grabbed a piece of paper. If God was whispering to her, it was in the dreams that she would find out what it was she was supposed to hear. She began to write down as much as she could remember about the three dreams, starting with the first one.

The Loft. Fig is painting. Baby crying. No one hears it but me. Alley. Cold. Dark. Moonlight. Dumpster. Fig's cat. Baby crying. Can't find the baby. Alley. Cold. Cat. Cat scratches me. Baby crying. Can't find the baby. Marcie screaming.

She stopped. Even as she wrote, she felt tension rising within her. She remembered the pull of Trace's arms around her as she pounded on the bedroom window, and as she stood poised at the top step of the loft stairs. The dreams had to mean something. They had to. But what?

Her eyes fell on the word *cat.*

Why had she dreamed about the cat Fig had drawn? Twice she had dreamed it.

She circled the word, frowning as she did it.

"Bad day already?" a voice said.

Rachael flinched and looked up. Kate was standing in front of her.

"Kate. You scared me."

"Just wanted to say good morning and to tell you you have a call on line two. You're here early. I almost told them to call back at eight-thirty."

"Yeah. Just thought I'd beat the traffic this morning. Thanks, Kate."

Rachael reached for her phone and pushed the flashing button. "Rachael Flynn."

She heard a muffled sound, as if the person on the other end was handing the phone to another. She heard the sound of cars in the background. Whoever was calling her was standing outside.

"Hello?" Rachael said.

"Um. Hey. I gotta message for you."

"Who is this?" Rachael didn't recognize the woman's voice. The tone sounded Asian.

"I gotta message. You ready?"

"What?"

"Okay. Here it is."

Rachael heard the crinkling of paper. Then the woman continued.

"Stay out of stuff that's not your concern. You've got a sweet little girl. It'd be a shame for someone at the county to hear you beat on her."

Rachael felt her blood rush to her ears. "What did you say?"

"You want me to read it again?" Was the woman speaking to her? She couldn't tell. Rachael thought she heard another voice in the background say, "Just hang up."

"Yes, I want you to read it again!" Rachael said. She looked beyond her desk to the hallway past her open door. No one was walking by her office. She put her hand over the phone's mouthpiece. "Kate!" she yelled.

She heard more muffled sounds on the other end of the phone.

"Stay out of stuff that's not your concern. You've got a sweet little girl. It'd be a shame for someone at the county to hear you beat on her."

The line went dead.

Kate appeared at the doorway. "Did you call me?"

"When you answered that call, did the person ask for me by name?"

"Well, yes."

"Was it a woman?"

"Yes."

"Did you ask what the call was in regards to?"

"Rachael, what is it? What's the matter?"

Rachael stood and grabbed her purse. "Did you?"

"Yes. She said it was a private matter."

"Was she Asian? Did she sound Asian?"

"No, she didn't. Rachael, what's going on?"

"See if Will is still in, will you? Have him call me on my cell phone."

Rachael dashed out of her office.

"Rachael, what was all that about?"

Rachael turned her head but kept walking. "I think someone was paid to give me a message. Whoever asked you if they could speak with me wasn't the person I just spoke to. She'd been handed the phone by someone else."

"Who?" Kate called out.

"Just call Will, please? See if he's in. Have him call me on my cell phone."

Rachael was sure she hadn't heard the Asian voice before. But she thought she recognized the muffled voice who had said, "Just hang up."

Traffic was still heavy in downtown St. Paul as Rachael headed to Ivy's duplex. Rachael spent the time taking deep breaths and calming herself. The caller hadn't threatened to harm McKenna. She had to keep telling herself that. They had threatened to file a false report of abuse.

She didn't want either one to happen, but one was certainly worse than the other.

As she turned down busy streets that would lead her to South St. Paul, she let her reasonable side berate her for even going to Ivy's. She should just report the threat and let the police handle it.

The thing was, if it was Ivy, her motivation had to be fear—pure and simple. Fear of a threat, or fear of exposing a girl she had sworn to love and protect. Ivy surely needed a way out. Longed for a way out. Rachael wanted her to see that she had one.

She pulled up alongside the duplex and got out of her car. She noted that Ivy's garage was closed. Rachael wondered as she mounted the steps to Ivy's front door if a warm car was parked inside. Or had Ivy been on foot when she found a pedestrian willing to read off a message into a pay phone for a few bucks?

Rachael rang the doorbell and waited. The curtains at the living room window parted slightly for a second and then fell closed again.

"Ivy?" Rachael called loudly. "It's Rachael Flynn. Can I please just talk to you for a minute. I'm alone."

Silence.

"Ivy? Please?"

The door slowly opened. Ivy stood on the other side of it. She looked pale and cautious.

"Ivy, are you all right?"

"What do you want?"

"I just want to talk to you."

"About what?"

"About a phone call I just got."

Ivy said nothing. Her expression didn't change.

"May I come in?" Rachael asked.

Ivy shrugged and stepped aside. Rachael walked into the living room. It seemed dark and unwelcoming compared to the other times she had been there. She took a seat on the couch. Ivy sank into the armchair. The woman reached for a tissue up her sleeve and dabbed at her nose.

"Ivy, I got a phone call a little while ago. Would you happen to know anything about that?"

"How would I know anything about your phone calls?" Ivy muttered. She stuffed the tissue back up her sleeve.

"You would if you had made the call."

"I didn't call you."

Ivy didn't look at Rachael when she said it.

"Ivy, I want to help you. I can see that this situation with Leo and Marcie is eating away at you."

"I don't need any help with anything. I'm fine."

"If you're protecting someone who has threatened you or is blackmailing you, what they're doing is illegal."

Ivy shook her head. "You people always think you know exactly what's going on. Like you know everything."

Rachael leaned forward, seeking eye contact with Ivy. But Ivy continued to stare at her lap. "Then tell me how I've got it wrong," Rachael said. "Are you trying to protect Liza? If she's mixed up in this, it's because she's sick. She needs help, not protection."

Ivy raised her head to look at Rachael. "You really don't get it. You'll never get it. You don't understand their world. I do. I've lived it. What do you know of this kind of life? You were born into a normal family. You went to college. You went to law school. You got married first and then had a kid. You made all the right decisions. You've no idea what it's like to live day after day, hour after hour in a world that wants to see you fall. How can you even begin to think you understand any of this?"

"Help me understand, Ivy. I want to understand."

Ivy said nothing.

Rachael was silent for a moment. "Don't you want to know what the person who called me said?" she asked a few seconds later.

Ivy shrugged. "It's none of my business."

"What *is* your business?" Rachael knew her question sounded like it was laced with a challenge. Maybe it was.

Ivy rose. "I can't help you. I'm sorry."

Rachael stood also. "I can help *you*."

Ivy walked to the front door and opened it. "I don't need your help."

Rachael walked to the door slowly, giving Ivy extra seconds to change her mind.

She didn't.

The last thing Rachael saw as Ivy closed the door behind her were the double-framed pictures of Ivy's grandchildren on the bookshelf.

Outdated portraits of grandchildren Ivy said she hardly ever sees though they live only an hour away.

Rachael hurried to her car. Notes from her second visit with Ivy were crammed into her briefcase lying on its side in the backseat. Somewhere in those notes she had written Ivy's son's name.

And where he lived.

THIRTY-THREE

Rachael's cell phone began to trill as soon as she got back inside her car. She pulled the phone out of her purse and looked at the tiny screen.

Will.

"Hello, Will," she said. Rachael reached behind the seat and began yanking out the loose contents of her briefcase.

"What's going on? Where are you?"

"I'm just leaving Ivy's."

"Ivy's? Why are you at Ivy's? Kate's been frantic trying to reach me. She said you got a strange call, and then went tearing out of your office in a panic yelling at her to call me."

"Well, I was a little panicked at first. I probably should've waited to call you myself." Rachael continued to sort through the pages of notepads in her briefcase.

"About what? What's going on? Who called you?"

"I think maybe Ivy paid a passerby on the street to call me this morning to give me a message. I didn't recognize the woman's voice who talked to me, but I'm pretty sure I heard Ivy in the background. I think it was from a pay phone."

"Message? What kind of message?"

"The threatening kind."

Rachael heard Will say something under his breath. "You get a threatening call from someone and you decide to *go over to their house?*"

He sounded mad.

"Will, it's not as bad as you think."

"Just how bad is it?"

"The woman who gave me the message was reading it off a piece of paper. She said something like I shouldn't get involved in matters that didn't concern me. I've got a sweet little girl. It'd be a shame for the county to hear I abuse her."

"That's exactly what she said?"

"Well, maybe not exactly. I think she might've said it'd be a shame for the county to hear I beat her."

"And you think it was Ivy in the background? And that she got someone to read this message to you?"

"I do."

"So why go over there and talk to her, Rachael? Haven't we been over this before? You keep trying to do my job. I'm the one with the badge, remember? I'm the one who carries a gun."

"She wasn't threatening to kill me, Will. She's desperate. She's having to choose between her girls. She's letting Marcie take the fall for one of the other girls and it's killing her."

"You don't know that."

"Then why get someone to pass on a threat to me? Are you telling me your guys asking all those questions on Friday doesn't have anything to do with this? Ivy knows I don't think Marcie did this! I was with her on Thursday. She knows I think she's either protecting Liza or under some kind of threat from Sharell. She knows I told you you've got the wrong girl in custody. She wants me to back off and let you send Marcie to prison."

"And why would she want to do that?"

"She doesn't *want* to, Will. She had to choose! She had to choose between the girls! I think she had a suspicion of who took Leo the first time. When he was taken the second time, she knew for sure. And it's because she said nothing that first time that he got hurt so bad. That's why she started throwing up when I told her what had happened to Leo. She was sick that her silence led to that."

"And you're saying the real perpetrator knows that Ivy knows."

"If it's Sharell, she knows. If it's Liza, I don't even think Liza knows what she's done."

Will paused for a moment. "All right, listen. I am sending a unit over to Ivy's neighborhood to see if anyone saw her hanging around a pay phone this morning. And we'll go over Marcie's apartment again, with a fine-tooth comb if we have to, looking for evidence we might've missed. In the meantime, will you *please* stay away from Ivy? And Sharell and Liza. Please?"

"I'm not trying to make things difficult for you, Will."

"You don't make things difficult, Rachael. You make me worry. If you want to be a cop, go to the academy. I'll put in a good word for you."

"I don't want to be a cop. I just don't want Marcie going to prison. And I don't want her to lose her kids." Her eyes zeroed in on a name and a city written in blue ink on a mini yellow notepad.

"Go back to the courthouse and be an attorney, okay?" Will said.

"Goodbye, Will." She purposely didn't say okay. She had no intention of going back to the courthouse just yet.

Rachael pressed her speed dial to call Kate back at the prosecutor's office. She told her assistant she had an important visit to make and she'd be gone the rest of the morning. She'd work late to make up for it if she had to. Before she hung up she had Kate look up on an Internet search engine the name Dallas Judson.

The drive to Wabasha was an easy one. The morning traffic had dwindled to an easy pace and Rachael found herself pulling into the riverside town within an hour of leaving St. Paul. Kate had put Dallas Judson's address into Mapquest and as Rachael followed the instructions she had been given, she prayed that the man either worked nights or that his wife was home and could tell her where he worked. She didn't want to leave Wabasha without having spoken to him.

Rachael found the one-level home without any trouble. It was a modest tract home with a less-than-tidy yard. The open two-car garage revealed an aging Ford Explorer on the left side. The right side was empty.

A dog began to bark from within the house when Rachael rang the doorbell. She said a silent prayer for wisdom, direction, and protection as she heard the doorknob being turned from on the other side.

The man who opened the door looked to be in his late thirties. He was of medium build and sported a goatee that needed trimming. He wore sweatpants and a faded Twins T-shirt and held a coffee mug in one hand. He stared at her through the screen of his storm door.

"Can I help you?" he said.

"I'm looking for Dallas Judson." Rachael said it as amicably as she could.

"I'm him. What's this about? If you're selling something, you're wasting your time."

"I'm not selling anything. I'm an attorney with the Ramsey County Attorney's Office. My name is Rachael Flynn. I know your mother, Mr. Judson, and I think she may be in some trouble."

It seemed Dallas Judson hadn't heard her. He said nothing at first.

"What kind of trouble?" he finally said. "If it's money trouble, I can't help her. I'm in between jobs and we're just making do on my wife's income."

"This isn't about money. I think your mother is withholding information from the police. She also may be the target of blackmail."

"Is she in jail?"

"No."

Dallas just stood there holding his coffee mug.

"Mr. Judson, may I come in?"

The man hesitated for a moment. Then he reached for the handle of the storm door and swung it wide, holding it open as Rachael stepped inside.

Dallas Judson's front room was smallish and decorated with cheap knickknacks and bargain furniture pieces: wood veneer tables scuffed at the corners, stiff polyester-covered sofa and chairs, fake chrome pole lamps, and knock-off prints in metal frames. A huge flat-screen TV dominated the room, followed by a collection of magazines, piles of junk mail, and trios of empty Mountain Dew cans that vied for control of the room. Dallas Judson muted the TV and moved a pile of newspapers off a sky-blue recliner.

"Have a seat," he said.

Rachael sat down in the recliner. Dallas slid onto the sofa. A little black-and-white dog Rachael hadn't noticed before jumped onto his lap.

Dallas waited for Rachael to speak.

"Do you mind if I ask you what your relationship is like with your mother?"

Dallas patted his dog. "Yeah, I might mind."

"Forgive me. What I mean is, if you're not particularly close, I'll understand if you're not able to help me help her."

"What kind of help does she need?"

"She needs help telling the truth. I think she knows something about a crime but she won't say what she knows."

"Maybe she doesn't know anything."

"I think she does."

Dallas said nothing.

"I think your mother is perhaps protecting one of the young mothers she is helping," Rachael said.

"What young mothers?"

"Do you know about the support group your mother started?"

"No."

"Mr. Judson, how often do you see your mother?"

Dallas looked down at his dog. "I don't see how that relates to your problem here."

"The photographs your mother has of your children are outdated. She says she doesn't see her grandchildren very often."

Dallas continued to stroke his dog. "And your point is?"

"It just seems a little odd to me that she sees so little of her grandchildren. Your mother has started a support group for struggling single mothers. She provides them with child care, helps them with their troubles, and offers them advice and acceptance. And she dotes on their children."

Dallas looked up at her and laughed.

"You find that funny?" Rachael said.

"Yeah, I find that funny," he said, nodding his head.

"How come?"

Dallas looked back down at his pet as he scratched the dog behind its pointed, silky ears. "Because she's just not what I would call the doting type."

"Why is that?"

He raised his head. "Because I lived with her, that's why."

"I don't get it."

"No one's asking you to."

"Mr. Judson, your mother told me she is able to help these girls because she understands the tough life of a struggling single mother. She told me she raised you and your sister by herself while working two jobs. I got the impression she held it together for the three of you during some really difficult times."

Dallas scratched his neck. "Look, I really don't know why you're here. If my mother is in trouble with the law, that's her problem, not mine. If you want to know why I don't visit her more often, why don't you ask her yourself?" Dallas gently removed the dog from his lap and stood. The interview was coming to a close.

Rachael stood as well. "I'm asking *you*. Was she a good mother, Mr. Judson?"

Dallas crossed his arms in front of his chest. "I'm sure she'd say she did the best she could."

"What do you say?"

Dallas held Rachael's gaze for a stretched moment. Rachael got the distinct impression he was about to tell her something he didn't often mention.

"She used to lock Amber and me in our room when she was angry at us, without food or water. She wouldn't even let us out to use the toilet," he said tonelessly. "If she was angry and there was something available to throw, that's what she would do. Amber and I dodged a lot of flying dishes, books, and bottles. If she was really mad, she'd slap us so hard you could see the imprint of every finger on her hand."

Rachael felt her mouth drop open. She couldn't picture Ivy doing the things Dallas was describing. The images defied logic, defied all that she knew about Ivy Judson. But Dallas would have absolutely no reason to lie to her. None at all.

"Ivy did those things to you?" she murmured.

Dallas smiled. It was a pitiable smile. "Only when she was mad."

THIRTY-FOUR

Rachael's mind was spinning in a million different directions as she drove the seventy miles back to St. Paul.

At the forefront of her somersaulting thoughts was the notion that Ivy wasn't who Rachael thought she was.

Rachael had assumed Ivy had bravely absorbed the blows of an unkind world in her early mothering days and had carved out a secure life for her two children despite steady misfortune.

She thought Ivy was a kindred spirit to Elizabeth McKenna, determined to rise above bad decisions and make a haven out of havoc.

But what Dallas told her had turned everything on its head.

Ivy had not only lived the tough life of a struggling single mom, but she'd made the worst kind of mistake a mother could make.

She had abused her children.

If Sharell somehow had found out about Ivy's past, then it was suddenly very clear the leverage Sharell had over Ivy. If Ivy had fallen back into an old bad habit, if Sharell had seen Ivy hit or mistreat a child in her care, and if Sharell knew Ivy's background, Sharell could end with one word the idyllic new life Ivy had made for herself.

"That's it," Rachael whispered to no one. Ivy stood to lose her new identity. Her new role as benevolent mother figure hung in the balance. That's how Ivy had decided to pay for her past mistakes. She'd begun the support group. She'd dug down deep and found the store of protective mother-love she'd been unable to tap into when Dallas and Amber were little. And she was doling it out to others, a generation too late.

Ivy had sought to atone for the abuse she had heaped on Dallas and Amber by reaching out to young mothers who, when she looked at them, reminded her of herself.

If Sharell really had it out for Marcie, if she felt so threatened by Marcie that she would end Leo Shipley's life to hurt her, was it possible Ivy had been pressured into silence by the weight of her past alone? Or had Ivy fallen back into an old habit?

And Sharell would have to be on the verge of being a sociopath to wish a child dead to ruin its mother. Sharell didn't appear to be homicidal in the least. Rachael had met homicidal thinkers. Sharell didn't fit the mold. Sharell didn't exhibit a hint of mental illness.

But Liza…

If Liza had taken Leo, why would Ivy protect Liza over Marcie?

Unless…

"Oh, Lord," Rachael said aloud, as near a prayer as it could be.

Unless Sharell knew Liza had taken and abandoned Leo. And she wanted Marcie to be sent to prison for it.

And Sharell had bought Ivy's silence, as Ivy also knew it was Liza, with the threat of exposing Ivy and shattering her beautiful new world.

"That has to be it!" Rachael said aloud. She reached with her right hand for her cell phone, tucked away in her purse on the passenger seat. When she had it in hand, she scrolled down the numbers in her contact list for Will.

He answered on the first ring.

"Will, it's Rachael."

"Why aren't you at the courthouse?"

"Oh, hush and listen to me. I've just learned something about Ivy that might explain why she'd be willing to lie to us."

"What are you talking about? Where are you?"

"I'm on my way back to St. Paul. I was in Wabasha."

"Wabasha. What's in Wabasha?"

"Who. *Who's* in Wabasha."

"Rachael, who's in Wabasha?"

"Dallas Judson. Ivy Judson's son. Will, he told me his mother was an abuser. She used to lock him and his sister in their rooms without food or water. She threw things at them. Hit them and left marks. What if Sharell knows about this? What if Ivy slipped up one day when she was taking care of one of these girls' kids and abused one of them and Sharell saw it? Sharell now has leverage."

"For what? What does Sharell have leverage for?"

"For letting Marcie, whom she can't stand, and who threatened her, take the fall for who really took Leo. Liza."

Will was silent for a moment.

"So you're saying Ivy knows Liza took the baby," he said. "Sharell knows Liza took the baby. Liza doesn't know she took him. Sharell wants Marcie to be blamed for it. Threatens to expose Ivy if Ivy comes clean and says it was Liza. Ivy regretfully decides to let Marcie take the fall, but comforts herself with the knowledge that she gets to keep Liza *and* her new identity as compassionate supermom."

"Well, yes. It makes sense, Will. It's the only thing that does."

"Okay, I admit it's as plausible an explanation as anyone's come up with. But how did Marcie wind up with ketamine in her bloodstream? And how did Liza get in? No forced entry, remember? Plus, we've talked to Liza's roommate. She says she was at home with Liza both of the nights Leo was taken."

"But it's not like this person stayed up all night. How does the roommate know Liza didn't slip away in the middle of the night?"

"And the ketamine?"

Rachael sighed. She hadn't thought that far. "I don't know, Will. Did you check that Tylenol bottle?"

"It's clean."

She pursed her lips together, deep in thought. She was onto something. She was sure of it. But she was still missing something.

"Will, can you have someone do a background check on Ivy? Go deep. Go way back."

"I'm already on it."

"Keep me in the loop?"

"If you promise to go back to the courthouse."

"I promise."

"I'll keep you in the loop."

Rachael was thankful for the amount of casework that needed to be done that afternoon. Her mind would drift to the puzzle tumbling around in her mind, but each time it happened she'd refocus on the petitions on her desk, preparing for an ordinary day at court for the following afternoon.

A few minutes before five she called Will to see if he'd learned anything new about Ivy Judson.

"I said I'd call," Will said.

"I know, but I'm getting ready to leave work and I want to be able to sleep tonight."

"We've not found a lot, Rachael. If Ivy was an abuser, she was good at hiding it. We traced her back to Nicollet County, but the only activity there is a complaint against her for having a trashed yard, which she cleaned up, and some intervention when Dallas started skipping school. We're not finding any court activity other than speeding tickets and one DUI. We'd need to get a court order to go through the kids' school files to see if their teachers had any suspicions of abuse, but I don't know what grounds to use to get it. A hunch doesn't work. Not even when they're yours, Rachael."

She sighed. "I know, I know."

"Go home. Let it rest for tonight."

"Right. I'm going home. Thanks, Will."

She hung up the phone.

There would be no rest.

Fig was at the loft when Rachael arrived home a little before six. He was at the stove, stirring a saucepan and wearing one of McKenna's bonnets on his head. McKenna was nearby in her high chair, jabbering and pointing to the hat.

"Kumquat! *Bienvenida!*" Fig looked up from the pot. One of the bonnet strings slipped into his mouth and he huffed it out.

"Hey, Fig. Nice hat."

"Oh. That." Fig raised his eyes as if to study the top of his own head. "The heiress insists." He pointed toward McKenna with the wooden spoon in his hand. Brownish drops of liquid splashed on the tile floor.

"What's that you're making, Fig?"

"*Mole* sauce, Kumquat. We're going Mexican tonight. Tracer and I are making you dinner. You've been looking tired, used-up. This is a great recipe. I use Chilean chocolate. It's my secret, though. You tell anyone and I'll have to run you through." He winked and began to stir again.

"Mum-Mum!" McKenna called out and Rachael went to her daughter and kissed the top of her head.

"Trace around?" she said, looking past Fig to the loft's living room.

"'Sent him to the store for a ripe avocado. You two have no food in this house. Have I not taught you anything?"

"We have some stuff," Rachael said defensively as she grabbed a dish towel and blotted the spilled drops. She'd been to the grocery store on Saturday. But she had been uninspired when she walked the aisles, her mind on Leo Shipley.

"Bread and sweet pickles. Fudge pops and saltines. A regular nursing home smorgasbord," Fig chided. "I'm taking you shopping this weekend, Kumquat. And we're not going to your boring grocery store. We're going to *mine.*"

Rachael smiled, tossed the towel onto the counter, and then stepped into the open dining area to set down her briefcase and purse. As she set them on the dining room table, her eyes were drawn to the little table directly under Elizabeth McKenna's drawing of the sparrow. Atop the little table's polished surface lay the artists' sketches of the alley. Fig's was on top.

She walked over to the table and reached for the drawing. Her eyes fell on the cat that sat and watched Fig's Cruella-like Koko speed away like a demon.

The cat in her dreams.

She stared at the drawing for several long moments. The animal seemed to hold her spellbound.

The cat in her dreams.

Then she walked back into the kitchen with the drawing.

"Fig?"

"*Sí, señora.*"

"What made you draw this cat?"

"Hmm?"

She showed him the drawing. "This cat. What made you draw him?"

Fig shrugged. "It's an alley. He's an alley cat."

"But what's he doing there?"

Fig peered at his drawing as if to refresh his memory.

Again he lifted and lowered his shoulders.

"I guess he's watching."

THIRTY-FIVE

Rachael fell asleep, afraid to dream.

She had enjoyed the dinner Fig and Trace had made and had spent the rest of the evening playing with McKenna, and then reading and sipping a cup of chamomile tea.

But her mind kept falling on troubling images.

She feared she would dream of Ivy hurtling objects at her or of being chased by a monstrous version of Fig's alley cat or of actually finding the crying baby but discovering that she had found him too late.

As it was, she awoke Tuesday morning having dreamt nothing she could remember.

Rachael arrived at the courthouse physically ready for the petitions that she would present to the judge, but mentally she was a million miles away, focused on seemingly tangled thoughts that pricked her all afternoon:

Marcie is innocent.

Ivy knows who took Leo.

Sharell has motive.

Liza is a ticking time bomb.

Ivy has a terrible past she wishes to hide from.

Ivy's reaction to Leo's wounds was genuine.

There was no forced entry.

Ketamine was found in Marcie's blood.

Marcie insists she locked her door and took nothing but Tylenol.

By late afternoon, after Rachael had returned to her office from several hours in court, she was nursing a colossal headache.

She called Will.

"It's been a day and a half, Rachael," he told her. "I don't know any more today than I did yesterday. We don't have any solid leads on Ivy or Liza or Sharell. Nothing beyond your very interesting hunch."

Rachael exhaled heavily. "All right."

"You haven't been toodling around St. Paul ferreting out more clues have you?"

"No."

"You've done all you can do, Rachael. You might need to let this one go and let the chips fall where they may."

"Those chips are going to send an irresponsible but innocent mother to prison."

"I know that's how you see it. Believe me, if there was something concrete to go on, we'd be all over this. Right now all the evidence is stacked against Marcie. That's just how it is."

"The crime scene guys have gone back to her apartment?"

"They're going back on Thursday."

"Okay."

"Sorry, Rachael."

"It's all right. Goodbye, Will."

Rachael hung up the phone. She began her usual post-court tasks. But every other thought was of Leo Shipley and the faceless person who had tossed him into the trash.

That evening, Rachael was restless and unable to concentrate on any one task. She tried to watch a movie with Trace after putting McKenna to bed but her mind was a jumble.

She rose from the couch where she had been sitting next to Trace and headed for the dining room. She grabbed the artists' sketches and laid them out one by one on the table.

Rachael pored over each image, waiting and willing for insight to fall on her like it had other times. She had never had to fight for clarity like she was doing now. The first time she felt divinely empowered to discern fact from deceit was when her brother had been on trial for murder. The truth at last came when a young Hmong teenager decided to trust her. The same thing had happened earlier that year with another case that had her reeling with perceptions she couldn't explain. Again, the truth came to light when her poking and prodding prompted a confession.

No one was confessing this time. She was going to have to figure this out without a confession or do what Will suggested and just let it go.

She didn't want to go there.

She didn't think she was meant to. The dreams were somehow a clue.

And it suddenly occurred to her that she was afraid of them.

If she was going to get to the bottom of this, she had to kill the fear inside of dreaming the alley, the crying baby, the feeling of hopelessness.

She would have to embrace the dream.

Be ready for it.

Go to sleep and await it.

Rachael was suddenly reminded of something her brother Josh had told her about this strange gift she had, when knowing she had it was new and her first response was to somehow control it. She had wanted to get inside it, to master it. Josh, who had insights of his own, told her she was meant instead to let the gift get inside her.

Okay, God, she silently prayed. *Show me. I'm not afraid. Show me the truth.*

Rachael had been standing at the table for several minutes when Trace came up behind her and wrapped her in his arms.

"Why don't you put those away and come to bed?" he said.

She leaned into him. "I'm ready."

The dream came as the last rays of moonlight fell across the loft's hardwood floors. A rosy sun was just beginning to peek over the bend in the horizon. Rachael lay in her bed. Trace was close to her. A ticking wall clock was the only sound in the room.

Behind closed eyes, she began to dream.

Rachael was in the alley. Alone. It was dark and cool.

I am dreaming, she thought. But she did not awaken.

A ripple of fear began to course through her and she tamped it down.

I am not afraid.

The baby's cries began softly at first. She heard them all around her: in front of her where the alley opened onto a damp, empty street; behind her, where she could see nothing; and at her side, where rotting boxes teetered on broken pallets. The cries were everywhere. She felt something on her arm and she turned. The cat was sitting on a box, half-hidden in the shadows, flicking its tail. Its whiskers had brushed her elbow, but it didn't look at her. It was looking toward the front of the alley. Watching. Rachael followed the cat's gaze and saw that there was a Dumpster at the end of the alley. The baby's cries now seemed to echo only from within its metal sides.

Leo, Rachael said.

Then Rachael heard a voice. It was Fig.

He was in the alley, too, behind her on one knee, practicing his proposal to Jillian.

Twenty thousand days, twenty thousand hours, Fig was saying. *Twenty thousand minutes.*

A garbage truck appeared at the entrance to the alley. The cat meowed.

Wait! Rachael yelled. *There's a baby inside!*

She wanted to scream but she couldn't. She tried to get Fig's attention but he didn't seem to hear her. He just kept saying the same thing over and over again. *Twenty thousand days, twenty thousand hours.*

Wait!

But her voice wouldn't carry.

She ran toward the Dumpster but it suddenly disappeared. So did Fig and the cat. Rachael was now alone in the alley. In her closed fist she felt something cold and firm. She opened her fingers.

A key.

There was a sudden blast of sound and light and Rachael sat up in bed with a start. Her heart was pounding and the skin under her pajamas was beaded with sweat. She looked down at her hands. One clutched the blankets. The other was curled into a fist. She opened her hand. There was nothing there but heat and moisture, as if she had just moments ago held something there tightly.

The key.

Despite Marcie's assertion that there was no spare key, the fact remained that someone had to have a key to get into Marcie's apartment.

Who would Marcie trust with a key?

There was only one person Rachael could think of.

Ivy.

Rachael sprang out of bed and walked to the window, her hands on her hips.

That made no sense! she scolded herself silently. *Why would Ivy let someone into Marcie's apartment to take Leo knowing he would be thrown into a trash bin?*

It was inconceivable that Ivy would allow harm to come to Leo. Simply impossible to believe. Even knowing Ivy's past. Not after seeing her vomiting into her toilet.

Rachael began to pace the bedroom. She had to be missing something. What was it?

Images and sounds from the dream fell all around her as she paced. The cat watching. Fig repeating the lines from his proposal over and over.

She suddenly stopped.

The cat, watching. Fig and his days and hours and minutes.

What was the difference between a day and an hour and a minute?

And what would that difference mean to a baby abandoned in a trash bin?

It meant everything.

It meant life and death.

And what if someone *was* watching?

Rachael dashed over to her closet and pulled out slacks and a sweater.

She had to get to the jail to talk to Marcie.

She was one question away from knowing the truth.

THIRTY-SIX

Marcie looked both hopeful and cautious as she was led into the jail's interview room.

She took a chair across from Rachael, clearly searching Rachael's face for the reason why she was there.

"Marcie, I think I might know what happened to Leo," Rachael said. "I think I've figured out who took him. I'm not exactly sure why they did. But I need your help. And I need you to be completely honest with me."

"I didn't do it," Marcie said, as if she were still in the courtroom.

"I know you didn't."

Marcie's eyes widened and she seemed to flinch in her chair. "You believe me?"

"Yes."

"Who did it? I want to know who did this to my baby!" Marcie's voice trembled. Relief at being believed was quickly being replaced with anger.

"I said I *think* I know, Marcie. I'm not sure. And until I'm sure, you're going to have to trust me."

"Tell me who did it!"

"You need to tell me some things first."

"Like what?"

"First you have to swear to me you'll tell me the truth. I can't help you if you don't."

Marcie hesitated, frowning. She sighed. "All right. I swear."

"You told the police that no one came by the apartment the night Leo was taken the second time. But that's not true, is it? Ivy came by."

Marcie said nothing.

"She gave you the Tylenol, didn't she? You had a headache and she gave you Tylenol."

"So?"

"Did you see the bottle? Did you see her take the Tylenol out of the bottle you keep in your bathroom?"

Marcie hesitated. "No."

"Why did you lie to the police about Ivy having been there? I need the truth, Marcie."

Marcie looked away for a moment. Then she turned her head back. Her tone was defensive. "Because she brought me some booze. I wasn't going to get drunk. And I didn't get drunk. I just needed something to calm my nerves. I had two drinks. That's it. And I didn't say anything to the police because *you* made me sign that paper that I wouldn't drink any alcohol."

"Ivy brought you alcohol?"

"Yeah. So?"

"Why do you think she did that?"

"Because she happens to understand people! She knew I just needed a little something. She even told me she was taking the bottle back with her so I wouldn't have more than I should." Marcie narrowed her eyes. "Why are you asking me this?" Her tone switched from defensive to doubtful.

For a moment Rachael said nothing. The picture was becoming clear. Very clear. Ivy had slipped the ketamine into the Tylenol capsules. Ivy had wanted Marcie to test positive for mind-altering drugs. Ivy *wanted* Marcie to lose custody of Leo, maybe of all three of her kids. Motive escaped her still, but Rachael knew she would soon know that as well.

"Ivy was there the day you had your new locks put in, wasn't she?" Rachael said.

Marcie tipped her head. Her narrowed eyes began to widen. "What're you getting at?"

"Did you give Ivy the spare key?"

"There was no spare key."

"What?"

"Ivy said the new lock didn't come with a spare key."

"Ivy said that?"

"Yeah."

Rachael stood.

"Wait. Where are you going? Who took my baby?" Marcie whimpered as she stood as well. Alarm coated her words.

"I promise I'll come back and tell you everything." Rachael turned to walk toward the door. She knocked on it.

"Tell me now!" Marcie yelled.

A uniformed police officer appeared from on the other side to let Rachael out.

Rachael turned her head to look at Marcie. "You need to trust me. I promise I'll come back."

"Wait!" Marcie yelled.

But Rachael was through the door and its heavy thickness swallowed Marcie's voice.

Rachael made her way out of the jail and back to the main entrance to the courthouse. She pulled her phone out of her purse as she stepped outside into the parking lot between the courthouse and the police department. She searched the lot for Will's car. It wasn't there.

She pressed the speed dial for Will as she got back inside her car, but wherever Will was, he wasn't picking up. Rachael waited for his voice mail to kick in.

"Will. It's Rachael. It's about eight-thirty in the morning. I need you to meet me at Ivy's as soon as you hear this message. I'm leaving the courthouse to go there now. If you get there before me, please wait for me. Don't go in."

Rachael clicked off the phone and started her car.

She was finally at the end of the puzzle.

Ivy had taken Leo. Both times.

But Ivy had never counted on him getting hurt. And that's because she had been watching. Ivy had been watching to make sure Leo would be found before anything happened to him. Leo had spent only minutes in the trash bin, not hours.

Ivy was the cat.

But something had gone wrong the second time. The cat had to flee before Leo was found. No one was watching when Ivy's plan backfired horribly.

Rachael put her car in gear and slowly drove out of the parking lot.

She had solved the riddle but within she felt only sadness.

Will's car was nowhere to be seen when Rachael pulled up alongside Ivy's duplex. June, Ivy's neighbor, was tending to some flowerpots on her porch when Rachael walked up the sidewalk on Ivy's side.

"Good morning!" June said brightly.

"Hi," Rachael said.

"Come to see Ivy, have you?"

"Yes."

"Oh, that's good. She has seemed so down lately. She could use some cheering up. She's such a sweetheart. I hate to see her sad."

June brushed her hands on her pants, smiled, and stepped back inside her front door.

For a moment, Rachael considered asking June to join her. She had no desire to confront Ivy with what she knew. She could wait for Will, but somehow she knew it would be easier on Ivy if she talked with her without Will being there. Rachael sensed no fear for her safety, but she had to admit she was glad June had seen her.

She rang the doorbell and prayed.

A few moments later Ivy swung the door open. Rachael could see that Ivy's demeanor hadn't changed. She looked exhausted.

"What do you want?" Ivy said tonelessly.

"We need to talk."

"We've already talked. I've told you I can't help you." Ivy started to close the door.

"I don't need your help anymore, Ivy. I just want to talk to you."

Ivy stopped and looked up. "You don't need my help?"

"No."

Ivy held the door open for Rachael wordlessly. Rachael stepped inside and immediately had to dodge a stack of boxes. Ivy had removed the contents of her bookcase. Rachael looked up at her.

"I'm leaving St. Paul." Ivy's voice was toneless.

"What about your support group? Your girls?"

Ivy shrugged. "I tried to help them. It didn't work."

"What were you hoping would happen, Ivy?" Rachael took a seat on Ivy's sofa.

Ivy paused and exhaled. "I was hoping for a miracle." She moved toward the armchair and the hitch in her step seemed like a painful limp. She sat down.

"A miracle?" Rachael said.

"When you start out messed up from the get-go, it takes a miracle to become someone other than who you were born to be. Some of these young mothers rise above it all and prove the world was wrong about them. But some don't. Some never will. They can't undo what's been done to them. They will never be able to undo it. They will take the children God has given them and they will do all the terrible things that were done to them, even though they don't want to, even though they swore they never would."

Ivy fell silent. She stared at her hands lying empty in her lap.

Rachael inched closer to Ivy and rested a hand on the woman's arm, purposely keeping her touch gentle, affirming.

"That's the way it was for you, wasn't it, Ivy?" she said. "You wanted to do right by your kids. You really did."

"I couldn't change the deepest part of me," Ivy said in a faraway voice, like she was speaking to no one. "I sat on a bed at a foster home when I was eight and I promised myself I would never be the kind of parent my mother was to me. I promised myself I wouldn't be. And that foster mother told me before I left her that I could be anything I wanted to be. Anything. She was wrong. I wanted to be a good mother. That's all I wanted. And I wasn't. The damage had been done. It was too late for me. It's too late for a lot of us."

Rachael sensed the moment was right. Ivy was ready to lay down the mask.

"That's why you took Leo, isn't it?" Rachael said softly. "You weren't trying to hurt him. You were trying to save him."

Ivy immediately raised her head to glare at Rachael. Rachael felt a prick of fear. For a second there was only tense silence.

"The jogger was supposed to be there at 6:20!" Ivy shrieked. "He always comes at 6:20! I had been watching. He always stops at the trash can to cool down and check his pulse. He always stops by the trash can! Always! I didn't know he'd be late that day! I didn't know there was a mean dog in the park. I didn't know!"

For another long moment Ivy's gaze was terrifying. Then all at once the tight muscles in Ivy's face seemed to come undone. A low moan erupted from deep within her.

She bent her body forward in her chair and began to weep. A car pulled up outside, but Ivy didn't seem to notice.

Rachael rose from the sofa, leaned over the armchair, and wrapped Ivy in her arms.

When Will walked into the room he found Rachael holding Ivy, whispering soothing words to her, and rocking her as the woman sobbed like a child in her embrace.

THIRTY-SEVEN

Marcie sat across from Rachael, dumbfounded. Will was standing in the interview room, too. His arms were folded across his chest as he and Rachael waited for Marcie to respond.

Finally the young mother opened her mouth. "You're telling me Ivy put Leo in the trash? Ivy drugged me? Ivy wanted me to lose my kids? Ivy wanted me to go to prison?" With each question, Marcie's voice rose in pitch and volume.

"None of this happened exactly the way she planned it," Rachael said.

"Exactly how did she plan it?" Marcie shot back.

"She thought a third baby was too much for you to handle, Marcie. Years before she'd been where you are and she thought she was saving Leo and you from a very hard life together. She was trying to save you from becoming the kind of mother she became. She took him the first time thinking you would simply lose custody and that would be the end of that."

"She came into my apartment and just…and just took him?"

"The first time she figured you'd drink the vodka. She left it out so you would," Will said. "You had already given her the key to your apartment a long time ago because you were always losing your keys. But you forgot to mention this to the police when Leo came up missing the next morning."

"And you're saying she actually threw Leo in that Dumpster?" Marcie was incredulous.

"She didn't throw him," Rachael said. "She was holding him in her arms in the alley, waiting to hear the garbage truck. She knew it came at 5:50. She'd been watching it for days. When she heard the truck coming, she took off Leo's sleeper and diaper so he'd get cold and awaken and start crying. Then she put him on top of the garbage in the Dumpster. She made sure he was making noise when she hid herself behind boxes in the alley. He was in the Dumpster just minutes, Marcie. Not a day. Not even an hour."

Marcie frowned as she processed what Rachael was telling her. "Then how could she let him get hurt the second time! That makes no sense!"

"She didn't expect him to get hurt," Rachael replied. "She'd been watching a runner who comes to that park every weekday morning. He stops near the same trash can every morning to cool down after jogging. She thought he was just a little late that day. The sun was coming up and she knew you'd be waking up and that the minute you saw Leo was gone, you'd be calling her, which you did. She had to get home to take the call. She left the park thinking Leo would only be on his own for mere minutes. She was sure the runner was coming because she thought she saw him at the far end of the park as she left. Only that was a different runner. That man didn't jog by the trash can. The runner she was expecting was late that day. By almost an hour. By the time he found Leo, he had already been attacked."

"And the drug? She gave me that drug? And put the crack in my bathroom?" Marcie said, looking more hurt now than angry.

"She wanted you to be found incompetent to keep Leo. She knew if drugs were found, you'd be in violation of your case plan and the county would likely begin a TPR."

"That's what she wanted all along? For me to lose Leo? To go to prison? To lose all my kids?" Marcie's eyes were glassy.

"What she wanted was for Leo to be adopted out," Will said. "She wanted him to have what she didn't have. What you didn't have. A normal upbringing. But things get messy when you try and play God. And she didn't count on Rachael here insisting you were innocent."

Marcie turned her head toward Rachael. "You did?"

"It just seemed like we were missing something, Marcie. Sometimes I sense things like that. I dreamt about it this time. Yes, I believed you were innocent."

"Thank you," she said softly, tentatively. It was almost as if she was testing the phrase after not having said it in a long while. "I can't believe Ivy did this to me," Marcie continued. "I trusted her. I told her everything. She's the only one who knows how much it hurts that Koko blames me for my parents' marriage falling apart. It wasn't my fault. It wasn't. Ivy's the only one who understood that. I thought she was my friend."

"In her skewed way of thinking, I'm sure she thought she was your friend," Rachael said. "And she never for a moment wanted anything bad to happen to Leo."

Marcie was silent for a moment. "So can I go? Am I free? Can I have my kids back?"

"The charges against you are being dropped. You'll be free to go within the hour," Will said. "Your mom's coming for you."

"She is? And I can have my kids back?"

"J.J., Hallie, and eventually Leo will more than likely be returned to you, but not before we go back over your case plan, Marcie," Rachael said. "You simply have to abide by the conditions. You have to."

"Yeah, yeah. I know."

"I'm serious, Marcie. Ivy had pretty much given up on you as a mother. She took matters into her own hands, broke the law, and made a mess of things."

"No kidding," Marcie interjected.

"But if you don't get your act together—and I'm talking about your children, about giving them a safe home where they're fed and warm, and where you're sober and clean—then the law is on *my* side, not yours. Do we understand each other?"

"Okay. Fine." Marcie was obviously annoyed at the shift in the conversation. "I want to see Leo. Is he all right?"

"I talked to your mother," Rachael said, sighing inaudibly. "She'll take you over to the hospital to see him when you leave here. If you want to."

"Of course I want to. Why wouldn't I want to? I'm not a bad mother, you know."

"Sure. Sorry," Rachael said. She stood to leave.

"So are we done here?" Marcie said.

"Yes, we're done." Will walked over to the door to knock on it.

"Cool," Marcie replied. "Can I have a smoke?"

Will and Rachael emerged from the courthouse into late-afternoon sunshine.

"You win again, Sherlock." Will said, as they started to walk across the parking lot.

"I don't feel like a winner," Rachael replied, half-smiling.

"You kept that young woman from losing her kids. You figured out who the real perpetrator was."

"Yeah."

Will stopped. "What is it?"

"I don't know." Rachael shrugged. "What Ivy did was wrong, but I can see why she did it. Marcie's as unprepared to be someone's mother as they come, but you don't send someone to prison for that. She still has such a long way to go. I have this feeling the county hasn't seen the last of Marcie Shipley. Ivy had that feeling, too. She could see down the road, Will. She could see J.J., Hallie, and Leo growing up the same way Marcie did, pretty much at a loss as to how to parent a child but having children anyway. It's a scary thought."

"Just because it happens to some, doesn't mean it happens to them all."

"True."

They were silent for a moment. "You're not headed back to your office, are you?" Will asked. "It's your day off."

"Nope. I have a couple apologies to make. One to Sharell, one to Liza. Then I'm coming back. I've a letter to write."

"You don't need to apologize to those girls."

"Yeah, I do."

"So who's the letter of apology to?"

Rachael swallowed. "It's not an apology letter."

"No?"

"I'm going to resign, Will."

Will tilted his head. He was smiling, but his eyes registered sadness. "You're kidding me, right?"

Saying the words out loud caught her in a tender place. She shook her head without saying a word.

"How come?" Will's voice was gentle.

Rachael mentally shooed away the emotion that crept over her. This was what she wanted. "I don't want to spend so much time away from McKenna. I don't want an overpriced, fussier-than-me nanny getting to spend all those wonder hours with her. She's so precious to me, Will. Before I know it, she'll be starting school. And when she does, I'll have all kinds of hours to meddle in your affairs."

Will grinned. "You won't be able to stay away that long."

"No, I won't. I'll do pro bono stuff here and there. Maybe volunteer at Legal Aid or do some consulting."

"I could use a consultant now and then. You're pretty adept at sleuthing."

Rachael blinked away a few tears that threatened to spill down her cheeks. "Well, keep my number in your Rolodex. I'll do my best to solve all your tough cases."

Will laughed and then fell quiet. He looked fondly at her. "I'm going to miss you, kid."

Rachael held up her hand. "Don't even think of saying goodbye. It's *not* goodbye. I expect you to call on me for my keen insights at least once a week."

He smiled. "That won't be hard to do. You've got a gift, Rachael. I've always thought so. Be a shame to waste it."

She smiled back. "I don't plan to."

Will was probably right.

In the great scheme of things, Rachael probably wasn't required by social graces to offer Sharell an apology.

But she found herself knocking on the woman's door nonetheless.

If nothing else, Sharell needed to know Ivy wouldn't be hosting the support group anymore.

The door opened and Sharell stood before her, expressionless.

"Hello, Sharell."

"Why are you here?"

"To give you some news and to tell you I'm sorry."

"What news?" No inflection, no sign of interest.

"Can I come in?"

"What news?"

Rachael exhaled heavily. "Ivy's been arrested for abducting Leo. Both times. She's confessed to it, actually."

Sharell said nothing. A second later she opened the door wide, silently inviting Rachael inside her small living room. A little boy was sitting on the floor in front of a television with a bowl of banana slices. He looked up at Rachael for only a moment before settling his eyes back on the cartoon in front of him.

"You wanna run that by me again?" Sharell pointed to a tattered brown couch, littered with Matchbox cars and X-Men action figures.

Rachael pushed aside a few cars and sat down. "It was Ivy who took Leo and left him. She had an elaborate plan for him to be found right away each time. What happened to Leo the second time was an accident. Ivy hadn't planned on him getting hurt. She expected him to be found right away."

Sharell folded herself onto a love seat next to her boy. "I'm having a hard time believin' you, girl. That doesn't sound like the Ivy I know."

"I know. I didn't want to believe it at first myself. Ivy thought she was doing Leo a favor. She thought there was no hope for Marcie as a mother, and that the best thing for him was to be adopted. Marcie had no intention of giving Leo up on her own, so Ivy decided to orchestrate it herself."

"Marcie *is* hopeless as a mother," Sharell murmured.

"I don't know if Ivy will post bail," Rachael said, ignoring the comment. "I'm thinking she will disband the group."

Sharell inhaled deeply and looked at her son. "Ivy doesn't belong in jail. She's the only person who ever thought I had something to offer the world. The only one who thought I was worth something."

"She believed in you," Rachael said.

"Marcie was useless. *Is* useless. I don't even know why she came to the group. She never did any of the things Ivy told her to do. But Ivy just kept trying to knock some sense into that gal anyway. Guess she finally figgered out it was pointless. So she did what she thought she had to do and now there's no group."

"I'm sorry to have to tell you that. But I thought maybe you could tell the others."

"Yeah. I guess."

A few seconds of silence passed between them. Sharell looked back at Rachael.

"What's going to happen to Ivy?" The woman's voice was tender.

"There will be charges." Rachael sighed. "Serious ones, I'm afraid. Kidnapping's a federal offense. She'll most likely get a prison term. I honestly don't know for how long. Hopefully the judge will see she truly meant Leo no harm."

Sharell turned her head toward her living room window. She said nothing as she gazed at the world beyond her front door.

"It shouldn't be this way," she finally said.

"No. No, it shouldn't."

Another long pause followed.

"I owe you an apology, Sharell," Rachael said, breaking the momentary silence. "I thought you might've had something to do with what happened to Leo."

Sharell swiveled her head around to face Rachael. "I know that's what you thought."

"I just wanted you to know I'm sorry."

The woman said nothing.

Rachael stood. "And just so you know, if Marcie ever threatens you again with making false reports about you to Child Protection Services, I want you to call the police. I'll give you the name of a friend of mine."

Sharell was speechless for a moment. "How did you know?"

"Liza confided in me."

"I mean how did you know they were false?"

Rachael lowered and lifted her shoulders. "Because Ivy believed in you. I think she believed you were the one shining example in her group of someone who was throwing the engine in reverse and honestly trying to make it work."

The tiniest of smiles seemed to play itself across Sharell's face.

"You should keep the support group going, Sharell. I'm not saying you need to keep Marcie in it. It's obvious your personalities clash. But for Liza's sake, for Arden's. For the others. You might want to think about it."

Rachael turned and walked to the door. Sharell stood and opened it for her.

"Guess I owe you an apology, too," the woman said.

"Don't worry about it. See you around, Sharell."

"Bye."

The door closed softly behind her.

Rachael got back in her car and started it. It would take less than ten minutes to drive to the Apollo Tattoo and Piercing Salon. As she made her way there, she decided she wouldn't tell Liza where Ivy was and what Ivy had done. She would let Sharell do it, in whatever way the new leader of the group felt was best.

She would just make sure Liza was okay. At least for today.

Minutes later she parked in front of the parlor, got out of her car, and walked in. A woman in Goth attire sat in a chair, waiting. She glanced up at Rachael with heavily lined eyes. The multi-pierced woman from the day before looked up from the front counter.

"Whatcha need?" she said, cracking her gum.

Before Rachael could answer, hanging beads in the doorway to the rest of the salon parted and Liza poked her head through. "I thought that was you! I saw you getting out of your car! Did you come for a tattoo, Mrs. Flynn? They're just the temporary ones. But I do awesome flowers." Liza was smiling broadly.

Rachael smiled at her. "Sure, Liza. I'd love a tattoo."

"Sweet! Come on back!" Liza held the beads back for Rachael as she stepped inside.

"Do you do birds?" Rachael asked.

"Like, so cool! Sure I do birds! Which kind do you want?"

The beads fell back around Rachael like a tender caress. "I'd like a sparrow."

THIRTY-EIGHT

The plan was in place.

After Fig made dinner for Jillian at his loft and presented her with the blue-hued iguana he'd named Merlin, he would coax her up to the roof of his building where a starry, moonlit night would be the backdrop for his proposal.

Brick, Sidney and Molly, and Trace, Rachael, and McKenna were to sneak up to the roof via the studio at a quarter to nine and wait for him and Jillian to appear on the hour. A harpist would begin playing Bach's "Sleepers Awake," one of Jillian's favorite pieces. The friends were to stand in a semicircle around Fig. Not too close, but not too far away.

Fig had seen to the comforts of his friends while they waited for him. He had brought in heating lamps to warm them and provided linen-covered tables laden with hors d'oeuvres and candlelight, and of course, the harpist, who played near the lighted easel bearing Fig's masterful drawing of Jillian at play, backlit by twenty-four standing candles.

By ten minutes to nine, all was in place.

McKenna had been tricked into an extra long nap that afternoon, so she toddled about the pea rock roof, happily allowing herself to be held by the hand by a watchful Trace.

"So what's the plan if she says no?" Brick asked as he spun a truffle-stuffed cherry tomato on its serving plate.

"We toss her off the roof and hold her by her ankles 'til she says yes," Sidney replied, popping a peeled lychee nut in his mouth.

"This is so embarrassing," Molly said. "If you had done this to me, Sid, I wouldn't have spoken to you for a week."

"It'll be okay," Trace said, letting McKenna lead him to a collection of imported palms Fig had dragged up to the roof. "Jillian's not the conventional type. If she was, she wouldn't be dating Fig."

"Well, would you have liked to be proposed to this way, Rachael?" Molly said.

Rachael slipped into a chair next to her. "It wouldn't have been Trace's way. And if Jillian's really in love with him, I don't think she'll care."

Sid stared at her.

"I don't believe it," he said. "Rachael Flynn, is that a tattoo? Did Fig make you get a tattoo for tonight?"

Rachael looked down at the little brown sparrow on her arm. "No, Sid. He didn't. Fig actually adores my new tattoo and he's pretty bummed it's only temporary. But I didn't do it for Fig."

"Trace?" Sid turned to Trace.

Trace winked at Rachael and swooped McKenna up into his arms. The little girl squealed. "Nope."

"I just did it, Sid," Rachael said. "I did it for a friend. It made her day. And I did it for me."

Sid looked unconvinced. "So have you become some kind of bohemian rebel? Is that why you're quitting your high-heeled county job and getting tattoos? Did you let Fig corrupt her?" Sid tossed this comment to Trace.

"Yes to all of the above," Trace said, kissing McKenna on the tummy.

"No and no," Rachael said. "I'm still the rational, über-analytical, over-achiever I've always been, Sid. Don't worry. The world is still as you know it."

"I think it's kind of cute," Molly interjected. "Though I think I would've gotten a hummingbird or a parrot. No offense, Rachael, but sparrows are kind of...kind of..."

"They're boring, Rachael," Brick said.

Rachael gazed down at the soft brown bird Liza had painted onto her skin.

You like sparrows? Are they your favorite? Liza had asked her.

Sparrows just remind me that God is always watching. It's nice to know someone is always watching over me.

Liza had paused for a moment, her tiny painting tool poised above Rachael's skin. *I really like that,* Liza had said, a smile slowly building. *I like that a lot. I am going to paint a sparrow on me. I want someone to see me, too.*

"They're coming!" Trace whispered hoarsely, and the remembered conversation slipped away.

The friends fell silent. The door to the roof opened and the harpist began to play the melodic first stanza of "Sleepers Awake." Fig emerged first, then Jillian. She was wearing a flowing, gauzy gown of sunset pink. Her long blonde hair fell freely about her shoulders. Delicate silver jewelry hung from her ears, neck, wrists, and ankles.

Her eyes fell on the gathering of friends and she smiled.

"You're all here!" she said. "Figgy, what are you up to?"

Rachael had never seen Fig look so nervous. He took Jillian's hand. His was shaking.

"I asked my friends to be here tonight, Jills, because they're my family. They are a part of me. They know me and love me and I know I can trust them. I know you can trust them. There's nothing in the world like the love of people who love you for *you.* Nothing like it in the world."

Fig sank to one knee. A smile blossomed on Jillian's face.

"I want you to be a part of this divine circle, Jills. I want you in the deepest part of it. I promise you that you will never know what it is like to be alone. You will never be loved by any man like I love you. This love has no parallel. Whether God gives us twenty thousand days together or twenty thousand hours or even just twenty thousand minutes, I will be there for you, Jillian. Always. Marry me."

He held out to her the ring he had made with its blue and green gems.

For several long moments, the only sound on the roof was the serene plucking of the harp. No one made a sound. Even McKenna seemed spellbound as Fig waited for Jillian to answer. Then without a word, Jillian slowly reached out her hand as if to take the ring. Her fingers closed around Fig's fingers instead, the ring now enveloped in the tangle of their entwined fingers and pressed palms.

"Yes," she whispered, the widening smile spreading fully across her face.

"Yes?" Fig whispered back. A shining tear trickled down his right cheek.

She knelt down in front of him, making within the circle of friends an inner circle of just two. "Yes!" she murmured.

He pulled her to him and kissed her.

Trace handed McKenna to Rachael and then began to applaud. The rest joined him. Fig slipped the ring on Jillian's finger.

"Oh, come, come, come!" Fig called out, standing and helping Jillian to her feet. He motioned for the others to come to them, wrapping his arms around his friends in a giant group embrace.

There was laughter and tears in the circle as hugs were shared.

"This is what it's all about," Fig said, his cheeks glistening as they stood in a huddle, arms entwined so that it was hard to tell whose arms were whose. "This is *everything*."

Sid and Brick clapped Fig on the back and began to tell him how pale he looked. Molly leaned in to admire Jillian's ring. As the huddle became more animated, McKenna pointed a chubby finger at the little sparrow on Rachael's arm.

"Loo!" the little girl said.

"Little bird," Rachael said.

She kissed her daughter on the cheek and leaned into Trace, who was laughing at something Brick had said.

This *was* everything. For now. For always.

Pearly radiance from a porthole moon fell upon the roof as she stood there with her family, bathing them all in a tender flood of light as it spilled from the eye of God in roving, white splendor.

A WORD FROM THE AUTHOR

I am privileged, dear reader, to have shared this story with you. The power of deep, unconditional, and selfless parental love is indeed stunning. It amazes me to think how different the world would be if every child knew that kind of love and lived under its protection. I would love to hear what you think of *Days and Hours*. I learn so much from what you share with me.

You can reach me by e-mail at susan@susanlmeissner.com or by mail at:

Susan Meissner
c/o Harvest House Publishers
990 Owen Loop North
Eugene, OR 97402

You can also visit me on the Web at www.susanmeissner.com

Grace and peace,

Susan Meissner

To learn more about books by Susan Meissner
or to read sample chapters, log on to our Web site:

www.harvesthousepublishers.com

ABOUT SUSAN MEISSNER

Susan Meissner is an award-winning newspaper columnist, pastor's wife, and novelist. She lives in southern California with her husband, Bob, and their children.

If you enjoyed *Days and Hours,* you'll want to read these other excellent books by Susan Meissner...

THE RACHAEL FLYNN SERIES...

WIDOWS AND ORPHANS

Widows and Orphans is the debut novel in the new Rachael Flynn mystery series by critically acclaimed author Susan Meissner. It is the perfect new series for readers who enjoy CBA authors Dee Henderson, Angela Hunt, and Brandilyn Collins.

When her ultra-ministry-minded brother, Joshua, confesses to murder, lawyer Rachael Flynn begs him to let her represent him, certain that he is innocent. But Joshua refuses her offer of counsel.

As Rachael works on the case, she begins to suspect that Josh knows who the real killer is, but she is unable to get him to cooperate with his defense. Why won't he talk to her? What is Josh hiding?

The answer is revealed in a stunning conclusion that will have readers eager for the second book in this gripping new series.

STICKS AND STONES

Critically acclaimed author Susan Meissner's Rachael Flynn mystery series started with the popular *Widows and Orphans.* In the second serving of intrigue, *Sticks and Stones,* lawyer Rachael Flynn receives an unsigned, heart-stopping letter:

"They're going to find a body at the Prairie Bluff construction site. He deserved what he got, but it wasn't supposed to happen. It was an accident."

When the body is uncovered, Rachael and Detective Will Pendleton discover that the fifteen-year-old victim, Randall Buckett, had been buried twenty-five years before. Are the letter writer and the killer the same person? Why would someone speak up now? And why are they telling Rachael?

...N INCLUDES...

A WINDOW TO THE WORLD

Here is the story of two girls, inseparable until one is abducted as the other watches helplessly. Years later the mystery is solved and the truth confirmed that God works all things together for good. Named by *Booklist Magazine* as one of the top ten Christian novels of 2005.

THE REMEDY FOR REGRET

Tess Longren is 28, single, and at a crossroads in her life. She finally has a job she enjoys as well as a proposal of marriage from a man she loves, but Tess can't seem to grasp a future filled with promise and hope. Her mother's long-ago death remains a constant, though subtle ache that Tess can't seem to move past. Here is a masterful novel about finding the courage to change a painful situation and bearing what cannot be changed, about understanding the limitations of an imperfect world and the vast resources of a perfect God.

IN ALL DEEP PLACES

Mystery writer Luke Foxbourne lives a happy life in a century-old manor house in Connecticut. But when his father, Jack, has a stroke, Luke returns to his hometown of Halcyon, Iowa, where he reluctantly takes the reins of his father's newspaper. Memories of Norah, the neighbor girl to whom he gave his first kiss, cause Luke to reflect as he spends night after night alone in his childhood home. Soon he feels an uncontrollable urge to start writing a different story altogether: Norah's story...and his own.

A SEAHORSE IN THE THAMES

Alexa Poole intended to spend her week off from work quietly recuperating from minor surgery. But when carpenter Stephen Moran falls into her life—or rather off of her roof—the unexpected happens. His sweet, gentle disposition proves more than she can resist and now she's falling for him.

Her older sister, Rebecca, has lived at the Falkman Residential Center since a car accident left her mentally compromised. Now, 17 years later, she has vanished, leaving Alexa fearing the worst. After Alexa places a call to her twin sister in England and despite a strained separation from her family, Priscilla agrees to come home for a visit.

As Alexa begins the search for Rebecca, disturbing questions surface. Why did the car that Rebecca was riding in swerve off the road killing her college friend, Leanne McNeil? And what about the mysterious check for $50,000 found in Rebecca's room and signed by her friend's father, Gavin McNeil?